The
Belonger

The
Belonger

a novel

Mary Kathleen Mehuron

SPARKPRESS

Published by SparkPress, a BookSparks imprint,
A division of SparkPoint Studio, LLC
Phoenix, Arizona, USA, 85007
www.gosparkpress.com

Published 2023
Printed in the United States of America
Print ISBN: 978-1-68463-206-0
E-ISBN: 978-1-68463-207-7
Library of Congress Control Number: 2022918604

Interior design by Katherine Lloyd, The DESK

For all my friends on Grand Turk Island,
Turks and Caicos, in the British West Indies—
a magical land of beautiful, formidable women
and idiosyncratic, fascinating men.
This is my love letter to all of you.

"You never know how strong you are until being strong is the only choice you have."

—Bob Marley

 # Chapter 1

Holly put both her hands flat on the deep sill of the hinged window of her bedroom and leaned out to see the morning light. Then she pulled on shorts and a T-shirt over her head. Flip-flops and bare feet were a common option, but this morning—like most mornings, in the early hours when it was cool—she put on a pair of sneakers so she could walk along the entire length of the seawall before the sun rose too high in the sky.

The top of the wall was as wide as a sidewalk and had the most beautiful ocean view she'd ever seen. At points along the way, the waves crashed spectacularly upon the cement pilings before taking a back dive toward the Caribbean. Each big surge made a great *brumpfasshh* sound that made her heart feel light.

Holly loved how the locals smiled their hello as she jogged by. How in the grocery store, shoppers often burst out singing together when a favorite song came on the radio, broadcast by the shop's sound system. How music seemed to be everywhere. As constant as the competing crash of the waves.

She wanted all of her guests to enjoy the island the way she did. She counseled her visitors that climbing up to the top of the wall at the start of the walk was a bit of a challenge, as was jumping down when they reached the far end.

She also told them, "Don't try it if you mind getting seafoam in your hair."

After her exercise, like most locals, Holly used the cool mornings for physical work, as the salt air and seasonal storms created a never-ending array of maintenance projects. On the extensive fencing, for example, which was needed to keep the wild donkeys, horses, and dogs out, a fresh coat of paint was always wanted. When she got back from her run, she painted a section white; then she dropped the brush in a bucket of water to soak. Anyone with any sense at all went inside or found a spot in the shade by midmorning.

Holly sat in her favorite place under an enormous *Lignum vitae*, sometimes called a "tree of life." It draped over one ocean-facing corner of her deep, stuccoed front porch. A high, thick, white limestone wall that was plastered to match the main house snugly fenced her small yard off from the street. On its opposite ends, two bright blue wooden gates rattled with each strong gust of the trade breeze.

The roof of the porch blocked the morning sun as it rose from behind her. The high wall in front would soon provide her some protection from the hottest rays when her work hours eased into the late afternoon. Holly kept a small table and chair in the spot under the cascading tree; it was there she now worked, hunched over her computer in the heat of the day, lost in the details of the orders she was placing, her troubles far, far away.

The restaurant needed new cloth napkins. She wondered about color and the quality of the fabric. *This time should I find a product with some texture? White is classic, but maybe it's time for a change.* It was the details that absorbed her imagination. The joy of creating something new.

A cruise ship was in port for a few hours and one of their trolley-shaped buses rolled slowly by with its loudspeaker blaring: "Though Grand Turk Island is the capital city of the Turks and Caicos, it has remained the quiet coastal village you see today. To your right is the historic Roseate House built in 1832. Though built as a family home, it's now a popular inn."

Holly shifted in her seat and acknowledged the mention of her business by waving to the bus. Many others in town complained about the almost daily invasion of tourists, but Holly's response to that was, "It's good for business and they're gone by three in the afternoon. Not exactly a bother." The temporary influx of Americans soothed her, too, as she was one of the very few who lived on Grand Turk Island.

This was a particularly large bus group. She stood up for a minute and peered across the street to make sure her head chef, Sameera, was opening the restaurant. The kitchen was wide open; she let out an assured sigh. *Business will be good today.* She sat down and allowed her attention to return to her computer's screen.

As the tour director squawked, his voice brought her back to the real world again.

"Across the road is a beach restaurant called the Sand Dollar, which was converted from an old garage. A beach bistro with signature cocktails, it's known in town as a fun place to hang out. And please notice the architecture of the inn, which was built in the British Colonial Bermudan style."

She tried to push the sound away. Return to her work. But she found she was marveling about how many centuries had passed since this town was built. She never ceased to be amazed that so many of the old homes on Duke and Front Streets had survived despite their low-lying coastal location. Much of the island had to be fixed or rebuilt every decade or two as the result of a direct hit from a major hurricane, yet the oceanfront road remained largely intact.

With the exception of her fingers clicking on the keys, she sat almost frozen for a long time. Holly was used to hard work. In the early afternoon, she got up and briefly went across the street to ask for a sandwich, then took it back to eat at her desk while she worked. For only a few minutes at a time that afternoon did she jump up and run into the office—to sharpen her pencil, grab her notebook, or pour a glass of water—and each time she was back on task quickly.

By the time she was answering emails, her shoulders and neck were beginning to ache.

She finally stood to stretch, staring out across her yard toward the sharp, deep blue line of the coral reef. In stark contrast to the turquoise water, the sharp drop-off of The Wall was a kilometer from shore.

Day is nearly over, Holly thought. *Why does it always make me feel so melancholy?*

The sun had fallen away from the peak of its arc and was inching closer to the western horizon. It seemed oddly quiet with the cruise guests gone. Resigned that the hours were gathering toward nightfall, she picked up her paperwork and laptop and went inside to shower.

Since Holly had come to live permanently on island, she'd ceased to see any point in trying to "do" her hair. The high humidity of the Caribbean air and the constant winds made her various attempts at styling irrelevant. Following her shower, she simply ran a wide-tooth comb through her wet tresses and let them air-dry.

To dress for the evening, she reached for one of her cotton sundresses, all of which were organized by color on their hangers. Because of her fair coloring, saleswomen tended to steer her toward pale shades of pink and blue. But there was that pastel green outfit too.

I'm not convinced about the green. I shouldn't have let her talk me into that.

She pulled one of the pink dresses over her head and looked into her bedroom mirror. *I suppose I should make more of an effort—but do I even know how?*

The Belonger

She twisted her hair up and held it back with both hands as she looked into the mirror.

Maybe I'll fuss with it after it dries. She shook her head and snorted. *Who am I kidding? Once I set foot in the restaurant, I won't have time to think about how I look.*

Over time, Holly had also accepted that makeup wouldn't stand up to Grand Turk's climate, either. *You can always tell a woman is a tourist here by her melting mascara and eyeliner.*

Locals did occasionally get done up for a special event, but it was rare. Most women on island presented faces that were scrubbed clean, with only a natural glow from the sun to enhance their looks. The benefit, as Holly saw it, was that this lack of pretense made dressing for dinner easy.

By this time of late afternoon, when the day surrendered to dusk, whole families positioned themselves to watch the sun go down. A keen observer of the island would take note of the extreme lengths each household went to in order to create an outdoor space for the ceremony of night's onset. *Like something holy.*

Everyone in Cockburn Town seemed to be pulled out of their doorways to stare at the horizon and bear witness to another end-of-the-day miracle. And Holly was no different from her neighbors. The sunset was always beautiful, but there were also exceptional nights when the colors in the sky could leave you breathless. Sometimes those nights made her feel joyful. Sometimes, when the tall clouds were rushing across the huge expanse of sky, she felt small and alone.

Air pollution was nearly nonexistent on Grand Turk, so there was usually a clear, unobstructed view across the distance—one of the reasons the island had the occasional green flash when the sun set. All that witnessed it were inevitably awestruck. More than once, Holly had scanned the faces of friends at such a moment—illuminated by the flattering light, expressions slack-jawed to the point of striking her as comical. In those moments, she knew they must feel the way she did: blessed by the divine.

She recalled that the great author Jules Verne had written about such an event. He'd said the color was "a most wonderful green, a green which no artist could obtain on his palette . . . the true green of hope."

The true green of hope.

She let this sink in. *The color of my hope for a fresh start here on Grand Turk.* Her hope that the small community of expatriates from Britain and Canada might come to accept her. And that the Belongers, who comprised the vast majority of the town, might give her a chance to prove herself. Though Byron's father's family was historically a pillar of the community, she worried they only politely tolerated her. As marginalized as she had been in Vermont, she prayed for something better in her new home on island. *I am just going to try to do the next right thing and hope against hope they will warm to me.*

Though Verne's idea about the green flash was marvelous, Holly thought his bold sentiment didn't quite do the phenomenon justice. The few times she'd witnessed one, it had felt powerfully significant—like a portent, a harbinger of things to come.

She held her breath until the last of the rays of the sun were swallowed by the ocean and darkness took up its reign. Even then she remained rooted as, one by one, the stars slowly popped out and her eyes adjusted to the changing light.

Wild donkeys were the only living creatures on Grand Turk that weren't watching the sunset in the precious, waning moments at the end of the day. They had noticed long ago that the humans were distracted during this time, so for them it had become an opportunity to steal food off a picnic table or take a drink from their outdoor footbaths. She often heard people hissing, shouting, and clapping their hands to drive them off as the sky turned pink.

The Belonger

She never bothered; she knew from experience the animals would eventually leave on their own, ambling away in their dallying fashion. Their loose hips rocked as they made their way up the hill with a punctuated *clomp, clomp, clomp* to the lighthouse, where there were easier pickings.

At the sound of their braying, Holly's stomach growled. Suddenly ravenous, she splayed the fingers of both hands across her tummy. *What has Sameera made for dinner tonight?*

Chapter 2

Holly would have done anything for her son. Given where she started her life, and her unexpected pregnancy, she had already moved heaven and earth to make something of herself. *I did it for Byron. So he would have a better life than I had.* Seeing how excited he was about the purchase of their inn and restaurant had left her with few qualms about moving from Vermont. Though she'd been giving up the only home she'd ever known, she knew her real home was wherever Byron was.

Leaving her chosen career had proven more difficult to do. It had taken her six years to work her way through college and finally get her license as a school counselor. She'd done it so she could help teenagers who were having a difficult time of it, like she had—and it seemed she'd succeeded. At an assembly given to celebrate her retirement, she'd been gifted a decorative box filled with letters from students and former students, each one moving in its own way. She now started every day by opening the box and reading one of them.

It had been meaningful work. But it was time to go. She separated her work life from her real life. Byron was her only family.

She stood gazing over the counter of the bar at the Sand Dollar toward the ocean with a soft cloth in her hand. It was hard to believe, but here she was. Not even a year after she and Byron had started talking about the purchase of the businesses, she was in Grand Turk, working at the restaurant.

Polishing the silverware gave her a comforting feeling. She rubbed and rubbed the bowls of her spoons, where she'd found that moisture could sometimes pool and create a stain. It was a simple thing. *But when these babies gleam, it makes me happy.*

Given the forecasted time of sunset and her view of the ocean, she knew a total and complete darkness would descend any minute. There were few electric lights to soften the dark of the night around the borders of the property. The staff jumped into action, lighting torches and candles on the tables.

Since there were few customers yet, Holly seized the chance to approach her head chef. She and Byron had inherited her from the restaurant's previous owner, who had described her as "Sameera Chetrit—the fiery Moroccan woman."

Sameera was alone in the kitchen, prepping for the dinner crowd. Holly went in and held up a bottle of her bartender Fabienne's "Green Flash" hot sauce. "Look at this, Sameera. Fabienne is making them. See the label? She makes every single one different and by hand. Cute, right?"

Sameera pursed her lips. Her eyebrows shot up toward the sky.

Holly's psychology background came in handy when working with this particular employee. She folded her arms and waited patiently.

It took some time, but Sameera eventually shrugged in begrudging agreement. Yes, the bottle was cute. But she wasn't happy about it. Holly could feel her anger radiating off her in waves.

"Well, I like the product," Holly said. "So does Byron. We're going to carry it in the gift shop and put one out on every table."

Sameera sucked in her bronze cheeks, which made her already full lips protrude even more. "Anyone can make hot sauce. If that's what you wanted, you should have told me."

Holly remained silent to give Sameera the idea that she was considering the notion, but her brows were furrowed as she did so. After a few respectful seconds, she made direct eye contact with the chef. "I didn't think of it before. I'm sure you make a great sauce, but it's not only what's in this bottle, it's the artwork and presentation. Byron and I have asked Fabienne to consider doing a painting for us, too. We think she's quite gifted."

"As you wish." Sameera screwed up her face. "I do think Haitian art is much overrated. Ufff!"

Oh, boy, here we go.

Holly's feelings had cooled toward Sameera since the night she drunkenly held forth on the subject of America's first black president. With a sniff, she'd referred to President Obama as "that African," her eyes meeting Holly's in challenge.

When she heard this, Holly shook her head like she was trying to get something out of her ear. "He's not African; he was born in the United States."

Sameera waved her hand derisively in the air. "He doesn't come from America. You know exactly what I mean."

Holly assumed the woman was trying to say she believed the unfounded rumor that the President was born in Kenya. But she played dumb. "Actually, I don't have any idea what you mean."

"He only became president because he was black," Sameera slurred. "They wanted him in."

What was she trying to prove? Holly was seriously upset by Sameera's snobby facial expression and the certainty in her voice. She wasn't going to let it go. "Are you an American citizen? Do you have any idea what you are talking about?"

Holly wasn't actually sure what Sameera's citizenship status was; she only knew that she had spent much of her life traveling all over the world.

The Belonger

Sameera swept her hands from near her face down along the length of her torso. "I am *Moroccan.*"

Holly nodded. "I don't understand what you mean when you say, 'They wanted it.' Who is 'they'?"

"Oh, please!" The chef tugged off her white toque and threw it to the floor.

Holly stood up off her bar stool with her arms crossed and faced her. "Since you aren't from the United States, you don't get a say about who we vote into office. And just for the record, our former president is a self-made man from humble beginnings. We put a lot of stock in that where I come from. He worked his way up the ladder until he was elected editor of the *Harvard Law Review.* Do you know how few get that honor? Barack graduated magna cum laude. From Harvard."

Sameera jerked her head up—so forcefully, and in such a wobbly manner, that Holly thought it was possible she might fall out of her seat. "Barack?" she snapped. "Do you know him?"

"No, of course I don't know him," Holly said, "but I feel like I do. I'm really proud of him." *Why am I arguing with a drunk?* she asked herself, and then immediately answered the question: *Because I don't want her out in the world spreading this nonsense.*

"You misunderstand me, Holly," Sameera said. "I have nothing against Africans. In fact, I rather enjoy them." She raised her eyebrows and wiggled them with a knowing look. "But . . . for president?"

Holly was offended by both Sameera's sexual insinuation and her rant in general. But the next day, during a scheduled meeting to review food orders, Sameera didn't seem to remember the conversation. Holly asked her about it and she dismissed her rantings with an imperial wave of her hand.

"I had too much to drink. This job is a lot of pressure. Every now and then, I need to blow off some steam."

"Sameera, you called President Obama an 'African' in a way that sounded like an epithet."

"It's how we do it where I come from," she said with a sniff.

"Morocco is in Africa, too. *You* are an African."

"In the north. Very far north. It is not the same thing."

Holly sighed, as by then she'd already learned that she couldn't change Sameera's mind once she dug in.

Holly wasn't about to let the discussion about Fabienne's artwork and her hot sauce go the same way as many of her conversations with Sameera had in the past.

"This is a direction that Byron and I have decided to go in," she told her firmly. "We hope you'll support our decision. Frankly, this is a way for Fabienne to make extra money, and I'd like her to have the chance."

Sameera put both her hands on her slim hips. She always wore platform sandals, which Holly assumed was because she was only about five feet two inches tall. Her long black hair was tucked into her white hat, which framed dark eyes that were currently flashing with anger. "I'm the head chef of this restaurant. I could work anywhere in the Caribbean because everyone enjoys my food. So, I think you should consider this: It is I who am the creative force behind your success, not Fabienne. When you hold her up to our customers, you push down their opinion of me."

Holly took in a sharp breath through her nose. *Getting another chef would be difficult. I haven't heard of a qualified Belonger who is available at the moment. This woman grates on my nerves, but I have to be practical.* She knew that bringing an outside employee into the country could take months; the British government, which ran the territory of Turks and Caicos, made employers go through a lengthy process to do something like that. That long a wait could close the restaurant down. She cupped her chin between her thumb and forefinger.

"We disagree, Sameera," she said carefully. "Byron and I are proud of both you and Fabienne and the talents you've contributed to our success . . ." She braced herself, expecting an argument, but then she realized she'd abruptly lost Sameera's attention. The chef was turned away from Holly and peering out toward the sea.

Holly pivoted in the same direction and heard the roaring sound that had apparently distracted Sameera. A faint glow from under the horizon illuminated a shadowy shape moving on the surface of the water toward them—a rather large fishing boat, from what Holly could make out. She squinted her eyes to help her focus, and then immediately rolled them. She thought she knew who was heading into shore, and she wasn't happy about it.

As she craned her neck, she realized she was holding her breath too.

The engine died back. Sounds of splashing drifted toward them. Laughter.

"Oh shoot," a man hollered.

"Land ahoy!" another voice called, sounding inebriated.

There was bawdy laughter. Then she heard the first voice say, "Been single for forty-eight years. Never married. A fact I am very proud of."

Just as I thought. It's Lord Anthony Bascombe. Entitled bastard.

Chapter 3

As Holly let out a sigh of exasperation, Sameera's face opened up into a huge smile, showing off her almost perfect teeth. She untied her apron, lifted it up over her head, and ran toward the bathroom.

Holly had seen her do this before. She would go overboard checking her hair and applying some makeup.

The boat puttered closer.

Since purchasing the Sand Dollar, Holly had had many such invasions by Anthony Bascombe, a man of dubious royalty and reputation. Him and his ever-changing, unsettlingly young companions. With a groan, she awaited the impact of his arrival.

Sameera returned from her primping session and stood beside Holly patiently. Holly had to admit, her chef looked radiant. She'd let down her black hair, allowing it to fall halfway to her waist in a shining cascade. She had also put on a bit of lipstick, and the contrast of the red against her skin made it appear to glow. Sameera had also lined her eyes with black liner as dark as kohl— they looked huge—and thrown a flowy, light top over her black leggings that exposed plenty of her ample cleavage.

"How do I look?" Sameera asked. "Do you have any perfume I could borrow?" The woman was practically salivating.

"Perfume? No." Holly's tone was decidedly edgy. "I don't even own any." As she took in her own rumpled cotton dress, she tried to smooth out the wrinkles as best as she could, but it left her feeling dissatisfied and frumpy. "That kind of fragrance doesn't belong in a working kitchen anyway."

Sameera pouted.

Holly had put her hair up into a topknot to keep the wind from blowing strands into her eyes. This hairstyle was rarely a choice for her at this time of night, as the salt breeze had inevitably encrusted every blond tendril she had on her head and whipped it into an unruly mess by now. She usually made a joke out of it—"Beach hair; don't care."

Sameera sucked in her cheeks again and glanced down her nose at Holly. Uncertain as to what to make of the haughty expression, Holly chose to watch the near distance with a drink in her hand.

Some clouds parted and she could now make out the large boat. The moonlit outlines of two figures threw kayaks overboard onto the water, climbed down, and got into them. The sound of splashing paddles followed and grew louder as they bridged the stretch into shore. Next to the Sand Dollar's decking was one of the most easily accessible beaches on the island. The two men arrived, pulled their small rigs up on the sand, and walked around to the restaurant's entrance.

The gait of the guy on the right was familiar; Holly readied herself for the energy about to fill the room.

The duo strode in like they owned the place. Holly noticed both Anthony and his friend wore black bathing suits doubling as shorts, and waterproof sandals, though their shirts were different: Anthony sported a collared knit shirt that looked expensive, while his companion wore an impressive Cuban-style button-down.

Sameera practically threw herself into Anthony's arms as he entered. As he embraced her, he tossed an amused smile over his shoulder to his friend and then, like a character from an old

Hollywood movie, bent her backward for a kiss. Although he pulled off a dramatic vignette, which he seemed to thoroughly enjoy, he only planted a loud smooch on her forehead instead of her lips.

"You gorgeous girl," he said. "What are you cooking up for us tonight? I'm famished. When we are ready perhaps you can give us one of everything. You decide—a chef's tasting." With that, he pulled her back up and gave her a playful push toward the kitchen. "But wait till later in the evening. Cocktails first. Priorities, you know. Then we are off on a walkabout."

Sameera seemed a bit baffled and, certainly, furious as she slunk back through the kitchen door.

Anthony's attention now turned toward the bar. "Fabienne, my lovely!" he exclaimed. "You are a shining example of the beauty of the women of Haiti. What shall I drink tonight, my darling?"

She cast her eyes down, presumably embarrassed by the intimacy in his statement, but Holly couldn't help but notice she was smiling. It was a shy smile, but a smile nonetheless.

"What are you liking, Mr. Anthony?" She scanned from him to the man accompanying him.

Anthony held his hands high, like the conductor of an orchestra. "Oh dear, where are my manners? Fabienne"—he gestured to her and then to the man by his side—"this is my dear friend, James. We used to work together on the stock exchange in New York. What shall we have to drink, James?"

Holly's eyes widened at the disclosure. *How long did he live in New York?* She rested her shoulder against the support pole nearest to her and listened closely.

"I always say," James said loudly, "'When in Rome . . .'"

"So you'll have a rum punch? Excellent choice," Anthony said as if he didn't have a care in the world. "Fabienne, James will have a triple rum punch, but make mine a single, neat, with only three ice cubes. That's just enough to keep the drink cold without watering down the liquor."

He turned to survey the room and caught sight of Holly. When he bowed at the waist like an actor at the end of a Broadway musical, she did the opposite and straightened up, not knowing whether to laugh or curtsy in response. As he arose, he nodded his head, gave her a two-fingered salute, and called out, "Madame!"

She shrugged as if to ask, *Who, me?*—then countered his salutation by saying in a dry tone, "*Non monsieur, je suis une mademoiselle.*" She thought she was quite witty, putting together a sentence in French on the fly. For some reason, at this moment, she found it difficult to look directly at Anthony. The focus of his attention made her uneasy. Though there was nothing on her skirt, she reached down and brushed off an imaginary speck.

He purposefully pointed to his forehead with his index finger. "*J'ai oublié. Excusé.*"

This got her attention, though he staggered a little from the effort the gesture took.

He bowed again, though not as deeply this time, and, nodding his head, held her gaze. His eyes looked as if they were ablaze.

Holly blushed. She was undone by his boldness. *I mean. I'm the third in line after Sameera and Fabienne.* She felt invisible back there in the corner, though the moonlight backlit everything with luminescence.

At long last, Anthony broke eye contact, but as he turned away she noticed that he was wearing a satisfied little grin.

He thinks he's God's gift to women. Lord help us all.

She watched as he leaned over the bar and whispered something into Fabienne's ear. Whatever he said made her laugh so hard she covered her mouth with the palm of her hand. It only added to Holly's general irritation.

She walked toward them with great authority in her steps. "I'm going to get some fresh air while it's still quiet, Fabienne. It feels a bit oppressive in here right now."

Fabienne didn't react, and after a beat, Holly sighed. No one had heard a word she'd said. "And that, my dear," Anthony bellowed, "is one of the many reasons why I have never been married!"

As he'd intended, his comment caused an uproar.

Holly charged down the short path outside and opened the gate leading to the street. She slammed it behind her with as much power as she could muster, then headed toward Roseate, across the lane, and unlatched the second gate. *It's a perfect time to get some paperwork done. Despite what Anthony said to Sameera, he's too cheap to stay for dinner. They'll probably wander down to the food truck when they get hungry. I'll pay some bills here and he'll be gone when I go back.*

Byron was at his desk in their shared office when she sat down at hers. He was working on something so intently that he didn't even look up.

His concentration afforded her a moment to admire her son and how handsome he was. She never ceased to be amazed by it. Though everyone said he looked like his father, she knew he had her eyes. They were the exact same shape, though a different color.

The large room they sat in was in the front corner of the building facing the road. A powerful, cool ocean breeze blew through the windows at this time of night and the location allowed them to watch, and often hear, the comings and goings at the restaurant.

Byron glanced up from what he was doing.

"How are you doing, honey?" Holly asked. "Are you going to eat something?"

The color of his skin changed from a rich brown to a glowing gold as it stretched over his high cheekbones and neared his green eyes. When he sat back in his antique desk chair, it creaked. "Sure. Finish what you came in here to do and then we'll go over and have dinner. What's Sameera's special tonight?"

"The fishermen were flush with lobster today. She's made it two different ways." Holly stuck a pencil in her battery-operated sharpener. After it whirred for a few seconds, she removed the pencil and blew flecks of sawdust off the point. "What are you working on? You want some help?"

She could hear his long exhale. "Mom. And Dad, too. Do either of you ever consider that I actually have a degree in business? Why do you always assume I don't know what I'm doing?"

"Oh." She hadn't realized. *But is that really fair? He's still so young.* Her eyes watered, and he caught it.

"What a life we lead," he said with a laugh, his annoyance gone. "We think nothing of eating lobster while we sit on the edge of the ocean."

She was relieved the moment had passed. So much so that she chortled gleefully. "Don't think I ever take living here for granted. I want to sit for a few minutes and write some checks. Just long enough so I can be sure Anthony and his henchman have left before we go over there." She put the pencil behind her ear for safekeeping.

As she sharpened a second pencil, she noticed Byron could barely contain his urge to tease her. When she blew at the sawdust, he declared, "Anthony's harmless, Mom. I don't know why you let him bother you so much."

I don't understand it myself. "He's a-a blowhard," she stammered, "and . . . he's always hanging out in my restaurant, flirting with the girls."

"And spending good money." His eyes were crinkled with amusement.

"Not as much as he could," she snapped.

Byron snorted.

No matter what I say he's going to laugh at me, she thought, flushing. She was still holding the pencil point up in the air. She turned it 180 degrees and blew the shavings on the other side off. Only then did she turn to Byron. She found it hard to spit the right words out.

"It's his hair!" *Finally. I said it out loud.* It looked like she was explaining her opinion to the graphite point. Holly bobbled her head at Byron with comically wide eyes. "You know exactly what I mean." She stuck out her tongue for good measure.

Byron bent over guffawing. He couldn't seem to stop shaking his head. "That was the last thing I thought you were going to say." He was collapsed so far over the desk that he was talking into his lap.

She was rattled. How could she explain herself? It did sound silly. "It's far too long for a man his age. Does he think he's in a glam band from the eighties? And all those different-colored highlights . . . he must go to Providenciales to have it done. The gas alone must cost a fortune."

"The gas?" That set Byron off again. He was slapping his leg. At one point he actually hooted. "Okay . . . well . . . Mom . . . of all things to worry about . . ." Now he was wiping at the tears streaming down his face.

Holly's lips pursed. "I don't know what you find so hilarious. You never saw anyone like that back home in Vermont. A grown man dying his hair?"

He was holding his belly now. "I'll admit it's over the top. But he's not hurting anyone. This island draws idiosyncratic types. From what I can tell, the whole Caribbean does." He pulled a tissue out of its box and finished wiping his face. But when he looked her directly in her eyes, he cracked up again.

Apparently, he was struggling to get control of himself. He

turned away and started busying himself with items on his desk. He sounded quite reasonable when he said, "I guess we all have our things that set us off. I know I do." But when he looked up and met his mother's eyes, he lost it again.

She threw her hands in the air.

"I'm sorry," he said, "but compared to other character flaws it seems so harmless. Maybe one of his girlfriends is a hairdresser and she got carried away, you know? A few drinks, and things got out of hand."

"That's another thing, now that you brought it up. Why is he running around with girls half his age?"

Her face was flushed already. When Byron answered, "Because he can?" she thought her head would burst.

"I can see you feel differently. He just bothers me—okay? Like how you can't stand the sight of any beverage that's red. You're not perfect either, mister."

His smile faded and his posture straightened; he clearly understood that it was time to change the subject. He paused to gather his papers together and tap the bottom of the stack against the desktop. Once the documents were righted, he put them in a blue folder. Then he cleared his throat. "On another, much more important matter, the band will be setting up soon."

"Mark my words," Holly continued on as if Byron had just confirmed he shared her contempt for Anthony, "he will walk down the street to eat a sandwich at the snack bar and then saunter back to listen to our music. Cheap bastard."

He shook his head, though ever so slightly. "People are free to come and go on this island. There's nothing we can do about it. He likes to go place-to-place and visit. To say hello to everyone."

Holly didn't even bother to answer him. They worked in a tense silence under the golden lights of their green glass desk lamps until a very old cuckoo clock struck seven o'clock. When it quieted down, they both heard Byron's stomach growl and laughed.

He swiveled his chair sharply and stood up. "That's enough work for today. Let's head over."

Yes, Holly thought. *Time for a drink.*

Chapter 4

The sky was pitch dark and the bamboo torches around the perimeter of their pavilion were ablaze. Byron and Holly took a table overlooking the pounding surf. Suspended in the crests of the waves, phosphorescent algae glowed like fireflies flitting around on a summer night back home in Vermont.

Neither of them said a word when they first sat down; Holly assumed it was because he, like she, didn't feel the need to. At this moment, she was proud of herself—and Byron, too. Somehow, they had pulled it off. They were living their mutual dream, and—for tonight, at least—it felt great.

Anthony was, indeed, gone. Holly settled comfortably into her chair and let the sound of the waves calm her. The surf sprayed up a mist that washed across her face, making her close her eyes and smile. She didn't change her expression at all when she started talking to Byron. "Since there are two lobster specials, let's each order one of them. That way we can taste both."

This was standard operating procedure for Holly. Since Byron was her child, she felt she could take great liberties with him in any restaurant.

He chided her in an even tone, "You're assuming I want to share."

Holly ignored his comment. She deliberately turned the corners of her lips up and tried to make her eyes twinkle at him. She knew he was used to her picking off of his dinner plates. When the waiter, Kel, came over, she asked him, "Can you bring us some small plates? We will want to divide everything."

"We can split the servings for you in the kitchen, madame."

"Please—mademoiselle." *Why is it so hard for everyone to remember I'm single?* "And don't bother; we like to do it ourselves."

Byron laughed at her, apparently over her use of the word "we."

Fabienne appeared at the kitchen door. She seemed timid and out of place standing there. For some time now, Holly had observed the way she watched Byron and hung on his every word. She felt a bit sad about it, because there were so many other girls coming and going from his life these days. Every new week brought with it an influx of tourists who were out to have a good time. Byron was still so young; he was in the phase of his life where he liked nothing better than to have a late night out with a new woman.

She supposed it was easy pickings for him. He could easily take a tourist off the beaten path—to meet a famous artist, to a local bar on the other side of the island, to hear music at a place that always made him get up and play guitar with them. Byron was a great guitar player. Holly thought that alone must make him something of a girl magnet.

I wonder what song he sings to the ladies when he's asked to sit in with the band?

Holly was sure her son would be horrified to know she also wondered if he had sex with these girls on those first nights out. She hoped against hope he was using protection. She would never dare bring that up with him, of course, as he was now a grown man. Still, she sometimes worried; she didn't want Byron to sacrifice his youth the way she had. Her employers in Vermont—the Trombleys and Montez's parents, Coralyse and Sanford—were what had saved her from complete ruin when she got pregnant. Them and good old-fashioned hard work.

Byron, seemingly immune to Fabienne's presence, called to Kel, "Please bring the conch salad out for a starter, but we won't order our entrees until Monsieur Curry gets here."

Holly gulped and then blinked at him a few times as she rolled his words around in her head. "Your *father* is coming? Why didn't you tell me?"

Byron shrugged. "I forgot. It was a last-minute thing. Dad called and wanted to meet to discuss some land we own up by the lighthouse, so I invited him. I thought we could talk about it after dinner. Is that okay?"

The wheels had already been set in motion, so it would do no good at all for her to argue with him. Once again, she felt disheveled and tired—and, alarmingly, she found her heart was suddenly pounding like a jackhammer.

"Why does everything having to do with Dad have to be a big deal?" Byron asked. "Can't he just come over once in a while?"

Holly shot up from her chair. "Of course. He's your father." *And the last person I want to see right now.* "You just surprised me, that's all. Do you want anything more to drink?"

He held up his beer to inspect what he had left, then shook his head.

Holly flew through the kitchen entrance to the area behind the bar and poured a healthy amount of single malt scotch into a rocks glass. She tossed it down, then poured a second and carried it back out to the table.

Tears stung her eyes as she sipped her drink. *When on earth am I going to get over Montez Curry?*

Chapter 5

S itting across from Byron, Holly blinked back her tears and
tried to appear nonchalant about Montez's arrival, but she
was suddenly deeply troubled that she hadn't brushed her hair
since she'd gotten out of the shower.

*If only I had known he was coming tonight. Maybe I should excuse myself
and go freshen up.*

The only thing that stopped her from doing so was that
she'd found it pitiful when Sameera had done the same thing for
Anthony earlier in the evening. So instead she hung her head and
took another sip of whiskey. The plain truth of the matter was,
she had known Montez for over two decades. No shade of lipstick
or hair brushing would change how he felt about her now.

She'd pretty much tried everything from flirting to ignoring
the man. Nothing had worked. Resigned, she sat back and tasted
the conch salad, moaning quietly with pleasure. It might be the
last pleasure she would have tonight. *Maybe ever again. I don't want
to love Montez, but I do. I'll just have to accept the fact he was the one for me
and I blew it. I'm not sure what I did wrong, but I lost him.*

Holly was a young woman when Montez arrived in Vermont for
a seasonal job. She wondered then if all men from the Caribbean
carried such a light inside of them. He reminded her of a rare
mineral sample she'd studied in science class—a volcanic glass that

had hardened with fine brown minerals trapped inside. Held to the light, it glowed through with a warm color, the chocolate at the center feathering into deep hues of honey at the edges. So seemed Montez to her with his shining eyes and easy laugh. She was spellbound.

Although Montez spoke English, he did it with a lilt in his voice that sounded almost like he was singing when he spoke. It was beautiful to hear and prompted her to ask him, "What do they call people from Grand Turk?"

"Belongers," he explained. "My family and I are native to the island and have historical ties in the West Indies going back many generations. In some of the other British Territories, they use the term Belonger as well."

He then flashed a smile so bright she could still recall all these years later how it had made her tremble.

Holly couldn't believe that after all these years just the memory of that smile still caused her to shiver. She ran her hands up and down the goose bumps on her arms.

"Do you want me to go get a sweater for you, Mom?"

Byron was a good son, but it wasn't like him to be so attentive. She wondered if he felt a bit guilty about asking his father to dinner without consulting her and thought he might do a good deed to compensate for it.

Dragged back into the present, Holly shook her head as she put another spicy morsel into her mouth. She glanced to her left and spotted Montez as he swept into the dining area and then doubled over laughing out loud.

What is he doing?

Holly scanned the darkness near the entrance, only to see Anthony Bascombe join Montez.

Dear God, no!

While it was no surprise that Anthony had been drinking heavily, it appeared that Montez had as well, which was uncharacteristic of him.

Heaven help us all. Holly started to stand up—then thought better of the idea and plopped back down in her chair with one hand over her heart. She was nervous, no question about it.

The sauce of her first course had contained chunks of spices and large flecks of fresh cilantro. She immediately set to exploring the surfaces of her teeth with her tongue in preparation for Montez's arrival.

If Holly had known Montez would be walking in with Anthony, she would have removed one of the chairs from the table so there were only three places available. As it was, the two of them approached rapidly and occupied the two empty seats at her table before she could do anything about it.

Byron's eyes lit up and he tightened his lips together—to keep from laughing at her discomfort, Holly suspected. She grunted when she noticed her two unwanted guests had carried drinks from outside—plastic cups and straws—with them into *her* restaurant. Although she thought it rude to carry in a cocktail they hadn't paid for at the Sand Dollar, it eliminated the need for the waiter to hurry over to the table just as the dinner service was becoming quite crowded, so she resisted the urge to say something about it.

Anthony impishly peered across the table at Montez and then to Byron on his left. They both leaned toward him.

"I'm sorry, lads, but this has to be said . . ." With that, he stared at Holly, though his eyes weren't quite tracking together; the right one seemed to be wandering off a bit.

Confused, she lifted both hands out of her lap and held them up. *What?*

"Christ but you are a beauty, Holly Walker," Anthony said.

"If you were standing up, I would smack you right on the ass, you luscious thing."

Everyone at the table seemed startled, not the least Holly. *Terrific. The guy who wants me is this jerk.* She was fuming, but she pretended to be deadly calm as she leaned forward on her elbows, hoping venom shot out of her eyes, and said, "Then I am thankful I'm sitting down, Mr. Bascombe. Something else needs to be said as well: Did you know I keep a very large aluminum baseball bat behind the bar? In two steps, Fabienne could reach over and hand it to me, and I could knock you out cold." Feeling avenged, she returned to a more comfortable position and added, "By the way, Anthony, I was a regional softball champion in middle school. I led the league in home runs. Most of them sailed right over the fence and into the crowd." She punctuated her not-so-veiled threat with a wink and a hitching noise.

Anthony burst out laughing.

Holly watched him, wearing an imperious expression. She'd always found that making someone crack up was the best revenge.

She took another bite of her salad, which only made him laugh all the harder.

Through his howling, he was somehow able to get out, "What a . . . saucy . . . wench." He wiped tears from his eyes and put a hand on Byron's shoulder. "Again, my apologies, son. I sometimes get carried away."

Byron didn't seem angry at all. In the tone of a man far older than his own years, he said, "That may be true, Anthony, but this is a family gathering in my mother's place of business. There are plenty of other women on this island who actually look forward to your attention. Mom is not one of them. I won't tolerate any more disrespect toward her."

Holly grabbed one of Byron's hands and squeezed it with gratitude before letting go. *I can't believe he has to witness this. His father will never love me—it's not going to happen—and he flaunts it by flirting with other women. The only man I can seem to attract is an old beach bum like Anthony. I always wanted Byron to have a family. A real family. Something I never had.* She tried very hard not to betray her feelings. Her roiling sense of guilt. And shame. Tears, once again, stung her eyes. Thank God no one was paying attention to her.

Montez had a proud look on his face as he patted Byron's shoulder, but it was Anthony who he addressed. "My son handled that well, don't you think? He put you in your place without spoiling a perfectly good evening. Now, don't make me sorry I invited you, Anthony. I do know you can behave when you want to, I've seen you do it. Only last week you were showing off your social graces at the governor's party."

Anthony appeared chastened. "That is true, Montez. Again, my regret is heartfelt. I fear that perhaps I have lived the bohemian life far too long. I shall try to remember how a gentleman behaves." He then turned to her. "I do apologize, fair Holly. I'm sorry."

Sure you are.

Like performers sometimes do, he wiped the palm of his hand in front of his face and waved it back and forth to indicate he was changing character. Then he cleared his throat efficaciously and asked, "How is business doing? I bet you wish you were this busy every night."

She tilted her head to one side. She wasn't as willing to let Anthony off the hook as her son and his father seemed to be. Yet, in the end, she didn't see an easy way out of this meal. *Let's just move on and get this over with.* Without betraying any obvious resentment, she acquiesced to Anthony's attempt to shift the conversation in a new direction.

"Fridays are great, it's true," she answered politely. "We get dinner guests, and then a crowd for dancing."

"Mom and I have been thinking about adding some special events during the week—like a trivia night," Byron added.

Anthony's enthusiasm for the idea was written all over his face. "That should be on Wednesdays. Everyone is ready for a little socializing by midweek. And trivia is good because anyone can join in. I like the sound of it."

"I'm so relieved to know we have your permission," Holly said, her tone dripping with sarcasm.

It only made him laugh again.

The worse I treat him, the more he seems to like me.

Montez held up his beer and they toasted. "To trivia night!"

Chapter 6

When Sameera brought over an order of cracked conch appetizer, Montez stood and kissed her on both cheeks. He held on to her hands as he scanned her up and down. Holly saw Byron roll his eyes in embarrassment. He often said his father sometimes went too far when he was flirting.

"You are so kind," Montez said. "Thank you. And you look so beautiful tonight." He pinched her cheek gently, making her giggle and flip her hair as she turned to go back to the kitchen.

Holly blanched. *Since when is Montez Mr. Affectionate?*

But it was Lord Bascombe whom Sameera gave a long and simmering look over her shoulder when she reached the doorway.

Byron had told Holly many times he considered Anthony to be an authority on the island night scene. He seemed sincere in drawing him in for further consultation about their business when he squared his shoulders and addressed him directly, "Obviously we should do a barbecue night with music, too. That's easy money."

Anthony took a dramatic slurp of his drink. "Yes. Yes. But, Bohio has Saturday night locked up. It would have to be another day . . . what about poker?"

Montez's gaze never left his plate, where he was cutting up a large piece of the conch, as he asked, "What about it?"

"The guys like to get together and play," Anthony said.

"Maybe do it twice a month." He waited silently as they mulled over the idea.

Now Anthony's the quiet one? What on earth is going on around here tonight?

"Mom's a good poker player," Byron informed Anthony, at which Anthony's face lit up like a jack-o'-lantern.

He tilted his head flirtatiously and batted his eyelashes at Holly. "*Is she*, now?"

Montez affirmed his son's statement with a grunting, "Uh-huh." After he finished chewing, he added, "She taught me how to play."

Holly was indeed excellent at poker, and the thought of making money momentarily smoothed over her resentful feelings toward Anthony. Suddenly overcome by a strong urge to prove the extent of her abilities, she got up and went behind the bar to retrieve her poker chips. She'd collected many throughout the years. Two outrageous sets had been given to her as gifts: one had been customized with her name in fuchsia, and the other had a variety of completely naked male models on them.

She returned with her arms stacked, the naked men front and center. "How many people are you talking about? I've got plenty of chips."

Anthony recoiled from the sight of naked men, but he managed to reply smoothly, "That depends. Should it be invitation-only or open to the public?" He popped a morsel of his appetizer into his mouth.

"Why can't we do both?" Byron asked. "We could have a special table for invited guests and then walk-ins could join the other tables randomly or come in and play with friends. Here's a good idea . . . the walk-in players could be offered a chance to earn their way up to qualify for a seat with the experienced group. We'll create a tournament. That might bring them in week after week."

Holly's glance shifted across the three men. "Twice a month on Thursday? We do have a dinner crowd those nights, but it tends to thin out by eight. If we set up the tables afterward it could get to be a late night. A group like that is going to be a drinking crowd." She placed the tip of one index finger to her lips, deep in thought.

Byron looked excited by the idea. "That means big money, Mom."

She loved it when he was this engaged about a project, but she still had her doubts about where the venture might lead. "It also might bring big trouble," she said slowly. "It's not like there are alcohol control laws here on Grand Turk, except on Sunday. The later it gets, the more unruly it could become, especially since we don't really have a closing time."

"You are only saying that because it was Anthony's idea," Byron said, rolling his eyes. "There's such a thing as being too cautious. I like this plan."

"I just like to think things through," Holly countered.

"Let's try this: You be in charge of the big barbeque night and buffet. I'll stay late on Thursdays. Let me handle it. I'm more than capable."

Once again, Montez appeared to like the way Byron was taking charge. He put his hand on his son's shoulder and said, "You might want to hire my cousin Howard as a bouncer. You're going to want a big guy who's tough."

"Two of the men I play poker with are police officers," Anthony added. "As long as they're in the restaurant, I don't see much trouble brewing. That should be some comfort."

Montez gave his son a look. "Call Howard."

Holly chewed on her thumbnail—an old nervous habit. After some mental calculations and reflection, she nodded. "We'll try it out."

Byron gave her a look. "Isn't that what I just said?"

Holly laughed. "Maybe give it two months and see if it's profitable. Whether or not it's worth the trouble in the end. Montez, can you give me Howard's phone number?" She pulled her cell out of her pocket and handed it to him. He punched in the contact information.

Anthony seemed genuinely pleased. He began to spin a yarn about what Holly suspected was his fantasy for the endeavor. "And you, Holly, will play at the head table. Your beauty will be the centerpiece of every Poker Night. And no worries about the late nights—just play until you get tired, then you can bow out."

A light bulb went off in Holly's brain when he said this and her face opened into an open-mouth "ah" expression. "Please don't tell me you expect me to dress up." She took in a breath of air, then blew it out loudly. "I've already worked a long day by eight o'clock at night."

"I think it will set the right tone if you do." Anthony looked at her with obvious admiration and Holly watched both Montez and Byron avert their eyes from the sight of it.

Holly turned toward Montez, whose lips were pinched in thought. "What do you think Montez?"

It took a few moments before he begrudgingly agreed, "I think Anthony's right, Holly. You want to make it a special affair. If you wear a nice dress, everyone else will take notice. The staff should make an extra effort, too."

Byron surveyed their dining room. "You know what else, Mom? Let's switch out our white tablecloths for the red ones on poker night. Maybe red could be a theme. On poker night, everyone tries to wear something red. If it catches on, we could have merchandise made with a logo."

The three of them looked to Anthony expectantly for his opinion. "Red, yes . . . and black. That's very Las Vegas."

"Have you been there?" Montez asked as he leaned back on one arm and put a toothpick in his mouth.

"Of course—I am a civilized and educated man!"

"I consider myself civilized and educated and I've never been to Las Vegas," Holly said.

Anthony sat up straight and, sounding like an emperor, he decreed, "Then your education is not complete. You must go for the experience of it. In the meantime, we will recreate some of Vegas's special magic here every other Thursday night at the Sand Dollar."

With that, Anthony gestured to their waiter, indicating with a circular motion that he wanted another round of drinks.

The foursome had already finished their meal when the band began to play.

They started with a few soft instrumentals as a way to do a sound check without disrupting the patrons' conversations. On that cue, Byron got up and wandered from table to table, saying hello to everyone. He also gave a thumbs-up or down from each position to the front man, who adjusted his soundboard accordingly. When it came time to push the tables back for dancing, the music would be turned way up, as it had to be quite loud to compete with the roar of the ocean.

Local diners outside of the high season tended to be professionals involved in the tourist trade, government workers, and retirees from every country imaginable, though Great Britain's territories were largely represented. English, Australian, and Canadian accents abounded.

As dinner plates were collected and carried away, an announcement was made from the main microphone. "We've had a tradition over the last year here at the Sand Dollar, ever since Holly and Byron took over. We wish to honor it again tonight. Byron Curry has selected a song to get the show going."

Holly had always marveled that Byron never suffered from stage fright. He hopped onto the makeshift stage area, slung a guitar strap over his neck as if he were born to it, and, fiddling with a tuner and turning his guitar pegs accordingly, he began to speak to the crowd.

"You all know my mother, Holly Walker." Two stage lights shone in his eyes as he looked up from the little digital screen of the tuner and tried to find her in the dim light. "Mom? You out there?"

Holly froze at the sound of his voice. She wasn't comfortable being the center of attention—Byron knew that—and yet now she was literally in the spotlight as one of the musicians swung a beam her way. *What is he trying to do?*

She sat alone. Montez and Anthony had migrated to the bar after finishing eating, and were now flirting with Fabienne and Sameera.

Holly had seen Byron play music many times, but this was the first he'd ever acknowledged her from the stage. Not knowing what response was appropriate, she raised her hand like she was back in elementary school. Her mouth was suddenly dry; she reached for her glass of water.

"I've been thinking a lot lately about all that my mother has done for me," Byron told the audience. "I hope she knows how much I appreciate it."

Wasn't he annoyed with me, like, two minutes ago?

"Tonight, I thought I'd do a song to show her how very grateful I am."

With that, he launched into Bob Dylan's "Forever Young."

Holly sat through the lyrics as stoically as she could, though she had to lift the corner of her cloth napkin to one eye and then the other repeatedly. By the time Byron was done and the audience was applauding, she longed to break down and have a good cry.

The problem with that was that all her customers were staring at her with big smiles on their faces. So instead she just blew a trembling kiss to her child and waited until the applause completely died out, at which point she ducked back into the kitchen and filled her scotch glass to the brim.

There was a brief break as the band figured out their set list.

Whew! Holly shook her head. *What a day. What on earth is going to happen next?*

When Holly emerged with her glass of scotch, she stood near the door and watched the band from behind Fabienne, who was tending to the patrons at the bar.

Improbably, Anthony toasted Sameera and Fabienne with his drink by shouting out, "Sorry, ladies. I've never been married—a fact I'm quite proud of."

His proclamation, which had become a refrain, rankled Holly. Though she had never been married either, she didn't brag about it.

As they all clicked glasses, however, the girls hooted as if his exclamation was the most brilliant sentiment ever spoken.

Anthony then held forth with a monologue so long Holly started to time it with her watch.

". . . You see, my father was the great Lord Graham Bascombe and so, I, too, am technically a lord, though I've never lived in England. I'm a much lesser lord than my dad—I think we can all agree on that fine point. Lesser is the very thing that I aspire to be." He held his glass aloft and finished with, "To all the lesser lords everywhere!"

While he took a long pull from his beer, Holly glanced down at the sweeping hands of the tiny oval face strapped to her wrist. Her mouth opened in surprise as she realized his speech had lasted a full two and a half minutes.

Did he take a breath in all that time?

Montez stroked Sameera's cheek playfully and she pushed his hand away, laughing.

The band launched into another song, but Holly could still hear Anthony droning on in a self-aggrandizing manner. From time to time, he stopped to clarify a point in fluent French—the second language of Morocco and the basis of Haitian creole. Both Sameera and Fabienne's postures relaxed at those moments and they beamed at him with adoration. In response to their pretty white smiles, his face became a study in smugness, and it made Holly want to smack him.

Pompous ass.

Her fingers worked quickly, shredding the napkin she was using as a coaster.

Three separate times, she heard him bellow, "What do you expect from me? I'm the descendant of pirates."

Over many years of visits to Grand Turk Island, Holly had seen Anthony gallivanting around with a great many young beauties. Sure, she got that he was charismatic as hell and had the wide-set eyes and high cheekbones of Ernest Hemingway—but he also had a thickening waistline. With each passing year, it stretched a little farther over his belt.

He must live on a steady diet of rum-punch, beer, and fried food. It does not serve him well.

Still, she had to acknowledge that the size of his biceps was impressive. He had great chest muscles, too, though it irked her that he often wore a skimpy tank top to show them off. If pressed, she'd also have to admit you could bounce a quarter off the man's ass a mile high.

Thankfully a Canadian woman shouted out, "Do some Neil Young for us, Byron," interrupting this disturbing line of thinking.

Byron was known for his spot-on imitation of Neil Young. He knew Young's voice. His guitar tone. Harmonica. It was uncanny, really. Canadians loved their Neil, and Byron had the man down pat. When he went into "Harvest Moon," nearly the entire audience crowded the dance floor—including Montez, who grabbed Sameera and threw her hat into the air. You could say what you wanted about Montez, but the man could dance.

An older gentleman who lived on Duke Street motioned to Holly to come out from behind the bar. When she did, he grabbed her hand and led her out on the floor. Even though he moved around with a walker in front of him, he was a pretty good dancer. Despite his enthusiasm, however, he tired quickly, and about midway through the song Holly had to help him to his chair.

Once he was safely seated, she stepped out from under the pavilion and walked down to the beach. There was a cloud of stars above. As always, this made her feel very small indeed . . . and extremely fortunate. A sense of well-being filled her heart.

When she peeked back inside to the gathering, she could see Montez watching her with a smile plastered across his face. He nodded to her and lifted his drink in a toast. He made a big point of singing along with Byron as he bopped his head and stared straight into Holly's eyes.

I'm still in love with you? Really, he sings that part to me?

Holly staggered backwards two steps. *Now I've seen everything.* But then Montez turned his stool back toward the band and their son, leaving her mystified.

She took a few extra moments to step back out to the beach and watch the rushing clouds in the sky. A glorious yellow moon mocked her, as if saying, "Have you seen *everything*, Holly Walker? Have you really?"

She crossed her arms, as the night air was growing cooler. Her blond hair blew behind her as she watched the crowd under the pavilion. The glow of the torches and hurricane lanterns was flattering to everyone present. She wished she'd thought to bring a camera to capture this moment.

Byron and I are creating something beautiful here. Putting our personal stamp on a long-standing business. The events we put on bring people out week after week. And the best part is, the numbers look impressive.

We made it. We moved from the United States and started a whole new life on Grand Turk. We did. My son and me. What could possibly go wrong now?

Chapter 7

Poker Night started at the Sand Dollar the very next week. For three months, a regular group of idiosyncratic characters showed up and bonded with Anthony and Holly over a spirited game of cards. Nothing had ever given her greater pleasure than did lording a good hand over Anthony Bascombe.

By the third event, she found she was growing bolder in her play.

"All in, Lord Bascombe," she said as she pushed her chips toward the center of the table. With a cocky expression on her face, she laid down her hand: a six-high straight.

Exasperated, Anthony threw his cards down, but his banter never faltered. "Wasn't it the great Dutch Boyd who said, 'Poker is a lot like sex. Everyone thinks they are the best, but most don't have a clue what they are doing'?"

Holly put a smirk on her face by way of reply. "And wasn't it the great Paul Newman in the iconic film *The Color of Money* who said, 'Money won is twice as sweet as money earned'?"

He shrugged. "Touché." He appeared only slightly upset by her victory. "I concede your point." He gave her a salute. "Well made."

"Gentlemen, will you please excuse me?" Holly asked as she stood. "I will call it bedtime now. See you next time." She took several steps away from the table, then stopped and spun around with her long red skirt in one hand. "Oh, and Anthony—keep it down out here. That voice of yours carries a country mile."

Montez's cousin Howard opened the gate for her as she headed out.

"Good night, miss."

"Goodnight, Howard."

A light had been left on in the office. Holly went in and turned it off—and then, instead of leaving the room, sank down into her chair and sipped the bottle of water she'd left on the desktop. The darkness and the quiet helped her wind down. She wasn't quite ready for bed.

She could see a couple strolling down the street, hand in hand. There was a security floodlight attached to the roof of the Sand Dollar, but it merely illuminated their outlines. They stood before the gate and Holly couldn't help but wonder if she knew them. It was already so late.

The man turned the woman to him slowly. So excruciatingly slowly. He bent down to kiss her.

Though his face was in shadow, Holly knew it was Montez. Her heart stopped. She remembered his kiss well. Nothing else had ever compared.

Holly collapsed into her cream-colored armchair, then got up and closed the blind.

Chapter 8

It was late May, and high season was over. Holly had just returned from a short trip to Vermont, where she'd had to attend to some paperwork. She'd used the opportunity to spend time with her old employers, whom she'd known since she was a girl. They had become like second parents. She'd stayed on a few days to catch up with them.

It was revealing, to say the least, to hear herself tell them, "Things are great. I can't imagine living anywhere else now. Working with Byron is, mostly, a joy. He's still my kid. We butt heads sometimes. But we're having a lot of fun. We put in long hours, but most of the time it doesn't seem like work."

"Is it hard being around Montez all the time?" Sally asked.

"It's better for Byron."

"That's not what I asked you. How is it for you?"

They were sitting at Sally's kitchen table. Holly was suddenly fascinated by her cup of tea. When she didn't respond Sally said, "Just what I thought."

"Okay. It's taking some getting used to, seeing him out and about. But I don't have many regrets about moving. I'd like to see you and Toby more. Byron and I miss your Sunday dinners."

"Well, one of these days Toby and I are going to figure out how to get away from the farm. You know how much he loves to scuba dive. And I've got about fifty books I have been meaning to read. Can you imagine? Just sitting outside and enjoying the sun?"

The many generations of the Trombley family had lived in Vermont for over two hundred years when Holly, then a teenager, met Sally and Toby. Their original farmhouse was one of the most historic buildings in their town of Woodberry. It was initially built to be on the main road outside of town, but over two long centuries, the city had grown out to meet it. Though the family still maintained enough acreage on the hillside to graze a hundred head of cattle. Across time, the outbuildings were converted to diversify the family's businesses.

They had a beautiful facility where they produced high-quality maple syrup. Their open dairy stand and cafe used both their own fresh milk and syrup to make the soft ice cream Vermonters referred to as a "creemee." They sold their artisan cheeses in their gift shop, where they also carried other Vermont products and crafts. The cheeses were also sold nationwide. Many of their repeat customers came to them with stories of finding their brand name in some of the finest food shops across the United States.

A full-time employee was needed just to handle Trombley's online orders. Every year, the demand was so great around the holidays that they had to hire a second staff member to help. Holly so wished she could get their cheddar cheese on Grand Turk. She'd eaten plenty during her visit.

She put the palms of her hands across her stomach. *I can see all that cheese right there. I have to work on that little roll. Maybe I can dance it off tonight.*

Sally and Toby had turned the main floor of the original Trombley farmhouse into a successful restaurant for serious farm-to-table "foodies." On the second story, there was a two-room office and a separate small apartment. They'd renovated the enormous attached barn into a huge, now thriving, saloon. It was the hot spot in town all year long, but in the high seasons of summer and fall foliage, they took it up a notch by featuring live music nightly and an array of local craft beers on tap. To take advantage of the lodging shortage in their area in the early '70s, the Trombleys had also built one- and two-bedroom cabins. During Holly's recent visit, they'd let her stay in one. What was once a family farm was now a complete tourist destination.

Holly first went to work for Sally and Toby the summer before her freshman year of high school. They still told stories about the Holly they knew back then.

Toby always said about her, "That girl never shied away from any job. Don't ask her to do something if you don't expect it to get done. Do you remember when she worked in the gift shop when she was fourteen?" At this point, he always took off with one of his favorite anecdotes:

"Well, business was slow. She said she needed more hours to make more money and she asked if I had any other work for her to do. So I told her I was trying to move a big pile of hay bales, if she thought she could carry some of them. I showed her where they were and where I wanted them to go. Then I went on with my day and forgot all about it. I finished my work and had dinner later with my family. Afterward, about seven or so that night, I went out to the barn to check on things."

He put the heel of his hand to his forehead every time he told the story, convulsing with laughter.

"It was dark out by then. I only had a few light bulbs going back where the hay was, so my eyes had to adjust to the low light. But I could hear something going on. I remember standing there squinting and trying to figure out what was happening. And what did I see? There's little Holly—still in her skirt and blouse from working in the gift shop—swinging the old cast iron bale hook into the hay. I couldn't believe my eyes. She must've moved close to half the pile by then. By herself, mind you. She was too young for me to even think about letting her use any machinery."

He patiently let the image sink in for those listening to his story. Toby was widely known as a great storyteller.

"Then . . . and this is the best part . . ." He couldn't continue, as he was bent over laughing again. When he eventually pulled himself together, he went on, "She looked up at me and said, 'What? You didn't think I could do it? That just proves you don't know everything.' Without even hesitating, I took out my wallet and handed her a hundred-dollar bill; then I drove her home. She couldn't have weighed a hundred pounds soaking wet at the time." He wiped tears from the corner of his eyes and finished with, "Lord, that girl just slays me."

Six years later, when she was a part-time college student, Holly worked her way up to head waitress in their fancy little restaurant. The Trombleys were accommodating to her class times, and since she wrote the schedule for the restaurant floor, it worked out to be mutually beneficial. Holly's two-year associate degree, which she had to work at piecemeal, took three years to complete. In celebration, Sally had taken her shopping for a dress to wear and insisted on paying for it. In the late spring, the entire extended Trombley family was present to cheer her on at her graduation.

As a gift, they presented her with one of their older family cars. She was moved beyond words. When she found her voice again, she used humor to temper the high emotion of the moment and her thoughts came out rougher than intended.

"I appreciate it, Toby, but I've gotta make sure you're not pulling a fast one," she said. "Do you expect me to take a pay cut in exchange for this vehicle?"

The family members roared at that.

An automobile was the answer to her prayers. In a few weeks' time, she began commuting out to Castleton State College to start working toward her bachelor's degree—all thanks to them.

Toby had learned how to scuba dive when he was in the service. He had gone down to Grand Turk for a vacation the year before Byron was born, and Montez had been his divemaster. Impressed with Montez, Toby had talked him into coming up to work for him during the summer and fall, which was low season on Grand Turk and high season in Vermont.

If not for that . . . Holly sometimes thought.

She hoped she could get Toby and Sally to start coming down to visit on a regular basis, and she said so often. "We have our own dive shop, Toby. And between the restaurant and the inn, Sally won't have to lift a finger. She deserves a real vacation."

Both Sally and Toby had promised to come down someday soon.

I'm going to hold them to it. If I get those two in the habit of visiting every winter I really will be living in paradise. Yes, Holly missed the Trombleys, but she didn't miss the harsh Vermont winters or the stress of her old job as a school counselor.

But the farm was so darn busy. When would there be a right time?

Chapter 9

In her new career on the island, Holly allowed herself two nights off: Sundays and Fridays. Sunday was for rest. This was when she loved to hole up on a chaise lounge and read. Friday was the opposite. She made every attempt to pack it with wall-to-wall fun.

Just a short distance down the street from the Sand Dollar was another inn called Salinas. They had a lush garden courtyard strung with party lights. For many generations, it had been where the traditional musicians would come to play ripsaw—the regional style of music, so called because an ordinary handsaw figured prominently as an instrument—for the public. Some called ripsaw "rake-n-scrape" because the musicians raked a metal scraper along the teeth of the saw to make the unique percussive sound that defined the genre.

When combined with guitar, keyboards, and drums, the effect was riotous, and nearly everyone broke out dancing once the band got going. All the generations came on Fridays. There was no need to worry if you didn't arrive with a dance partner; once the floor filled with people, the crowd moved as one. Many Belongers regularly attended, of course, but so did the smaller expat crowd. And a few tourists always figured out it was the place to be on a Friday night as well.

Over the decades, the musical genre had morphed to embrace popular songs in addition to the traditional tunes. Jamaican reggae was a staple in the Friday night sets, and the band always threw in a surprising and unpredictable array of rock songs for good measure.

It was said that the renowned North Caicos musician Lovey Forbes had come up with the name "combina" to describe a sub-genre of ripsaw that had come about in the early '80s, which blended ripsaw with popular foreign music. Holly liked to tell people, "You haven't lived until you've heard a Rolling Stone tune played on a handsaw."

When she went to Salinas to hear the band, she danced to the point of exhaustion. She also routinely indulged in one too many drinks. Byron had accepted early on that she slept in on Saturday mornings, and was careful to adjust their staff's schedules accordingly. He seemed happy that after all her years of backbreaking work, she was having some fun.

On most of those Saturday mornings, Holly awakened with a light heart, humming the music from the night before. Sometimes she hummed it all day long.

Because everything on Grand Turk Island was brought in by boat, goods there cost way more than they did in the States. Holly had seized the opportunity to go shopping while she was in Vermont, and she'd brought back as much as she could carry in her three "nesting" suitcases. Most of her purchases were linens for the inn, but she'd gotten four new sundresses for herself, too, and—her biggest coup—two semi-formal dresses she'd discovered in a consignment shop, perfect for poker night. She'd also gotten pretty new underwear.

It's interesting how quickly anything with elastic disintegrates in the Caribbean. It must have something to do with the salt air.

It was late afternoon on Friday, May 25th, when Holly stood before her full-length mirror in her brand-new, coral-colored,

The Belonger

A-line dress. *Lace pink panties and bra. My little secret. I don't know why, but they make me feel confident.* She brushed her hair and got ready for her night of dancing.

Since business was light across the island, she and Byron had decided to close down on Fridays for a while and let business fall to Salinas. They'd agreed the success of the music of ripsaw night was a win for everyone in their community, and that it was important to showcase the local culture.

The kitchen of the Sand Dollar had a small walk-in cooler where they stored perishable food. Any day of the week, she could easily carry a plate with her and assemble a meal off the wire mesh shelves, which she often did. Tonight, however, she was in the mood to be catered to, and she found it was good business to frequent other places on island—it encouraged them to come to her place in kind.

The smell of Salinas's special pasta sauce floated to Holly on the trade breeze, making her mouth water. She decided she would have dinner there before the music started. She knew better than to ask Byron to join her at the last minute, as he probably had a date. At some point this evening, she would inevitably see him bobbing across the dance floor with a girl in his arms. She cursed herself for not inviting a friend to come with her sooner, as she truly hated to eat alone and doubted she could find anyone to join her now.

As part of prepping for the night, she had gone so far as to paint her finger and toenails the same coral color as her dress. She thought it looked great with her gold-toned gilded sandals and deep tan.

Bracing herself for a solitary meal, Holly walked the short distance down the street and slipped into the back garden of the café. As she found the mere thought of sitting at a table alone depressing, she decided to take a seat at the bar. She cocked a hip up onto a barstool and set her small purse in front of her on the counter. Tucked in here against the wall, she felt much less conspicuous than she would have out on the open floor.

She caught the bartender's eye immediately and nodded. Before she knew it, a chilled martini arrived before her and she let out a relaxed sigh. The fluted glass was frosted, the party lights were shining, and music played softly. It was an almost perfect setting, until . . .

"Well, hello there, Sheila."

Of course, Anthony *would* take the seat right next to hers.

Holly turned away for a moment to recover from her surprise at running into him so early in the evening. The bartender knew how she felt about the man—as did most everyone in town—and he gave her a knowing glance. In response, Holly threw her hands up and shook her head.

"Sheila? My name's not Sheila." She leaned in and scrutinized Anthony's face.

He nodded knowingly—just as self-assured as always. "I lived in Australia for a while," he said cheerfully. "Haven't I mentioned it before, young lady? Some of the lingo rubbed off."

Holly snorted. "If you're calling me young, you've got the wrong lady."

Anthony chuckled, and it made Holly decide to be polite and make small talk. She liked that it was easy to make him laugh.

She took a sip of her drink, savored the juniper scent of gin. "So I know you lived in New York, and now Australia too. How long ago did you live down under?"

"During my misspent youth. You want to talk about feeling old . . . that was twenty-five years ago. Time overwhelms me sometimes."

"I know exactly what you mean. My child is twenty-three years old. The other day I was walking down Front Street, and as he turned the corner toward me I thought, *Oh what a handsome young man. He looks familiar.* You laugh, but I'm serious."

Still laughing, Anthony took his sweating beer, jumped off his stool, and went over to the shack that served as the kitchen. He began to taunt someone inside playfully, and did so speaking Creole. From inside the building, Holly could hear hysterical, if somewhat muffled, laughter in response. Everyone on her side of the patio was listening to the exchange and smiling.

He has a gift for languages, I have to hand him that.

Anthony wore an exquisitely subtle Hawaiian shirt with a fabric of such quality Holly longed to reach out to feel it between her thumb and forefinger. He was freshly shaven, and as he neared she caught the scent of his citrusy cologne. He carried with him a plate piled high with shrimp and a small ramekin filled with sauce. "This is a gift from Zeus—he's cooking tonight, and he insists we both have the house special as our entree. Are you alright with that? I swear, this morning, all the way over on Queen's Cay, I could smell the pasta sauce. I took a cruise here just for dinner."

"That's why I'm here too." Holly had her long legs crossed. She looked down at her new sandals; some of the beads that were sewn into them coordinated perfectly with her dress and nail color. Though it appeared she was wearing ankle bracelets, the straps were really designed as part of the shoe. She thought they were pretty sexy.

Anthony's head sagged—theatrically and for effect. "I didn't know which would be worse for you, luv: to have me sit down here with you or to have me leave you feeling ignored."

She gasped and blushed from being caught dead to rights.

Discreetly ignoring her discomfort, he continued, "I'm fully aware I can sometimes be rather a dolt."

Holly laughed at his refreshing honesty, although she was still a bit embarrassed that he knew of her misgivings about him.

"You're fine where you are," Holly said to quell her unease. "It's not like we haven't broken bread together before."

Anthony beamed at her. She didn't think she deserved the delighted look upon his face at all. "Bartender," he called out. "What's the best wine you have hidden away back there? Bring it and two glasses." Shifting his eyes back to Holly, he added, "My treat, dear."

"Why . . . well then . . . thank you." The bright red patches on her face took many minutes to abate.

When their plates were delivered, the sight of linguine piled high with chunks of red snapper and lobster—and the aroma that emanated from them—was a delight to Holly. Anthony leaned over, eyes closed, breathed in the rich scent, and grinned. She reached out and squeezed his arm. The sizzling scent of garlic was almost dizzying. On the side of their large crockery plates were fresh greens topped with grilled vegetables. It was a gorgeous presentation that made Holly suddenly feel like she was starving; her stomach even growled so loudly that Anthony looked up at her and let out a "ha!"

She covered her tummy with both hands. "Byron's usually the one who gets going like this."

Anthony nodded. "He's still so young . . . still filling in. That takes a lot of calories. He's a busy man, too. You must be proud of him."

Holly was always thrilled to hear praise about her son.

They both longed to dig into their meal, but it seemed everyone who walked into the cafe stopped by to say hello. Holly felt compelled to stand up every time, shake hands, and exchange pleasantries with each one. On this island, in this community, rudeness was not a thing easily forgotten. But giving every friend the greeting they deserved was time consuming—especially when Anthony was doing the talking, and the friend was a young woman who'd happened by to hug him hello.

The Belonger

The longer they chatted with new arrivals, the more apparent it became that the crowd would only get larger as the night wore on. Holly had no idea how to handle the situation. By now their server had even taken the initiative of carrying their plates back inside the kitchen to put them in a warmer.

Anthony took her arm and whispered in her ear, "There's a table in the side garden. Let's have them bring our meals out there." He swiveled toward the bar. "Bartend! Will you please open another bottle for us? We're moving to a quieter location."

Once he'd retrieved both of their plates from the kitchen, he led the way for Holly. She followed him down the stone path, both their stemware in hand, through the courtyard and over to the south side of the property.

It's quite lovely here, Holly noted appreciatively. And she discovered she was having a good time.

Chapter 10

Holly sat in one of the two wrought iron chairs placed at a matching table. She could smell the fresh white paint on them as she studied the yard. Her appreciation for the spot made her glow.

"I've never noticed how beautiful it is out here," she said. "These shade trees are huge by Turks and Caicos standards." Under their shelter, a cool breeze blew across the yard.

Anthony patted her hand and smiled at her. "As hard as you work, you probably never have a minute to sit still and enjoy the simple things."

Holly warmed inside at the realization that he understood that much about her. Yet she felt conflicted when she thought about him and his day-to-day life. *I wonder if he knows what hard work really is. Compared to my old job, running the Sand Dollar is a piece of cake. He wouldn't know how to do what I do. He's so entitled.*

To change the subject, she said, "Now that I know how gorgeous this garden is, I may ask Erica if I can bring a cup of tea over in the afternoons. It's so private. It can be a mini-getaway from my own business." She took in a deep breath and let out a contented moan.

Anthony nodded in agreement. "I've never had the knack for gardening, but it doesn't stop me from admiring those who do."

They sat together tranquilly, in a comfortable silence. She

thought this was unusual for him but she didn't feel at all compelled to entertain him, to be anything more than what she was at this exact second. She let her gaze drift, taking in the greenery surrounding them, and noticed something that interested her. "Look at those succulent plants. With their thick, shiny leaves, they look like they are bursting with something wonderful."

Anthony became suddenly quite animated, as if inspired to disclose an important thought. "For a bit of time, I was fascinated by reports of 'afterlife experiences,'" he shared. "You know . . . when someone is declared dead, but they're brought back to life. Many of these people go to what some would call heaven. The stories are remarkably similar. One observation given over and over again is that when you get to the afterlife, you can visibly see a life force surging through every living thing. Witnesses' descriptions of plants have always been especially fascinating to me. Now, don't laugh, but I think I feel the force they are talking about when I'm surrounded by nature like this. I'm rejuvenated. It gives me a charge of something. Look at my arms—I've got the chills just talking about it. I suppose that's why I love to scuba dive as well. To me, every creature that lives in the ocean pulsates with life."

Holly let out a tiny "ooo" and, nodding, said, "I've often said the same thing. Nature feeds me. I didn't know about the afterlife experiences . . . but that's so intriguing. You know, I've never been diving."

Anthony put his hand over his heart and leaned back in his chair. "How is that possible? You've been coming to Grand Turk for years. What economy exists here is driven by divers coming to explore our pristine coral shelf. How is it that you've never seen it?"

Considering this, Holly took a sip of her wine. "When I started coming to the island, Byron was a baby. As wonderful as his grandparents are, I didn't think I should just waltz off and leave them to take care of my infant for a big chunk of the day. Babies are a lot of work, you know."

"I don't personally know that from any extended experience." Anthony coughed. "I can imagine, though."

Holly drew a scribble in the condensation on her wine glass with one finger. "Money was always an object. Until very recently, I struggled to make ends meet. I had a mortgage to pay and a son to raise. Montez did what he could to help, but he didn't have much back then either."

Anthony leaned toward her, but he didn't comment. A blood vessel in his temple pulsed, giving the impression that he was thinking very hard. In the silence, with their unspoken but clearly shared intention to be at peace, they enjoyed the food, wine, and the magnificence of the garden in the fading early-evening light.

So maybe I'll never get married, Holly thought. *It's not so bad, is it? I'll enjoy the company I do have. Not expect anything more. Maybe I'm meant to be a loner, but that doesn't mean I can't have fun.*

After Anthony took his last sip, he held his glass in the air, signaling the end of their meal. "Let's step out front and watch the sunset," he suggested. "It will be any minute now."

He opened the gate for her and made a sweeping motion with his arm, indicating that Holly should step through. They sat side by side on the low seawall that ran along the other side of the street, facing west. There wasn't a cloud in the sky.

"Conditions are perfect tonight," Anthony noted.

She knew he was referring to the possibility of a green flash occurring, and she agreed. "Maybe we'll get lucky tonight.

"Legend has it," he began in a pompous tone, "once you've seen one, you'll never again go wrong in matters of the heart."

"You've seen at least one before, I'm sure," Holly said, giving him a smirk.

He nodded. "Of course. Many. I grew up here."

"So much for the legend about matters of the heart, then." She stuck out her tongue at him. *My gosh. I'm flirting.*

Anthony bulged his eyes out comically. "No need to spoil the moment."

She leaned toward him as they both laughed. He was fun. She had to admit it.

She gasped as the sun's rim turned that rare shade of green. Only then, in that fleeting moment, did she realize she'd been holding her breath. "Oh, oh, oh," she cried as the green faded away, throwing her hands in the air. "My God, it was like a movie. Like there was a director standing there with a megaphone, shouting, 'Cue the flash!' I watch the sunset every night, and it happens so rarely that it gets to the point where you think you must have been mistaken—that the green flash really doesn't happen at all."

She turned back toward him; he was still in an almost-squatting position on the low wall.

"Anthony," she said softly, her throat closing up—and then, to her surprise and his, she sat down next to him and hugged him.

He put his arms around her but faced straight ahead, his body stiff. "It *is* beautiful," he said, "every time. There's no doubt of that."

"I didn't expect to be so moved," she said quietly as she released him.

Her eyes filling with tears, she put her elbows on her knees and buried her face in her hands. Anthony patted her twice on the back. She straightened up, wiping her eyes, only to collapse back down again, now sobbing. He stroked her back slowly with one hand.

"Geez," she muttered, hiccupping the way a child does when they are spent. "Sorry to be so emotional. You know, the last time I saw a flash was when Byron asked me to move to Grand Turk and I came here to talk to him about it."

No longer stiff, Anthony gathered her into one shoulder and put his arm across her back. He pushed the hair away from her eyes and kissed her forehead gently. It felt so natural that Holly relaxed into him. He had a marvelous scent that had nothing to do with his cologne.

"Don't ever be sorry to shed tears of joy," he said. "We're all handed plenty of reasons for the other variety. The wonder of the great outdoors . . . frankly . . . is what I have always loved most in this world."

She leaned against him, spent but content. *He really has tried to become my friend. Mine and Byron's. He has a strange way of going about it, but he has tried.*

The strum of a major chord on an electric guitar filled the air. She heard an amplified voice call out, "Sound check. Sound check." A snare drum shot out a sharp crack like a lightning strike. Someone on a bass guitar played a long run of deep, punctuated notes, joining the overall clamor. Holly's entire body tensed, anticipating the start of a song . . . and abruptly, there was silence.

Until the band's drummer, who could clearly hear the crash of the ocean swells from across the street, began to mimic them on his cymbals. Every clang sounded like a wave crashing onto a sandy shore.

There were two Jamaican men in Cockburn Town who kept horses they took down to the cruise center in the mornings and rented to tourists to ride. They suddenly appeared on the street between Salinas and the beach next to the Sand Dollar. Just as Holly noticed them, the band's percussionist began playing a woodblock, echoing the sound of the horses' hooves hitting the ground.

The instant the horses had gone far enough away for the clomping noise to fade, the first verse of Bob Marley's song "One Love" burst forth—and then died out—on the evening air.

The Belonger

Anthony lifted himself up off the seawall with a groan and extended his hand to Holly, his eyes smiling down to where she was sitting. "They'll be starting soon. Shall we go in?"

She took his hand gratefully, thinking, *I'd better wash the tracks of my dusty tears off in the ladies' room sink before the dancing starts. I must look like a lunatic.*

Chapter 11

Holly sat at her restaurant with a cup of black Dominican coffee against her forehead. She was nursing a major hangover. A tall glass of water sat on the table before her, condensing droplets streaming down the outside and saturating the paper coaster underneath it.

I wish I could rehydrate myself as easily as that paper.

A flock of bright pink flamingos flew overhead in a V-shaped formation. The sight of them momentarily brought Holly out of her haze of misery. When a second flock sailed by, she stood and walked toward the gate to watch them. It was then that she saw her son, sauntering toward her from the south, and knew he'd spotted her too.

She couldn't even bring herself to nod to him. She simply dragged herself back to her table and sat down.

In a matter of seconds, Byron plopped down in the chair across from her. If she was not mistaken, he was laughing at her.

"*You* were dancing with Anthony Bascombe last night?"

Holly put on her large-framed sunglasses and turned away from him, toward the ocean.

Undeterred, Byron pressed her. "How exactly did *that* happen?"

She waved one hand in the air and stammered, "Well, um . . ."

It was hard to remember it all—let alone describe the evening to her son. Finally, she said, "We had dinner. I find he grows on you after a while. We watched the sunset . . . then the music started . . . Byron, please, you know I need some peace on Saturday mornings."

He was laughing so hard at this point his head was on the table. "But seriously—Anthony?" With his elbow up and the back of his hand pressed to his mouth, he waited patiently for his mother to say more.

Right now, Byron's mere presence annoyed her. *Look how hard he's trying to contain his amusement. Probably certain there is quite a story to be told here.* She took in several swallows of coffee without comment. Byron just sat there with an expectant stare. As always, she couldn't help but admire the color of his gorgeous green eyes.

Finally he asked, "So?"

"You obviously missed the part where he left with a gang of his young girls." Holly rolled her eyes. "You're not getting anything else out of me. Go away. No, wait, I have a better idea: Let's talk about *your* night last night. Where are you coming from at this early hour?"

It was rumored that Byron was spending time with a scuba-diving cougar from Texas over at Bohio. Holly knew perfectly well that he was not about to discuss such a thing with his mother. She'd hit the mark perfectly; she got the silence she was longing for.

Surrendering for the moment, Byron stood up and started walking across the road, still chuckling.

"I can hear you," she yelled at him.

He stopped in the middle of the road and started whistling a song.

Holly drew in a sharp breath at the sound of it. She knew the tune; it was Gershwin's "I've Got a Crush on You."

Byron stopped whistling, and started singing it. She couldn't see him at this point because he was blocked from her sight by the kitchen. However, she could hear his tenor voice clearly, if a bit muted, singing about a handsome Romeo.

Holly jumped out of her chair and started running after him, calling out, "You little shit! Stop. Someone is going to hear you." But she laughed as the words left her lips.

Byron's only response was a jaunty salute; with that, he ducked inside the inn.

Sunday morning found Holly feeling much better. She stepped out her front door and surveyed the ocean for boats. Was there a cruise ship gliding in? If so, she would keep the Sand Dollar open for extended hours during lunch today. Whose sailboat was anchored offshore? Was it . . . ? Yes, Henry and Kristin were back! She was sure they would be by soon to say hello. She made a mental note to check to make sure she had their favorite lager in stock at the bar. How many dive boats were running trips this morning? *Hmmm.* Business looked good. And there were already two groups of snorkelers out by the wall—a great place to spot the migrating turtles, dolphins, and humpback whales who used the passage next to it like a superhighway. The entire chain of Turks and Caicos Islands sat on top of a relatively shallow underwater plateau. The natural reef growth had led to the creation of many canyons and swim-through spots over the years—great for snorkelers and divers.

As she stared out in that direction, Holly saw a shiny new boat anchored nearby, bobbing and swaying in the water. She took in the cut of it proudly, for it was Byron's new boat *The Halcyon.* He'd named it after a mythical sea bird that never came close to shore and, according to legend, nested at sea about the time of the winter solstice. It was also said it had the power to calm the ocean waves.

Everyone on island commented regularly on the similarities between Byron and Montez. When he was Byron's age, Montez's parents had already inherited large tracts of land. Much of it was oceanfront, on some of the most beautiful beaches on earth. After several international travel writers fell in love with Grand Turk's unspoiled beauty, the real estate market suddenly picked up. But the Currys found the old expression, "You have to have money to make money," to be true. In order to develop their property, they needed cash—to hire surveyors and attorneys, and even just file with the government of Turks and Caicos for the necessary permits.

Montez was only twenty-one when he took Tobey Trombley up on his offer of high-paying work in Vermont and flew to the United States to make money. The only reason he strayed so far from home was so his family could work toward selling their land. Though he was horribly homesick, Holly watched him work determinedly that season to make his family's dream come true.

Coralyse and Sanford had told Holly many times that Montez had always been industrious. When he was only a child, his astonished parents listened as he described his observations of how, although business owners were the most prosperous people in town, dive masters did well too. He wondered aloud what he could do if he had a job like that. As his parents told the story, he had no problem getting hired on at the dive shop to wash saltwater off the equipment at just ten years old—and since they only needed him a few hours a day, he went to the place across the street and asked for work there, too. For two years he could be seen running between the two businesses every day, trying to please both of his bosses in a timely manner.

It was a town joke that he'd sent up clouds of dust behind him as he sprinted back and forth across the dirt road several times a day. The image of the little boy so captivated the locals' imaginations, his name became a catchphrase. If anyone seemed to be in a hurry, they would say, "Hey, *Montez*, you got to slow down."

By the time he graduated from high school, Montez was the manager of both of those dive shops.

Although it seemed to Holly that Byron was not as driven as his father had been at his age, he sent up plenty of his own dust clouds as he motorcycled his way from his father's building sites to Duke Street and back again. Between the projects he did for Montez, his work at the Sand Dollar and inn, and his new venture running excursions for scuba divers and snorkelers, he was a busy man. His grandparents got a real kick out of how similar Montez and Byron were, and when they talked about it in Holly's presence her chest swelled with pride at the man her son had become.

Smiling, she listened to the gentle knocking sound of Byron's anchored boat as she tightened the laces of her running shoes. She swept her long hair back in a ponytail and jogged in the direction of the seawall.

On her morning runs, she always passed the same small crew that was responsible for keeping the waterfront avenue—which, for some historic reason she didn't fully understand, changed names from Duke Street to Front Street to West Street the farther south she ran—clean and swept. She usually passed by three different portable radios as she went as well; apparently, the music helped ease the physical labor of the road cleanup. From Holly's perspective, it was a riotous soundtrack for her already beautiful morning routine. Merengue, bachata, and hip-hop Creole music were turned up as high as the little receivers could go; the effect was scratchy, but infectious and lively. Yesterday morning, however, she had noticed something different happening, and here it was again today: instead of music, the workers were listening to the news, and the reception was perfectly tuned in.

Over the panting sound she made as she picked up speed, she could only catch snippets of the reports as she passed by the wrought iron gates of the majestic Grand Turk Inn. The word "intensifying" jumped out at her as she swept by, followed by, "Huge storm . . . storm surges . . . strong winds."

The last radio in the sequence of three was usually placed at the crossroad where the biggest seawall began. As Holly climbed up onto the wall, the name "Nestor" was announced loud and clear on the breeze, though she couldn't make out anything else said by the announcer.

On her way back home, running down the shady side of the narrow lane, she noticed the laborers were gone. Holly knew her world on Grand Turk was something of a bubble, and it was one she embraced wholeheartedly. The consequence of her isolation was that she often missed big news stories—but if she were being honest, that insulation from world events only added to the tranquility she treasured on island. Ignoring the news was a big part of what had made her historically intense anxiety a thing of the past. But something important was clearly going on, and she should find out what it was; she made a mental note to look at the news online when she got back home.

Today, Byron was supposed to be hosting a boat party to celebrate the purchase of *The Halcyon*. He'd invited both his parents and grandparents to cruise with him over to Queen's Cay, where they would have lunch. Holly thought it more than likely that Henry and Kristin would be invited along, too, once Byron realized they were back in town.

She stopped short in front of Salinas and looked at the ocean. *The water level is high, isn't it?* Her internal clock unconsciously registered the frequency of the waves and they seemed off to her too. *They're moving . . . faster than usual.* She sprinted the rest of the way home to retrieve her cell phone and call Montez.

He grew up here, she thought as the phone rang. *He'll know if it's anything to worry about.* But Montez didn't pick up.

She glanced across the street and saw Fabienne standing in the middle of the restaurant's floor, riveted to the screen of her own phone, her eyes huge and her lips wide open in an oval shape.

Holly's heart leapt. She bolted across the lane and grabbed one of Fabienne's hands. Based on the woman's expression, Holly was certain that someone close to her had died; terrified, she pulled a hand to her heart in empathy and asked, "What is it? What happened?"

Fabienne's huge, dark eyes shifted to Holly's and her face grew slack. The voice that came out of her twitching lips was unfamiliar, wooden and deep. It made the hair on the back of Holly's neck stand on end.

All Fabienne could muster was two words: "Hurricane comin'!"

Chapter 12

"How will I *protect* you, Mom?"

Holly winced at Byron's tone. She couldn't ever remember a time when he'd raised his voice to her.

She arched her back and planted her fists on the backs of her hips. "I'm the mother here, let's not forget. It's *my* job to protect *you*."

She knew she was in the right. Of *course* she was right. She had been Byron's mother for many, many years. But the certainty of her position faltered when he stared down at her, an anguished expression on his face. As he reached out and drew her into a hug, Holly could swear he was sniffling, though she wasn't sure because his face was buried in her hair.

"You are a strong woman, Mom," he whispered. "Everybody knows it. But you are also just a tiny little thing."

What he said was true—and Holly thought he was kind to leave out the fact she was also growing older by the day. Only yesterday, she'd leaned in close to the mirror and noticed that some of the blond hairs at her temples had grown white. *Even so, I am more than capable of looking after him*, she thought stubbornly. Despite the uncertainty Byron's desperation caused her, she—as was her lifelong habit—consciously willed her backbone to become steel.

When she pulled away from her son and planted her feet wider, he threw his hands into the air and turned away with a gesture that said, "Come on!"

"I'm not leaving you, Byron," she said. "I won't back down."

In response, he folded his arms across his chest with his head bowed; he looked like he was barely managing to hold himself together.

Holly was embarrassed to spot Anthony across the dining area. He was near the bar, in the shadows, and he obviously could hear everything she and Byron were saying as they stood at the overlook to the sea. She thought perhaps he was trying to give them a moment to hash out their disagreement, but he was clearly restless.

The urgent problem, the dilemma, was Hurricane Nestor—a category five hurricane of potentially history-making power that was reportedly headed their way, although you wouldn't know it if you were to judge by the current weather. Except for the rise in sea level Holly had noted earlier, it was a gorgeous September day.

"Mom, Anthony's mansion has stood for centuries. The safest place you can be during the storm is over on Queen's Cay. You know it's always said that it's a hurricane hole."

Holly scrunched up her lips. "That's an old wives' tale. And just where will *you* be?" she challenged him. "During the storm, I mean."

"Dad's been staying with Mami and Papi until his new house is ready. It's being built to hurricane specifications and it's all steel-reinforced concrete. I sure wish we could go there, but . . ." Byron looked down, seemingly embarrassed, as he said this, though Holly wasn't exactly sure why that would be the case.

His grandparents' house on Middle Street was a fragile old thing made entirely of wood.

"Well, Coralyse and Sanford can't stay at their house," she said. "They're lucky it hasn't blown down already." Her eyes grew a bit misty. "They can all come here. We'll hunker down together. Why would I want to walk away from Grand Turk now, when everything is at risk? A good chunk of my life's savings is sunk into this place. Not to mention, you are my only child."

To her, this seemed like a reasonable sentiment, but deep down she knew that in addition to wanting to stay with Byron, she was comforted by the notion of Montez protecting her, just as he'd done in the past.

Holly had long idealized a particular night from her time working with Montez in Vermont all those years earlier.

She was having a beer in the Trombley's saloon after a long day when a man staggered across the room toward her. She put a hand up and said, "Look, buddy . . ."

"Drew. My name is Drew."

She would never forget his ravaged face.

The next thing she knew, she was overpowered by the stench of his hot breath on her ear. "You are one pretty girl. I can tell you're a natural blond. Natural all over, I bet."

As he let out a laugh that sounded like *gyuh, gyuh, gyuh*, Holly flung herself as far away from him as she could go—so far that she almost fell off the backless stool.

She shuddered when he picked up a lock of her hair and stroked it with his fingertips. "You've got blue eyes, too," he slurred. "You're every guy's wet dream."

Reflexively, she pushed him away, hard, though it didn't move him an inch. Frightened, she held her hands up, palms forward, as a sort of peace offering. "Uh . . . thank you . . . uh . . . Drew, but I'm visiting with my friend Jillian here." Holly motioned to the bartender. "I work for Toby and Sally Trombley. The owners of this place? I just came in to relax. I'm not looking for a date."

Drew let out a low chuckle and stepped back—to leave, Holly thought. But instead he just shifted his position to stand behind her. She didn't realize he was still there until she heard him growl, "I've got something that'll help you relax."

With that, he circled his powerful hands around her waist and yanked her rear end tightly into his crotch. He had some nerve, including the audacity to slowly push his groin into her backside.

In shocked silence, she locked eyes with Jillian, who wore an expression that said, *What the hell is he doing?*

As Holly gripped Drew's wrists and tried to pull his hands off of her, she saw Jillian dive under the bar—looking for the Louisville slugger she kept down there, Holly assumed. In the moments that followed, she and Drew engaged in an awkward struggle that set her hips rocking right to left and back again on her seat.

If anything, he seemed amused by her resistance. "You can fight all you want, little lady, but you can't get rid of me that easy."

It dawned on Holly only then just how drunk Drew actually was—and in fact she thought he might be high on something as well, because the one look she got directly into his eyes made her think that he was crazed. She began to hyperventilate. It was exactly like a recurring nightmare she'd had since she was a small child. As hard as she tried, she couldn't make herself scream. Though she gulped air in, no noise would come out. Her exhalations were short and spastic.

"Yum," Drew said as he slid his hands up her torso.

Holly saw stars and worried that she might faint. She struggled with him with all her might, though she felt the muscles in her arms tiring and giving way.

Instinct must have taken over, because she finally yelled out, "Jillian!"—and, with the help of the adrenaline coursing through her veins, managed to twist and turn away from Drew to keep him from reaching her breasts. Gritting her teeth, she glanced around the bar for help just as the couple across from her finally caught on to what was happening.

The man stood up but the woman with him put a hand on his arm, keeping him where he was. "Honey," she said, "don't get involved."

Holly felt crushed. *So much for women helping each other.*

To control her thrashing, Drew pulled her in tighter. Just as he lifted her off the stool in a suffocating backward bear hug, a piercing bang echoed through the nearly empty dance hall—the sound of something hard hitting the floor.

Holly later found out that Montez had been returning some equipment to a storage closet near the entrance door when he saw what was happening. In an instant, he was storming toward her aggressor—beating Jillian, who was coming around the bar with her baseball bat, to the scene.

With a powerful hoist, Montez threw Drew off Holly and the jerk flew forward and to their right. Drew landed on his stomach across the bar and a graceless "uhmp" sound exploded out of him. Holly numbly thought it was fortunate for him that he had missed impaling his face on one of the pointy beer taps. Before he could recover, Jillian let loose with the clear swing she had been waiting for. Her aim was good; she hit his left shoulder and also knocked him across his ear and the back of his neck.

Drew's friends were up on their feet. "Drew! Jeezum Crow! We can't take you anywhere."

Jillian held her bat up and stared at them in a way Holly thought was meant to be threatening, but Holly could tell her friend was trembling. At the same time, Montez reared up to his full, intimidating height of six foot three and pulled his shoulders back like he was daring the other men to come at him. Panting, he glared at Drew, who had now turned himself over and was holding a hand to the side of his head.

Holly was still on her stool trying to calm her breathing. *Don't you dare cry.*

She noticed that instead of confronting Montez, Drew screeched at Jillian. "You hit me, you goddamn bitch! My frigging ear is bleeding."

You deserved far worse than that, you ass, Holly thought. *Thank God Montez came in.*

"You're done here," Jillian jeered at Drew defiantly, clearly pleased with the outcome of her efforts.

Still mumbling curses, Drew peeled himself off the bar. Holly was happy that he looked foolish and weak as he slouched away. Though he scowled at her, she couldn't help but observe that he didn't dare look at Montez.

Coward.

"Let's get out of here before they call the cops," one of Drew's friends shouted.

Drew whined until the moment the heavy front door shut behind them with a clunk.

Except for the quiet gasping sounds Montez and Jillian were making, the bar was silent for a long moment.

Finally, Jillian recovered enough to state flatly, "Him lying on the bar like that—it was a bad angle for me to be able to really hurt him. If I'd had a better shot, I could've taken his head off. Montez! Lord, you should be on some kind of Olympic team the way you hurled him in the air." Her shoulders began to heave as she let out a nervous laugh.

Holly noticed that her fingertips and toes, which had been totally numb just moments earlier, were suddenly tingling. The roaring in her ears was quieting, too, and that enabled an array of thoughts to explode in her head. She leapt up from her stool. "Are we going to call the police?"

In response to the question, Montez frowned and Jillian grew thoughtful.

"I think that's up to you, Holly," she said. "I'll support whatever decision you make."

"Well, I don't want him coming back in here, but I don't want him arrested either. I don't want to turn this into a big deal . . . maybe Toby and Sally will somehow decide it was my fault." *Or, she worried silently, everybody might side with the local boys—and where will that leave Montez?*

Jillian picked up the bar logbook. "I'll record the incident so you'll have a paper trail if you need it later."

"We have to tell Toby what happened," Montez said with a nod. "It wouldn't do to keep it from him."

Although he sounded confident it was the right thing to do, Holly wondered if he was concerned about the security of his job just the same. She also felt nervous for Toby to hear about this.

"Really?" She made a face. "Oh, Lord. You know he's never liked me hanging around in here. This will just be more ammunition for him."

Montez asked Jillian for a beer. As they all watched her pour it for him, he spoke out of the side of his mouth toward Holly. "Toby sounds like a wise man to me."

She bristled. "Nobody is going to tell me where I can and cannot go," she said. "I didn't do anything wrong, Montez."

Holly never did stop coming into The Saloon at night. Instead, by some kind of unspoken agreement, Montez made it his habit to come over after closing the restaurant. When Toby thanked him for the extra hours he put in watching over the bar at night, Holly had a sudden thought that sent a thrilling chill down her spine: *He's not watching over the business. He's watching over me.*

Holly had observed that men tended to protect the ones they loved. After the experience with Drew, she assumed that Montez's feelings for her ran deep . . . that he was as crazy about her as she was about him. Yet when October came, he went back home and started his real estate project as planned, and she spent many years trying to rekindle his interest and attention.

▶▶▶

As Holly's mind came back to the present, to her grown son standing in their place of business and begging her to get off-island for the duration of the storm, her heart still raced at the memory of what had happened that night at The Saloon. She took a breath and told Byron in no uncertain terms, "I'm staying here. On island. With you."

He turned his eyes away. Was he blushing?

"If you asked Dad, he'd agree, Mom. Obviously, this is your home too, but . . ."

She noticed his averted gaze again. "What's going on?"

Holly could see he hated to be the one to give her the news. "Dad's got a serious girlfriend."

Holly received the blow with a lurch of her head and a sick feeling in the pit of her stomach. She knew Byron would assume she would be upset by the idea. When he was only five years old, he'd told her, "When Dad's around, your eyes are like a light bulb that got turned on." Since then, she'd tried to be less obvious about her infatuation with his father—but he was her son. He knew her better than anyone else in the world.

Montez had dated other women before, but the relationships hadn't lasted, and Holly had always managed to cope with the ups and downs. She'd thought things would continue on as they always had, indefinitely. Perhaps that had been foolish.

She'd heard some rumors recently, of course, but she'd refused to give them credence. Had she been silly to ignore the news on the street? Had she indulged in blatant denial?

Holly watched as Byron glanced over his shoulder to check on Anthony's position before leaning close and whispering, "Dad said, 'I'd like you to spend some time with her soon. Some time away from the business. Just family.' He looked at me so seriously. He said, 'She's a keeper.' That's something that's never happened before. I'm sorry, Mom."

"What did he mean about the business?"

"It's Sameera, Mom."

A single sob escaped Holly before she could stop it. She jerked away from Byron and walked over to another railing so her back was turned to him, one fist pressed to her mouth while the other wiped at the tears escaping her eyes as if they had a life of their own.

Holly turned her focus to her son and wondered how this must all make him feel. After what he'd just told her, she couldn't deny that Montez must really like Sameera. How could that be?

She suddenly remembered something a mutual acquaintance had said to her a week or two earlier: "Don't be surprised if there's a wedding coming. I've never seen the man smitten before."

Gee, thanks so much, Holly had thought at the time—and then she'd filed the comment away in her vast pit of denial.

She now realized how insulted she'd felt—how insulted she felt now. For twenty-two years, she had been the only long-term relationship Montez had had with any woman, although it had become platonic after Byron was born. Holly supposed she was proud of their long-shared history, but now, once again, she had overestimated his intentions toward her . . . to say the least.

She turned back to Byron.

He spoke his next words tentatively, as if he hadn't told her the worst news yet: "There's something more important than our family and our businesses, Mom. Have you heard the talk? People are saying undocumented workers will not be allowed into the shelters."

A moan escaped from Holly as her problems were quickly put into perspective. Many on Grand Turk lived in ramshackle shacks that could barely keep them out of the beating sun, let alone a storm.

"No, no!" she wailed, grabbing the sleeves of Byron's shirt. "That can't be right. The cabins they live in are no protection against that kind of wind. They are the most vulnerable among us."

"That's why, if it's true, I have to help out," Byron said firmly.

"We have friends and employees who came to Grand Turk to work and to send money back home to Haiti and the Dominican. They really have nothing. If they need a place to stay, I could secure the main house and they could camp out in the dining room. It's huge. But we don't know where this could lead . . . what will happen after? If things get bad enough, there could be looting . . . and I don't know what else. It's different for me: I'm a man, I'm young. I'll be fine."

"That doesn't even make sense; being young doesn't protect you from the power of a hurricane," Holly spat out, clenching her fists, although her fierce determination flickered when she thought of a young woman who helped them with the cleaning at the inn and her precious toddler.

"Byron, you can't make yourself responsible for everyone," she insisted. "What if something goes wrong? What if someone dies?" She couldn't get the image of a baby's frightened face, terrified by howling winds, out of her head. To her surprise, she dissolved into tears.

"Mom, the main part of our inn is solid stone," Byron said gently. "The new roof was put in after the hurricane of 1866; it has been almost impenetrable for over a hundred and fifty years. It's leaked, sure, it's been repaired and resealed, but it hasn't blown off even though we've had, what, fifty hurricanes and cyclones since then? Even if the outer parts of the building sustain damage, there's a couple thousand square feet of safe space in the core building."

He may have felt confident, but to Holly he looked smug.

She imitated his expression back at him. "I like your logic. I will stay with you in our perfectly safe space."

This is no time to leave my community behind. Or my businesses. And certainly not my son.

Chapter 13

Holly had her hands on her hips when her phone chimed. It was Montez.

"Yes?" Holly answered.

"Hello, Holly," he said. "I am calling to find out where you are riding out the storm."

She glared at her son. "I'm staying right here with Byron, of course. Where else would I be?" She stepped away so Byron couldn't hear the words they were about to have.

"Are you sure that's a good idea? He's going to have enough to deal with without having to worry about you, too. The old folks are saying Grand Turk will get the worst of it. You would be safer on Queen's Cay."

She was outraged to think Montez knew all about Byron's plan to send her away *and* that he would ask her to abandon her entire world based on the hearsay of folk tales. "They don't know where Hurricane Nestor will land or even if it will make landfall," she snapped. It seemed everyone, including Anthony, had been talking behind Holly's back—and she didn't like it.

"Let's not take any chances, Holly. Get off-island with Anthony and go to his house. I'd . . . consider spending the storm together, but . . . I've got my parents and my . . . girl . . . friend."

Holly clenched her teeth. She wasn't going to make this easy for him. "Your *what?*"

"Okay. I understand you're surprised. I should tell you, she's not just a girlfriend. I'm afraid I've fallen in love. With Sameera. You know I've always had a thing for her. It looks like I finally won her over."

Although Holly continued to listen, she did so bending over, with the back of one hand held up to her mouth. She felt like the world was spinning. "Why haven't you told me this before now? This is a small town. You've made me look like a complete idiot. In front of my employee, too."

Not only was she the last person to know he was serious about another woman, that woman was her head chef.

Montez sounded contrite. "Yes. I would've told you, but she and I haven't been dating long. Nestor has forced my hand, I'm afraid. I want her with me so I can keep her safe. I'm sorry, Holly. You've never lived through a big hurricane before. I'm sure you don't realize it would be awkward for her to have you in such close quarters, possibly for days on end."

"Even though the quarters that you mention are mine?"

He cleared his throat. "It's Byron's home too. And he is my son as well. The money he used to buy his half of the business was from a trust fund I started for him. I feel I do have some rights. Anthony is proud to take care of you over on Queen's Cay."

So everyone, including Anthony, had been talking behind her back. She didn't like that one bit. Her face flushed into what she knew were ruddy patches. "I have two hands, Montez. I can take care of myself." In her embarrassed state, she couldn't stop herself from adding, "Like I always have."

With that, she hung up.

Years earlier, when Holly had announced to Montez that she was pregnant, he'd told her he was overcome with shame. There couldn't have been a worse thing for him to say.

"I was lonely and far from home," he said then. "That isn't an excuse, but I see I've made a terrible mistake. Now, you will pay the price for it."

Fuming, she went back to her doctors and asked how it was even possible. She had done everything they'd told her to prevent pregnancy. She was committed to getting a bachelor's and then a master's degree . . . and she had to work full-time while she did it. How could she become a mother while trying to do all that?

In the end, she was left with an overwhelming decision: would she carry this baby to term, or not?

When Montez finally brought himself to confess to Holly that he wouldn't marry her, she pointed out, "We have bigger fish to fry than whether you love me or not." It popped out in anger, as the most blatant truths of her life often did.

It hadn't been easy. But Byron had turned out to be the best thing that ever happened to her.

Holly was torn away from her memories when she heard the sing-song ring of Byron's phone go off. He never really uttered a word. Instead, he kept repeating, "Uh-huh," until he said a final "bye" and pressed his red button.

She watched him closely, worried about how worried he looked.

He took a deep breath before he turned from his phone toward her. "Mom, we insist. It will all be over in a few days. It could even be fun for you. A nice change of scenery." He lifted his eyebrows in a look that was both hopeful and questioning.

As charming as Byron was being, Holly had no intention of caving on this issue. She pulled her shoulders back and crossed her arms—and, quite unexpectedly, a strange-yet-all-too-familiar sensation came over her and she lost her balance.

It was as if the entire planet had tilted. The line of the horizon was now vertical, and her field of vision was covered with flashing lights. She grabbed on to the back of a chair as the room spun faster.

Oh no . . .

And she was hit by a wave of vertigo that dropped her to her knees.

She bent herself in half and put her cheek down on the cool cement floor.

Anthony sprinted toward her. "What on earth?"

"Sometimes, when she's really upset, she gets dizzy," Byron explained.

From the floor, Holly watched Anthony lean down toward her. His mouth moved, but she couldn't understand a thing he was saying to her; strangely, the only things registering in her brain were the questions he was posing to Byron, and Byron's responses.

"How long does this last?" Anthony asked with great concern. "She looks like death warmed over."

Byron leaned over her too. "It doesn't happen often, but it can be on and off for a day or two."

Holly lifted herself up onto all fours, willing herself to hold in the contents of her stomach. After a moment, Byron handed her a bottle of water.

"I'm sorry," she whispered. "I'm so sorry." She swept away a couple of tears.

Anthony stood in front of her head, gesticulating wildly. "Byron, how do we help this poor girl?"

Her son got down and spoke softly into her ear. "Can we move you? Can you make it to the house?"

Holly nodded, though she had no idea how steady she would be on two feet.

To Anthony, Byron said, "She has to have calm and rest if it's going to pass."

Byron took one of her arms and began to help her up, but before Holly could find her balance Anthony swooped her up in his arms. Byron seemed to respect the efficiency of the move; without a word, he motioned for Anthony to follow him to the inn.

The three of them made their way across the narrow, dusty road, through the wooden gates, and through the tall double entry doors, which were flung wide open. Once in the foyer, Anthony followed Byron along the hallway that led to Holly's small apartment. She was mortified by all the fuss, yet she couldn't deny she was still feeling pretty helpless.

As Anthony laid her down gently on her bed, Byron opened her closet and took a look inside.

"Mom? Where's your suitcase?"

The weakness had overcome Holly to the point where she could barely speak. She had been sick like this many times before, and each time it was disabling for a while. She didn't have the strength to fight Byron any longer.

She motioned Anthony closer. "My physical therapist says that being in the water can help vertigo," she whispered. "She was always trying to get me to join a gym with a pool. Do you think it's true?"

He looked surprised. "I do. In my experience, it definitely helps seasickness. The coolness of the water, and something else to focus on besides the nausea."

"Will you take me out? I don't want to just lie here and have it roll over me again and again. I'll be happy to try anything."

Anthony put his hands on his hips and looked down at the floor in front of him. When he spoke, it was with certainty. "I'll handle this, Byron. I know you have a lot to do before the storm hits."

Byron didn't stop moving as he scurried around the room collecting things for his mother to bring with her. "I can't thank you enough."

Mary Kathleen Mehuron

As Anthony stuffed the items into a bag he said, "You better get to the Do-It Center soon, or all the plywood will be gone. I'm going to load your mum on the boat and head out immediately. You two best say your goodbyes now."

In addition to being nauseous, Holly suddenly felt horrified, "Byron," she said through a sob, "what if I don't see you again?"

He looked at her like she was crazy. Her son, at his tender age, still felt the misguided omnipotence of youth.

"Mom—for heaven's sake! Nobody is going to die." He sat on the edge of the bed, near her knees, and took her hands in his. "We'll both be fine. Just head across the passage to Anthony's house and get some rest. I'll see you in a couple of days."

She reached up for his face. "Honey . . ." She was not going to the other island. She was going to take a good long swim, and when she felt better, she would come home. But he didn't need to know that right now.

Her mattress was old and soft, and she was sunk down into the middle of the bed. Byron leaned over to embrace her.

If he's hugging me, he must really be concerned. Pull it together, Holly Anne Walker. Don't be such a baby.

Sameera appeared at the bedroom window, pressing her face against the screen. She made a monster roar and then laughed.

Holly barely reacted to her little performance.

This seemed to irritate Sameera so much that she hissed at them all before saying, "A hurricane is coming. Get your ass in gear, Holly."

She can't wait to be alone with Montez.

Byron gave Sameera a malevolent look. "You just go on and mind your own business. I'll take care of my mother." He gazed down at Holly with an expression so sweet that even in her distress, she couldn't help but smile back at him.

"Anthony's got a stash of food—probably rum, too, if I know

him at all," Byron said quietly. "His house will be quieter for you. One more hug and then I've got to run. There's a lot to do."

He leaned down again and she held him close for a long, long time. When she finally let him go, he patted her shoulder and then turned to Anthony. Glancing at the window, Holly was relieved to see that Sameera was gone.

"Thank you again for your generous offer to take care of my mom," Byron said, clasping Anthony's hand in a firm shake. "I'll see you soon."

Anthony pulled Byron in for a brief hug—which only alarmed Holly further. She knew full well that Anthony was the only one of the three of them who had survived a massive storm before. It was obvious he saw the situation as grave, and she noticed he wasn't promising they would all see each other again in a couple of days.

Anthony stoically clapped both of Byron's shoulders. When he let go, he cleared his throat several times and wouldn't look Byron or Holly in the eye.

Holly had heard many stories about the hurricanes that had passed through Turks and Caicos. Many lives had been lost here, and none of those storms had intensified to the level of a category five like Hurricane Nestor.

God help us all.

# Chapter 14

Holly must have briefly fallen asleep, because the next thing she heard was Anthony's voice saying, "Here. Suck on these ginger lozenges. They work great for nausea. Even though the water is shallow and fairly calm, it may still feel a bit choppy when we get out there. Especially if you already feel sick to your stomach. Maybe the ginger can settle it down before we reach the reef."

The gentleness of his tone was soothing. "Thank you."

"You are very welcome, my dear."

Holly sat up slowly and scanned the room for her bag. "Did you take my knapsack outside already?"

"It's safely aboard. I'm sorry to rush you, but do you think you can walk now?"

She nodded. "I can make it that far." Gripping the headboard for support, she stood up slowly, testing herself."

"Good. We should go." Anthony studied her with a doleful look on his face.

"Where did Sameera get off to?"

"I didn't ask her," he said. "Given the recent news, I assume to find Montez."

As hard as Sameera had chased Anthony in the past, Holly found it interesting that he didn't seem to care one whit about her. And even more surprising that Sameera had apparently changed from desiring Anthony to desiring Montez in a heartbeat.

The Belonger

"Did you know about her and Montez?" she demanded.

He nodded, though it was clear he took no pleasure in it.

"Why didn't you tell me? I thought we were friends."

"I didn't think it my place. And to be honest . . . I knew you would be upset. At my very core, I am a coward. Hate confrontation. I suppose I worried you might kill the messenger."

Holly stood and massaged her temples, hard, as if holding on to the sides of her head would help her keep her balance. Anthony's arm around her was surprisingly secure and she moved easily with him. Once they started walking, she clasped onto his shirt with one hand. Her body was so tense she took in a deep breath and exhaled slowly, to try to mitigate the feeling she was hanging on for dear life.

He must have felt the extent of her panic, because he asked in a coy voice, "Do you know what my T-shirt is made of Holly?"

She knew he was trying to distract her, but the oddity of his question amused her, so she played along. She scrunched up her face at him and guessed, "Umm . . . cotton?"

"No, beautiful girl, boyfriend material."

She let out a long laugh that nearly knocked her over. Anthony stopped walking and held on to her patiently.

Through a stifled chortle she said, "This is not a time to flirt."

"Nonsense. It's always the time for that." He gave her shoulder a squeeze as he led her down the beach.

If this hurricane doesn't get the best of me, this man just might.

Squinting against the bright sunlight reflecting off the white sand, Holly saw a tandem sea kayak at the shoreline. Handling her like she was made of fragile glass—which made her feel slightly foolish—Anthony steered her in the little boat's direction. After he helped her into the front cockpit of the kayak, he gave her a life vest.

She pushed it away. "It's too hot. I'm going to suffocate if I strap it on."

"Put it in your lap then . . . just in case," he said. "We don't know how dizzy you'll get when you're sitting on top of the waves and getting tossed around."

Snorkeling had better turn out to be a real cure. It's more trouble than I thought it would be.

She took the vest from him and he pushed the rig off the beach. It made a raspy, scraping sound as it slid into the water.

Just past the breaking surf, the shelter of the enormous coral wall surrounding the island kept the surface relatively calm, but they had to get past the crests first. Holly watched as Anthony waded in thigh-high, pushing her and the kayak ahead of him. He got batted around by the currents, but he had the strength to keep his balance. At one point, she saw him tilt precariously far to one side, threatening to topple over, but with a great push he managed to break through the crests and keep himself upright.

It looked like Anthony was still touching bottom, though he was now in chest-high water. He jumped and pulled himself up on his belly over his cockpit. After a few moments of recovery time, he got himself all the way on the kayak and into a sitting position, though the route there was neither elegant nor very athletic.

She was just happy he managed it without capsizing both of them.

They were sitting on top of the swells now, and with a few powerful strokes of his paddle, he easily got them the rest of the way to his boat, *The Angel Fish*.

Anthony used one hand to keep the kayak steady and one hand to help Holly along as she scrambled up the ladder. Once she was on deck she sat on a padded bench, gasping for breath, and watched as Anthony hauled up the kayak.

I am useless. He's doing all the work. The least I can do is make conversation.

The Belonger

"Are we going to Little Barrier Cay? Seeing it again will be one good thing about this mess we're in."

"It's the closest place to go," he said, nodding. "If you don't have some wildlife to study while you're swimming, I don't think my remedy is going to work very well."

He used a towel to dry his hands and face and then left her for a moment to go to the front of the boat. Her heart raced as she clutched the ginger candies and prepared for the worst. Although the trip was relatively short, she knew things could get rough once the boat crossed over the Great Wall. She felt exposed up on deck, but she knew lying down below would be a mistake, as it would make her feel the rocking of the waves more intensely—not to mention she would also be breathing the exhaust from the engine down below. For now, she would stick it out here on the bench.

The movement of the waves lulled her and made her eyelids heavy. She was spent and she longed to rest, but she fought against it. The bright sunlight caused intense pain behind her eyes. She could reach the railing of the boat from where she sat, and she clenched on to it as her stomach roiled.

Hold yourself together . . .

Over and over again in her mind, she recited, *Just ten more minutes. Just ten more minutes. Just ten more minutes.*

Monumental fortitude got her across the shallowest part of the water, but it turned out the grit she had summoned was futile. As the engine revved up and they moved farther away from the shoreline, gasoline fumes rose up and overpowered her. In the end, she couldn't fight the spasms that took hold of her gut: she stood and threw up violently over the side of the boat as she held on for dear life.

She was mortified to discover that in the process of getting sick, she'd also wet her pants.

Talk about adding insult to injury. I would say this day couldn't get any worse, but I don't want to tempt the universe.

Holly turned and saw Anthony studying her from the helm. As another retch threatened, she bent far over the side of the boat once again.

The sound of the engine changed; Anthony was slowing down.

He probably thinks I'll pitch myself overboard.

She raised her head in time to see a small, sandy, and very much deserted island come into view straight ahead of the boat. It was lovely. The water around it was a much lighter turquoise than the deeper ocean, making it possible to see the coral reef that encircled it. Anthony was heading right toward it.

A man—Anthony's buddy Matius, someone Holly had met before—appeared on deck. Anthony handed over the wheel to him and came down to join Holly.

"Point of fact, I couldn't picture myself alone trying to take care of a woman in distress," Anthony said, gesturing toward his friend.

Despite her temporary ill health, Holly had never thought herself as being defenseless. She fully intended to give Anthony a piece of her mind . . . when she felt well enough to do so. For now, she just offered him a half-hearted shrug.

"Matius serves as my first mate when I run fishing and whale-watching expeditions," Anthony explained. "He'll watch the boat while we swim."

Holly knew many accused Anthony of only working when he felt like it. It was an inside joke among the locals. She had some idea about the price of excursions he ran, since she had her own dive shop. *Even though he's working part-time, he's still doing pretty well. His tourist jaunts easily keep him in spending money for his nights out.* She smiled. *And cash for me to win on poker night.*

They reached the coral shelf surrounding the little island and Matius hurried to unfold a small anchor, which he tossed away from the boat and into the green-blue water with a great splash. Once the anchor was secure, Anthony brought a beaming Matius over to Holly.

"Matius knows the sea as well as anyone. Better than I do, in fact."

Matius was a virtual ray of sunshine. She guessed his demeanor had a tempering effect on the melancholy Anthony sometimes seemed to endure. And it was fun to watch how much Anthony enjoyed the opportunity to talk with Matius in Creole, Spanish, or French—depending on their mood, she supposed. *Handy way for them to communicate if they don't want me to know what they're talking about, too*, she thought wryly.

She caught them in the act when Matius asked Anthony in French, "*Est-elle une hystérique?*"

"No *she* is not in any way hysterical," Holly said. "*Je te comprends.*"

Though Anthony gave her a guilty look, he abruptly switched back from French to Creole for a few more words with Matius before ducking downstairs into the cabin.

When he reappeared only seconds later, he had two masks and two sets of fins.

"Let's hope this works," he said.

"Yes," Holly said, "there's so much work to be done. I hate being the little woman who swoons."

Though the sky was a brilliant blue, the ocean swells were higher than Holly remembered from the last time she'd been out that way. She could taste the tang of salt on her tongue and smell it in the air. She had tried to secure her hair back in a rubber band, but the wind kept pulling tendrils loose and whipping them into her eyes.

Still supporting her weight against the side of the boat with both hands, she was hit by another wave of nausea. It seemed as if her knees might buckle at any minute. She bent over the side with her eyes closed, praying for mercy. When she opened them, she fixedly stared down at the water until she sensed Anthony standing next to her.

He leaned close and whispered in her ear, "Let's try it. I've brought hundreds of people out on fishing trips and some always get sick. The surface of the water is kicking up already, but it should still be an easy swim in this shallow water."

"You think so?" Holly was hopeful, though her pulse picked up and her shoulders sagged at the thought of swimming in her condition.

"We'll start slowly," Anthony assured her. "I'll be right there with you. At the least, you'll feel cleaner once you swim." He handed her the mask and fins.

A small stain marked the crotch of the shorts she wore over her bathing suit. She was mortified that he knew she'd peed a bit when she threw up. She was grateful he didn't say more. She went toward the ladder, slipped off her shorts, and threw them in the water. Without a moment's hesitation, she jumped in after them.

Anthony followed her with a splash.

As Holly lowered her mask and put her face in the water, she smiled. *This is like a scene out of the most beautiful travel show you could ever imagine. That, or an expensive aquarium that's blown up to be larger than life. It's almost unreal.* Corals of various colors formed natural statues and rays of light filtered through the water in ever-changing patterns. As they drifted along in the turquoise current, three spotted eagle rays swam below them, close to the ocean floor.

Anthony took Holly's hand and pointed to the rays. He had a huge hand, like a teddy bear's paw. His touch created a surprisingly warm sensation inside of her. When Holly woke up every morning in her new life on Grand Turk, she felt fabulous—cozy, calm, free of aches or pains—and she realized with a thrill that she felt that way now. She could have held Anthony's hand and floated with the current forever. When he reached out and patted her on the cheek, she wondered if he felt the same way.

The rays moved as if they were flying; they resembled the eagles Molly had seen at home in Vermont—if an eagle had an extraordinarily long tail and a face like a stunted dolphin. One of them settled down in the sand with its entire body curved and cupped into the ground. Bulbous eyes protruded out of the top of its round, snouted head. It looked like an adorable alien sitting there. Maybe a creature from Mars.

It's just extraordinary.

Though Holly knew the rays had several venomous stingers they could use when threatened, she'd also been told they were quite shy by nature. She was more than content to float quietly above them, near the top of the water, and observe their behavior. The shifting beams of light were a mere backdrop to the animals' majesty. Turning her head for the best angle, the gentle swaying of sea fans and the hues and shapes of the coral lifted her heart. In fact, as time seemed to pass slowly below her, she filled with happiness.

She'd been horribly ill just moments ago; now she wondered, *Have I ever been more content?*

It took some minutes before reality invaded and she remembered this was not a travel show, or even a vacation. It was an outing designed to prepare her for an impending and dangerous storm. All of Turks and Caicos was bracing itself for the possibility of a state of emergency. They should be moving on as soon as possible.

She lifted her head from the water and signaled to Anthony. When he swam to her, they pulled their masks up to rest on their foreheads so they could talk.

Holly calmly treaded water. "You were right," she said—nearly breathless, but in a good way. "I feel much better than I did before."

"Happy to hear it," he said with a smile so bright it rivaled the sun overhead. It was a grin that faded as he looked up and searched the sky. Holly wondered if the weight of their predicament, with all its peril, had been suddenly thrust upon him too. He had a resigned look on his face.

He spoke so quietly Holly had to swim closer to hear him. All she caught was, "We'd best go back, then."

"Thanks for the offer to go to Queen's Cay, but I'm going back to Roseate House," she said. "There's just no point. I won't leave Byron. Or The Roseate, to be honest." She clenched her jaw.

He put a hand across his face and briefly began massaging it. His eyes were closed. "Obviously, I can't argue with you . . . you know your own mind. I've been weighing the options myself. My childhood nanny is still alive and on Grand Turk. I will want to check in with her when the storm passes. My house is already closed up because I've been over here for a few weeks. Matius has family here, but I'm not as fortunate. Might I stay at Roseate as well? You will find I'm a handy guy to have around. Handier than you might have imagined, given all the hurricanes I have lived through."

It's the least I can do. And the truth was, the idea of Anthony hunkering down with them sounded perfect to her. She had her own apartment, where she could separate herself from the group when she chose to. And when they were gathered together, Anthony could serve as a buffer between her and Montez. Friend to both. Great comic relief.

"That would be fine," Holly said.

With a nod, feeling confident, she repositioned her mask and took off toward the boat.

Chapter 15

The swim worked miracles. Holly felt completely restored to her usual self. How had she not known about this quick cure before? It could have saved her many hours of suffering. Of course, Vermont was landlocked. No turquoise ocean to jump into up there.

Thank you, Lord. She was going to need her strength to get through the next couple of days. But she could do it. She was suddenly sure of that.

After scrambling back on board, Anthony said, "I've got to go take the boat inland. Through the passage into North Creek. I'll take you ashore and you can rest, Holly."

"I'd rather come with you. I feel fine now. Better than fine." It had been a long time since she'd seen the interior of the island. She was always so busy. And she hoped she'd run into Byron, who was no doubt bringing *The Halcyon* into the creek right now as well.

She felt the opposite of helpless now. Instead, she was renewed. And interested in a bit of adventure, too. "I bet after we tie the boat up, we can catch a ride home from North Creek."

"But what if we have to walk back? It's a bit of a trek, truth be known. Are you sure you're up to it?" He stared into her eyes with what she read as genuine concern. The intensity did not surprise her at this point, but it was still a tad unnerving.

She nodded. "It's amazing, really. If I ever get vertigo again, I'm going to tell Byron to hand me a mask and snorkel and throw me in the ocean."

"Ha! Happy to be of service." He gave her a short bow. "As you wish, then. We'll drop Matius off on shore and head to North Creek."

Belying its name, North Creek wasn't a running stream but a 340-acre lagoon with a fairly narrow opening from the sea. At the southernmost end was a narrow channel whose shores were scattered with docks, posts, and platforms. Holly counted seven other, much smaller, boats already tied up. She wasn't sure why this area counted as shelter. "Are they really safe in here?"

Anthony shrugged. "Historically it's worked well for most middling storms, but there's no guarantee against hurricane destruction. But . . . it's all we have—isn't it? And certainly the best we can do against Hurricane Nestor. The boats are valuable, sure . . . but Holly? Only a few thousand people live here on Grand Turk. If I lose *The Angelfish* in the next days, it will be inconvenient for me. Absolutely. But if we lose a life . . . it will hit many people. Hard." He cocked his head. "By the way. That rumor we heard about undocumented workers not being allowed in the shelters? Just that. A rumor. One thing we can stop worrying about."

He secured his boat between four posts that were cut from old telephone poles and embedded into the bottom of North Creek. When he finished tying the ropes off at each corner, he jumped, tucked in a cannonball position, into the water closest to shore with a loud splash.

Three different varieties of pelicans scattered in surprise. The reddish and great egrets expressed their concern as they stretched their long legs and necks to warn him with their full height. Especially annoyed seemed a small flock of flamingos, who displayed the width of their wingspan at him. The terns that were present filled the air with a screeching *awwwkkeee!*

Standing in the water, Anthony motioned for her to climb down the back ladder. "Just watch for jellyfish. They sometimes make it up this far."

Holly made her way down quickly, but it was with some difficulty that they both waded through the chest-high water toward land.

Holly watched vigilantly for jellyfish as they trudged along. "I got stung once," she told Anthony. "Afterward, I did some research on jellyfish. Did you know they have thousands of stinging cells in their tentacles?"

Anthony made a wincing face as he laughed. "Oh, yes. They have laid me low before. Such intense pain. And the blistering—ouch! Did you get that striped pattern on your skin?"

Holly listed to one side just then, and he reached out and grabbed her hand. Once he got her righted, they plowed ahead.

"No," she said, "it wasn't that bad. Maybe we should stop talking about it—it's freaking me out. Just a little bit."

He let go of her hand—and reached out and gently pinched her on the back. She jumped and let out a tiny scream, but when he laughed she did too.

They both grunted from their exertion as they neared the bank. Groaned as well.

"We're in the clear," Anthony declared in a relieved voice. "Not to worry; we're almost there. The stripes I was asking you about? I got them once. They're actually punctures. The rash they caused made me weak for days. Fever and muscle spasms like I will never forget. It was miserable." A wasp started flying around his head. Ducking, he shouted, "I'm allergic to the damn things."

"Many people assume you are hard as nails," Holly said,

laughing. "But it seems Lord Anthony Bascombe is extremely sensitive to anything with a little venom."

He laughed out loud. "Including Homo sapien females. Don't you forget it. Women don't cause raised red welts—not most of them, anyway—but the way I feel when they are done with me is far worse."

Holly giggled. They reached the bank and she let out a whoop of joy.

As if they'd choreographed things ahead of time, Anthony wrapped both hands around her waist and she jumped as hard as she could at the same time. He pushed her up, she made it onto the high sand and scrambled to her feet.

"Let me help you now," she said, offering him her hand.

He shook his head. "I'm not taking us both down." As he climbed up the slick surface of the bank, Anthony's foot slipped and he crashed down face-first. "Jaysus," he cursed softly under his breath. "I am old, fat, and completely out of shape."

His biceps are rock solid though, Holly thought. *He's still a powerful man.*

Once he made it up on the bank, he shook his head and looked at his feet. "Walking home in these wet water shoes is going to give us blisters on the bottom of our feet. I forgot about that. I shouldn't have let you come."

Holly didn't argue with him, but she didn't say anything either. She had not gotten the encounter with Byron she had hoped for here in North Creek. When she finally got to announce to her child that she was staying put, she would be drenched in sweat.

The two wound their way around a narrow sand path through a buttonwood grove, which on a cooler day might have seemed quite lovely. The rapidly soaring humidity made her feel irritable as she slogged along after Anthony, one foot in front of the other.

The Belonger

They flagged down an elderly couple in a golf cart and hitched a ride on the bench seat in the back. They were about halfway home when the couple said they were turning in the opposite way of The Roseate.

After another thirty seemingly endless minutes walking in the baking sun, Holly's old mansion stood before them in the distance.

Chapter 16

The sight of The Roseate with the rows of stone-rimmed Salinas to the left of it, like formal gardens leading up to the house, perked her up a bit. As they drew closer, she couldn't help but admire the remnants of the wooden windmills that had once moved shallow water along to hasten the evaporation of their ancient salt crop. The beautifully made stone walls lining the giant, rectangular ponds were still intact, as were dividing walls that broke them into smaller, geometrically similar chambers.

She nodded her approval while she paused and took in the sight. "Anthony? How long have these walls held?"

"Almost two centuries."

She already knew this. She just wanted to hear him say it out loud. "Wow." Her eyes scanned left to right. A 180-degree view. "Now that's craftsmanship!"

Anthony seemed lost in thought. "The family that built The Roseate was never given an opportunity to come up with a name for the house because locals immediately gave it the name it has now, due to its similarity in color to the roseate spoonbill. Have you seen one?"

Holly shook her head.

"You may have and mistaken it for an extremely vibrant flamingo. They're not as common as flamingos. There used to be more in the old days, but they're still around. A few rather famous photographs have been taken with the birds in the foreground and your house rising behind it. I have a large framed print in my dining room; I'll show you sometime."

"I have one in my living room like that," Holly said. "I wonder if yours is the same one?"

As one might expect, there were beautifully shuttered windows and deep porches on the north and west sides of her inn. Holly had never given a thought to closing the shutters until now. "I wonder what kind of shape the hardware on the shutters is in."

"I suspect it's in good shape. The previous owner lived through his fair share of storms."

Where there was a door opening, it was built tall and wide and hinged in a way that its hand-carved doors could be left open to let in the cool morning air. Holly pictured herself coming out the front door to the porch with her morning coffee and she smiled. She was a long way from New England.

The first floor was built like a raised cellar—which, given the prediction for record storm surges, comforted her. Stone steps were built to each entrance, wider at the bottom and becoming narrower as they ascended. *Welcoming arms,* she remembered. Someone had told her years earlier that this was the term for them—and she saw the sense in that, because she did always feel they were welcoming her home. The crowning glory of the house was the stepped white mansard roof, which gave it the most classic of Caribbean lines.

"Almost there," she said.

"Brace yourself, young lady," Anthony warned. "The last thing Byron expects to see is *you* walking through the door."

She braced. "Not to mention Montez. This may be the first time I've ever really stood up to Montez Curry—but this is *my* house. And Byron is *my* son. I raised him pretty much on my own. Montez will just have to deal with the fact that I am staying here on Grand Turk."

Anthony snorted. "Dealing with it and liking it are two very different things."

Holly felt Anthony watching her gaze into the distance. Seeming to read her mind, he said, "Yes, that house is still glorious after hundreds of years. The family that built it came here for the fortune to be made in the salt trade. The shameful truth was no one in their right mind would choose the punishing work of raking salt, so our entire production was contingent on buying slaves. It is their 'illustrious' ancestors who brought the first African slaves to Turks and Caicos. Mine too. I have spent an entire lifetime carrying the weight of that inescapable fact. I am unceasingly conflicted about the glory of my old house and the fact that blood money was used to build it. It's a dark thought, I know, but if this hurricane is as massive as they claim, so be it. Perhaps it's time the slave-owners' houses are destroyed once and for all."

Rendered speechless by this disclosure, Holly was grateful she didn't have to say a word as Anthony went on with a pinched look on his face.

"I would like to take a DNA test to see if there's any part inside of me that isn't Caucasian English or Irish. How delighted I would be to find it was so. Most of the people I've grown up with—my closest friends on Queen's Cay—are black or of mixed race. What is most difficult, for all of us, I'm sure . . . is some are even related to the slaves my family originally brought with them. That's something to grapple with, believe me. I don't know whether to hang my head in shame all the time or pretend it never happened." He cast his gaze skyward. "In the end, the cost of the enterprise turned out to be far greater than any profits my family made. It was a complete waste—of lives, of effort, and, what is worse, of their dignity. Even so, our family came to love Queen's Cay and we could never entirely leave. As sullied as our name is, we now live as neighbors with the people we once exploited, side by side."

Holly staggered for a moment. She decided not to even presume she could come up with any kind of sage response to Anthony's disclosure, so she let her silence speak for itself.

She was dripping wet and tired now, but she reminded herself how lucky she was. *Many don't have the luxury of taking shelter in a building raised up twelve feet from the ground. I'm glad to be here to help where I can.*

A sudden gust of wind made the branches of a dead tree rattle. Small pieces of the brittle wood fell to the ground as if the tree was an old-fashioned fortune teller throwing bones. They landed in the sand by her feet in a spiral pattern. Looking down at them, she shuddered.

Anthony took her arm and surprised her by saying, "I need to rest for a moment."

It seemed a shame to stop now, as they were so close to the house and the shady interior with its thick stone walls. It couldn't be a good sign that Anthony was asking to halt out here in the blazing sunlight. She looked at him closely; he was bent over with both hands on his knees, turning green around the gills.

Uncertain as to her next course of action, she left him where he stood and ran ahead to her outdoor shower, where she saturated a small towel with water and pulled a bottle of water off the shelf where she stored a case of them.

Anthony had lost his sunglasses when he jumped into North Creek. He shielded his eyes with one hand against the brutal midday light and stumbled toward her and The Roseate, one slow step at a time. She opened the front gate for him and held it. Though he still seemed unsteady, he kept plodding his way along. When he got close enough to see her clearly, she held up the washcloth and water as motivation.

He managed a laugh. "What are you doing out here, girl? Haven't you heard there's a hurricane coming?"

Holly laughed in response. Just a little too loudly. Profound relief caused the borderline hysterical edge to enter her voice. For if Anthony was joking around, he probably wasn't having a heart attack. They'd made it home.

She rushed forward to greet him. "If you're fool enough to be walking across the island with a hurricane forecasted, I guess I can be outside too."

She opened the water and handed it to him. He gratefully accepted and gulped it down while she toweled off his face and the back of his neck with the wet cloth.

He pulled away and stared into her eyes in a way that made her heart race. "Never before would I have taken you for an angel," he said softly, and he kissed the back of her hand tenderly.

She felt the kiss deep in the pit of her stomach as she stepped closer. She embraced him, knowing full well he would be damp with perspiration, and whispered hoarsely, "That's an exaggeration and you know it. You helped me and I'm helping you. It's as simple as that."

Holly was seeing another side of this man, a side she very much enjoyed. *He's suddenly adorable. Once we got on that boat he turned into another person.*

"There's a bottle of shampoo and a bar of soap in the outdoor shower. Get in there, cool off. Give me your dry-bag and I'll lay out some clean shorts and a T-shirt for when you're done. Sorry if it's not the outfit you'd hoped for."

Anthony grinned wickedly. The weathered creases around his eyes cut deep. "Yes, because on this day, which will surely live in history, fashion is what is most important."

Terrified at this oblique mention of Nestor, Holly knotted her hands together. She found she could put the power of the hurricane out of her mind for long periods of time when there were tasks to be done. But then anxiety would come rushing back like a mental cyclone. More than once this afternoon she had prayed that she could stay strong—Anthony didn't need her to fall apart on him. Her internal agony about facing Byron was particularly daunting. She was thinking of her child when she asked, "How bad do you think this weather is going to get?"

"No way to know yet, lass."

A cryptic half-smile lifted one side of her face. "Lass? What's that all about?"

Her expression must have been what made him chuckle. "My family sent me off to Ireland to go to school when I was a boy. I've picked up habits everywhere I've lived."

"That explains a lot about your accent and speech patterns. I've been trying to place their origins for a while. I love to read about Ireland. Where exactly did you live?"

"Dublin, as one might expect. The compulsory education here in Turks and Caicos ends at age sixteen. My parents wanted more education for me, so off to Europe I went. For two long and lonely years."

"Why Ireland?" she asked, shifting her weight from one foot to the other.

"Mother has family there." He chugged another draft of water and wiped his mouth off with the back of his hand.

She thought of her own arduous journey to an education. The years she'd struggled to pay for school and keep a roof over her head had scarred her. Families who assumed it was their responsibility to pay their children's way in the world always fascinated her. "Did you go to college too?"

"Yes, of course. My parents wouldn't have settled for less." He gave her a wink and turned to study the horizon.

At this moment there was nothing more interesting to her

than where Anthony had studied. She wanted to know if he'd been able to stay at the school for all four years, and if he'd had to work at all or if he'd actually been able to participate in extra-curricular activities. When people talked about fraternities and sororities, she was stymied. How would it have felt to have that kind of time on her hands?

"Where did you go?" she pressed.

Anthony was distracted by something. "The flocks of birds that normally feed in the Salinas—they've all vanished," he said, his eyes as wide as she had ever seen them.

"So?" Holly asked, not knowing at all where his thoughts were leading.

"That's a bad sign. A very bad sign."

Once again, her first thought was Byron. Without birdsong, the air was filled with a deathly silence punctuated only by the sound of crashing waves. Her stomach tumbled in panic. It made no sense at all, but she swatted the back of her head wildly, like she'd just been stung by a bee. Trying to ward off the ephemeral threat of danger.

Holly longed to fill the quiet, to return to some kind of nor-mal, to be delivered from her paralyzing fear, so she latched on to the question Anthony had left unanswered. "Where was it you said you went to school?"

His nose wrinkled as if he'd eaten something rotten. "Har-vard," he nearly spat out. "Feckin' Boston."

He paled again, and bent over to put his hands on his knees for the second time that day.

We are both losing our minds over this.

A choking took hold of him; it seemed he couldn't find his breath, and he kept clearing his throat over and over again.

Holly reached out and rubbed the small of his back. It didn't help. She once again wondered, given his age, the heat of the day, and the stress of the situation, if he was going into cardiac arrest. In the interest of soothing him, she played her concern close to the vest.

"Go cool off. Get cleaned up and you'll feel so much better."

He nodded at her obediently, and when his choking calmed down to the point that he could stand back up, he finished the rest of his water.

Holly took the empty container from him. "I'm going to start securing the windows. If Byron hasn't started already. In which case, I'll help. Then I'm headed for the kitchen to do a quick inventory of food, water, and . . . I don't know what else . . . general supplies, I suppose."

Holly was eager to do something–anything–to relieve the thick tension they seemed to be steeped in at the moment. The volume of the alarm bell that had been ringing in her own head, on and off, for most of the day was deafening. She spun around playfully on her heels and shot a parting comment over her right shoulder.

"You might want to let yourself into the bar after your shower and start hauling bottles of booze up there."

He laughed heartily. "Priorities, my dear Holly!"

She tossed her hair. "Yes, I have heard you say it so many times: 'We must all have our priorities.' We'll all have a good, stiff drink when we get this place sealed up, Lord Bascombe. Let's look forward to that."

I hope I can get a shower in, too. I smell like fear. I'm lucky all the wild dogs haven't come running to get me.

Chapter 17

As Holly walked from room to room, she stood in the open doorways and ran her fingers down the dark, polished hardwood of the moldings—just appreciating the old house. She loved that it had "good bones," as she had heard builders and real estate agents say. And that it was filled with interesting architectural details and antiques.

To lose this place would be devastating. All of the work we have done on it. It was her home. Her business. The place where she had started over.

She circled back to the living room and dragged a chair up to a large window that was about four feet off the floor. Its hinged sashes were thrown wide open, and its sill was wide enough for her to stand on, as the limestone wall was nearly two feet wide.

Anthony showed up just as she stepped onto the sill. He climbed up beside her. Squeezed into the frame, side by side, they leaned out to examine the antique hardware of the shutters.

"They haven't had to shutter the place up in over ten years," Holly said. "But the hinges and latches look like they will hold just fine to me. What do you think?"

Anthony nodded. "Looks sturdy enough. But then, looks can be deceiving. I don't know, dear. We're going to be closed in here for a long time. Besides the occasional gust, there's no sign of the storm yet. Well, the birds leaving . . . granted, that's a big indication. But let's talk about our overall strategy before we seal things up."

She gladly deferred to his experience, since she had never been caught in a hurricane before. "I've been buried in snow before—one time we lost power for three days," she told him. "But hurricanes aren't exactly common up in the Green Mountains of Vermont."

In the end, they decided that as long as the sun was still shining, they would let fresh air circulate throughout the house. Only when the wind really began to blow and the sky was completely covered with clouds would they begin the process of closing it up. There were plenty of other things they needed to attend to until then.

Humidity and heat were a fact of life in the Caribbean. Anthony described vivid memories of the suffocating stuffiness he'd endured during previous storms. But there were other difficulties too.

"There's no avoiding it: you have to make the house as tight as possible, or it springs leak and the water streams in. After what we experienced with Hurricane Ike, it's good that you've sealed most of the window panes around the outside with silicone. If, in fact, this storm develops into a category four or five over the island, we'll have jets of water coming in everywhere with the wind and air pressure changes."

Holly stared into space, trying to imagine how this happened and what the living room would look like when it did.

Anthony climbed down from the window on legs that seemed stiff. Once he made it down to the old wood floor, he leaned against the wall and stretched them out like a runner, taking a moment. He stopped when he spotted Byron, at the same moment Holly saw him.

Holly suspected her son had been standing there for a while, waiting for them to finish their inspection. A dead quiet prevailed for several seconds.

"What are you doing here?" he asked them.

Anthony reached a hand up and helped Holly down.

"I told you I wasn't leaving you," she said. "I meant it." Though she accepted Anthony's offer of help—it was a long step down—she told him, "I'm tougher than you seem to think. I jump off the seawall almost every day, you know."

He shrugged at her with a wounded look on his face, and Holly regretted saying it. She knew he was only trying to be a gentleman. In fact, gallantry seemed to have been bred into him.

Anthony turned toward Byron, looking like a schoolboy who had just been reprimanded.

"Are you staying here too?" Byron asked him.

He nodded. "Put the boat in North Creek."

"It's going to get a bit crowded. Dad went to get Mami and Papi. And *Sameera*. Lord help us."

"Your grandparents can have the big bedroom at the front of the house," Holly said. "They should be on the first floor. Mami can't do stairs anymore. Your dad and Sameera can be with you on the second story. I really don't want anyone up on the third, just in case we lose part of the roof. Anthony? You can have the second bedroom in my apartment. It's small but right near the bathroom. That all makes sense, doesn't it?"

Byron looked at the ceiling. "Oh boy. I don't know what Mami and Papi are going to make of that."

"Make of what?"

"You having Anthony in your place."

"Seriously? How many girlfriends has your father had over the last twenty years?"

"Yeah, but they're used to that, and they seem to think it's different for a man. They're always telling me how grateful they are that you haven't brought another man into my life. Like I'm still six years old."

"Do you have any silicone around?" Anthony asked. "I don't like the look of a few windows at the back of the house."

Byron smiled. "Yep. And I bought them out of caulking cord, too. I'm going to start jamming it into any gap I can find between the windows and doorjambs and the old stone walls. We'll try to get the place as waterproof as possible."

Anthony looked like he was thinking things over. After some seconds, he asked, "We're just going to work up here on the first floor, right? For now, anyway."

Holly nodded emphatically. "Yes. There's no way to secure the cellar. It has those big loading doors all around; we can lock them shut, but flooding is something to be expected. It's the reason the main house was raised up in the first place. We should assume anything stored down there will be destroyed. Oh, shoot! I should bring up the gas grill."

Byron stopped her. "I already did it. I brought up anything I thought would be necessary and useful."

Holly winked at Byron. He was always telling her to stop acting like he was a child. Now here he was, proving how strong and capable he actually was.

"Thank you," Anthony said. "I'm sorry I haven't been of more help. I was feeling a little peaked for a while."

Byron shrugged. "Like my grandparents say, 'Don't hurt up ya head. One hand duz wash de odda.'"

Anthony laughed out loud. "Thank you, young man. But I really do feel I need to earn my keep. Feel free to ask me to do anything."

Holly clapped her hands together. "Okay. The caulking, then. We've got lots of caulking material. Before we do our own bedrooms, I think we should focus on the living and dining rooms. The government will shut the power off to the entire island at some point today. There's no telling how long we have to work."

Byron's mouth dropped open. "Why would they do that?"

"It's just common sense," Holly said. "There will be poles blowing down, and those live wires can cause all kinds of problems."

"Years ago, after another storm, an Islander was electrocuted even though he was thirty-five feet away from the downed power line that was still live," Anthony added. "It was a lesson we all took to heart."

The Nor'easters and blizzards Holly had weathered back home were crazy enough. *What kind of havoc will happen here?* She and Byron had been shocked the first time they returned to Grand Turk after Hurricane Ike: the island had been a mess, and they'd heard stories that had stuck with them. But neither of them had been trapped in anything like this before either.

Anthony must have sensed her tension, because he moved nearer to her. "No matter what happens, we can still cook, since you have a propane cooktop and oven. We'll have to light it with matches, but that's easy enough." He looked into her eyes with a tenderness that made her feel just a wee bit safer.

Byron laughed at him, interrupting the touching moment. "You going to worry about fine cuisine at a moment like this?"

"If we don't have electricity for days on end, we'll have to use up everything you have stored in your chest freezer. Guessing you two have a solid stock of meat in there, am I right?"

Holly nodded.

"Good. You don't want to be hungry like we were the last time. With your reserves, we won't starve." It sounded like Anthony remembered Ike well, though it had happened many years before. "Of course, I don't know if I'll have any appetite. It felt like we were imprisoned last time; it made me a little crazy. And sick to my stomach, to be true."

Byron slapped him on one shoulder. "But you survived, didn't you? And no worse for wear, from what I can tell."

"Nothing kills my appetite," Holly jumped in. "I'm always hungry. Except for . . . well, the vertigo . . . but that doesn't happen very often." She picked up two rolls of the white caulking cord. "So, we push this into any holes or gaps we come across? What about if we find older caulking that's already been done—do we pull it out and replace it?"

"Leave any that's already in place where it is," Anthony quickly answered. "It might be hard to scrape out, and I think you'd do more damage than good. Don't you?"

She nodded in agreement. "Do you want to start in here? Or the kitchen?"

"Whatever you want to do is fine, but I thought I'd start with the kitchen. Everything we really need is in there. If I don't have time to get to my room before the storm hits, I can sleep on the kitchen floor, but most things in there are irreplaceable."

She gave him a brief nod. "That's good thinking. Go ahead."

"Will do." Anthony gave her a smart salute. "And Holly? Thank you for having me."

She bowed her head. "You are most welcome, Lord Bascombe. Oh, and I wasn't kidding about the bottles of liquor. Before you caulk, why don't you haul some up and bring them to me in the kitchen."

"Certainly, madame."

"Mademoiselle. I have told you a million times."

The clock on the wall chimed three times. They all stared at it in a bit of a daze. The sound seemed to hang in the air.

Holly's heart started pounding wildly, as if a great weight had just descended upon her chest. "Time is short, guys. Let's move." She took off down the hall toward the kitchen at a dead run.

Chapter 18

The moon broke through the clouds racing across the sky from time to time as the evening progressed. But by the time Byron and Holly pulled the last of the shutters inward and threw their locks closed, it was getting dark outside. The howling winds made the old house groan and created a ghostly sound as it traveled down the chimney.

Holly followed Byron into the kitchen, where they found Anthony, Sanford, and Coralyse leaning against the gleaming copper kitchen counter, watching Sameera chop vegetables.

An exhausted Holly plopped down in the small breakfast nook to rest for a moment. *At least that dizziness is gone.*

She realized who was missing. "Montez?" she asked the room.

Sameera pursed her lips. "He went upstairs to take a nap. A nap!" She didn't seem happy as she continued chopping the garlic and red onion on the cutting board in front of her.

Holly shrugged at the others. "I keep feeling like there's still something to be done, although I can't think what it is. A couple of the shutters had locks that were a bit suspect, so we screwed them completely shut. We've moved everything up here. We're sealed up as best as we can be. Coralyse? Sanford? Are you settled in?"

"We are fine, dear girl. Can't thank you enough for having us."

"Byron would be worrying about you day and night if you

weren't with us here at The Roseate. Isn't that right, Byron? You are doing me the favor, believe me."

The group chuckled at this, but everyone quickly grew quiet. Nerves were taking over.

Holly didn't move at all as she watched Anthony. She was waiting for him to gather his thoughts. All that could be heard above the howl of the wind was his breathing, which seemed louder than usual. She thought he might actually be wheezing.

"Are you allergic to dust?" she asked, thinking about all the dirt she'd encountered in the tight spaces of the old house that day.

He waved away her concern. "I'll be fine. I'll step out on the porch in a few minutes and the fresh air will clear me out. First, I need to get back to something we talked about earlier. As I've already explained, if the storm is big enough and gets close enough, streams of water will shoot in. It's just something that happens."

"Why?" Holly asked.

"It's the air pressure," Sanford explained. "There's a noise like the sound a straw makes on the bottom of a glass—a great sucking noise. And that's what's happening. Any place the water can be pulled in, it is. Streams shoot in around the windows, along the plumbing and electric wires . . . through any path it can find."

Coralyse visibly shuddered. "Sameera, I need something to do," she said. "Shall I chop those carrots? Do we have another board?"

Holly put her fingertips to her forehead. "The combination of water and electric wires sounds really menacing. Honestly." A brainstorm hit her, and her eyes widened. "Should we move the beds as far away from the windows as possible?"

Anthony and Byron responded at the same time: "Absolutely."

"The old folks have always said this area of town is a hurricane hole," Byron added, "but direct hits have happened here before."

"You said Queen's Cay is a hurricane hole," Holly countered. "Are those even real? Or just a myth?"

Anthony held a closed fist to his mouth. His voice sounded grave. "We shall see, won't we?"

Holly's mind reeled with ideas. "Let's move the couches, too. You know what else? I'm going to put all the bathroom towels in the hall closet by the bathroom—that's as close to the center of the house as you can get. Best chance of keeping them dry."

Anthony nodded thoughtfully. "Excellent idea."

Bossy as an old schoolteacher, Holly continued, "Only take the towels out one at a time, as you're using them. We'll store them in garbage bags on the shelves. We can put our clothes in that closet as well; the shelves are really deep. There's plenty of room for everything." She turned her attention to Sanford. "Go take the easy chair in the living room, won't you? I can tell your bad knee is bothering you with this weather. Do you want some Advil?"

"Thank you, darling, I took some already." He started limping toward the living room. "You're right. I'll just rest a spell."

As if it were pre-agreed, Holly, Anthony, and Byron darted off on their furniture-moving mission, which seemed paramount to complete as soon as possible.

Moving furniture was easier than Holly feared. Within minutes, they were done and back in the kitchen.

Holly checked her phone. "I've gotten word from Erica that the power will be cut off at ten o'clock, which also means there won't be any cell phone reception."

She felt a pressing need to call the Trombleys in Vermont and speak to them one more time. They would be following the news and feeling a bit panicked. But she barely had one bar of reception.

Remembering that Anthony had been making calls throughout the day, she asked, "May I use your phone? It's to call the States."

He handed over his cell without question and she treated him with a small smile of thanks.

She thought to step out on the porch as the call went through, but she reconsidered when she caught the look on Byron's face. The Trombleys were practically family. She put the phone on speaker as Toby answered.

"Hi, Toby," Holly said. "Is Sally with you?"

"Right here," Sally's familiar voice piped up.

"We are still in one piece and everythi—"

"Love you guys," Byron jumped in, "but we're in a hurry. They're going to cut the power soon."

"Toby? Sally?" Holly felt her throat grow tight. "I just wanted to tell you one more time that I love you. I'm so grateful for all you did for Byron and me. I don't know where I would be without all your help. Especially when I was a kid."

"No point in being dramatic, Mom," Byron said, giving her an exasperated look. "It's bad enough as it is. We've shuttered all the windows, weather-proofed the house as best we can . . . we'll be okay. Love you guys. We will call afterwards. As soon as we can. Now we gotta go, right, Mom?"

Holly blinked back tears. "I'm not being dramatic."

"We're saying lots of prayers," Sally said. "The whole family is. Byron, you listen to your mother."

"Byron, give your mother a little room to feel something," Toby said. "I'm sure it's scary. Not everyone can say they've lived through a catastrophic hurricane. But that's exactly what you two are going to do. You hear me? You are going to get through it." His voice cracked. "I can't imagine a world without you two in it."

Holly started to cry. "Give my love to everyone. We will call you after it's over."

Tears became sobs when she pressed the button to end the call. Whatever comfort she'd wanted from the conversation, she hadn't gotten it. But there was no time to stew about it.

She felt a strain to get the meal on the table, since they wouldn't have water pressure once the electricity went out. They could still get water from the cistern in the ground level, but it would be a heck of a lot easier cleaning up with hot, running water instead of hauling buckets up to the kitchen sink.

She sighed and slumped over the stove with a hand on each side of it. So tired. "Anthony, could you fire up the gas grill? The side dishes are almost done."

"I'm going to get some fresh air before we eat," Coralyse sang out. Like they were having Sunday dinner instead of awaiting chaos.

"I'll come with you, Mami," Byron said. "We won't be too long, Mom."

Holly knew that no one was sure when they would eat again. What their reality would be in twelve hours. *Who will be left alive.* She said a prayer and moved on.

They still had the front and back doors open to provide some air. As the wind was already kicking up, Anthony lit the grill in the foyer and then carefully rolled it toward the door as far as the propane tank hose would allow. He repeated the same procedure three times before he got it outside and away from the house.

Holly had left seven steaks and a roast, a precious commodity on Grand Turk, on the counter to thaw while they were working earlier. Now Sameera was at the kitchen stove, searing the pork roast in a rub so aromatic that it made Holly instantly ravenous.

The Belonger

"The roast is for tomorrow," Holly told her flatly. "Chances are we won't be able to cook then, despite what Anthony says."

Anthony was in the dining room. She heard him open and close several cabinets and drawers as he gathered items—trying to make a special table, despite the circumstances. *Or maybe because of them.*

As if once again reading her mind, Anthony spun to face her through the archway. "I'm determined to make this night one of celebration. It's an approach that has served me well before."

One of Holly's brows lifted with curiosity.

"I know from unfortunate experience that the longer we are sealed up in here, with only buckets of water to use for washing, the crankier people will get. Some may even get a little crazy."

He held up three bottles of wine—good wine, Holly noted. Where had he unearthed them? She let out a nervous giggle. Though there was fear in the pit of her stomach, she was game to try to set it aside and have some fun. One thing the locals said about her was that she was always willing to give it a go.

Well, that's what the Brits and Canadians said. The Belongers put it this way: "She don't cut no dy-doh." Between cultures, a consensus had been reached. Holly was considered a go-getter.

Time to prove them right.

Chapter 19

Anthony opened one of the bottles. When the cork let go there was a loud pop.

Holly jumped, then laughed.

"I'll just let the wine rest for a few moments." He set the bottle down on a large coaster.

"Perfect. I'm going to check on Sameera and dinner. But let's have a drink before we call everyone in. I could use it right about now." She picked up a decanter of scotch and headed toward the stove, where Sameera was loading food onto platters. "Excuse me." Holly reached over her and pulled two short glasses out of the cabinet.

She heard a loud snap, and turned to see Anthony smoothing a heavy linen tablecloth over the table. He'd left a drawer of the sideboard behind him open. "I'll be back to finish the job after I pop out for a cig," he called.

Holly hurried over and handed him his scotch. With a small bow, he clinked his glass against hers before sliding out the front door.

Glass in hand, she walked over to the sideboard and took a sip. "Ahh. Now that's the ticket."

She closed the drawer, which was filled with linens, and explored the contents of the other five. Two dark wood rows of three. She found the heavy ornate silver they'd inherited when they bought the place. She hadn't looked at it in ages, as she usually ate at the Sand Dollar. She kept the pieces packed in large plastic bags so they wouldn't tarnish.

She sorted through the flatware and watched Anthony outside the front window, which was the last to be left open. As she counted out seven spoons, knives, and forks, he took a drag off his cigarette with his head tilted up toward the northeast. Judging by his stance and the fact that he was motionless for some minutes, she was sure he was once again studying the sky.

He threw his cigarette butt to the ground just as dusk was drawing to a close. She lit two candles, and the warm, fuzzy light they gave off bathed him as he reentered the room. Holly could swear he looked twenty years younger.

Anthony grabbed two pieces of crystal stemware from a glass curio cabinet and poured them each a glass of wine. They toasted each other silently. He stood at the head of the table and held up his own glass high in his right hand with his left tucked behind him at the small of his back. Standing ramrod straight, he said quite formally, "Holly, I wish you a safe passage through this adventure we're about to embark upon. If we stick together, we should be fine. To us beating Hurricane Nestor!"

"To us!" Holly repeated as she hoisted her drink.

"Dinner's almost ready," Sameera called from the kitchen.

Holly walked to the front door to check on Byron and his grandmother; they had not gone very far. "Byron," she hollered, "can you please wake your father and tell him dinner's ready?"

She sure wasn't about to do it.

Sanford roused from his armchair. She suspected he'd been dozing.

"Where do you want us, Holly?" He looked hungry.

"Wherever you are comfortable. We're going to try to have some fun."

"Wonderful. You and Byron should sit at the heads of the table. It's your home."

"Okay, Sanford. Thank you."

"Here's our boy," Coralyse said as she and Byron breezed in. She went to the kitchen to grab a steaming plate of roasted vegetables before she sat down. "This smells divine. Sameera knows how to cook; that is one thing we know for sure."

Sameera set a bowl of garlic mashed potatoes down and joined them just as Anthony brought in a platter with the sizzling steaks on it. Holly set about pouring ice water for each place setting. Bottles of red wine had been placed at opposites ends of the table. Everyone helped themselves. Just the way Holly liked it.

She heard Montez's heavy footsteps coming down the stairs. Though he was barefoot, he looked pretty crisp in slacks and a collared shirt.

"Hey, Mr. Sleepy Head," Coralyse said.

He scratched his head and laughed. "I was out like a light."

"You didn't hear me when I was caulking the window up there?" Byron asked.

Montez shook his head. "Didn't hear nothing."

Sameera made a face. "The rest of us didn't have time for a nap. So much to be done. Such a serious set of circumstances."

The tension between them was uncomfortable. Holly changed the subject.

"You know, no one is sure when this dining table was brought to Roseate House. It's just assumed that it was either carried on the original ship that brought the family, *The Revenge*, or made from the oak of the boat's exterior planking once they arrived. When opened to its full length, the table can seat twelve. Tonight I only put in two of the leaves. Our little dinner is a modest gathering compared to others that have happened here for hundreds of years. History is so cool, isn't it?"

"Are you giving us a history lecture, Mom?" Byron shook his head. "If you start explaining where all the old stuff in this house came from, we'll be here all night." He lifted his glass. "Drink well, everyone. God knows where we'll end up tomorrow."

The seven of them toasted and clinked their glasses.

Holly took in the expressions on Anthony and Sanford's faces. Both were staring at their plates silently. She bet they were worried to the point they weren't tasting a thing, though they both muttered, "Delicious. Thank you."

"Holly, why don't you tell us how you met Montez?" Sameera asked during the lull in conversation. "And how you came to have Byron."

Talk about a loaded question. The story's much different from my viewpoint than Montez's, I'm sure. Not to mention how his parents felt about an unexpected pregnancy, and me being an unmarried mother.

To be polite, she rambled out a generic version, putting emphasis on the fact that Montez had never abandoned her or Byron–that he, Coralyse, and Sanford had always stayed in touch.

"Good Lord," she finally declared, "I've dominated the entire conversation." She licked her lips and took another sip of her wine.

"Not at all, dear," Coralyse said. "It's nice to reminisce. Oh, how the years go by." She folded her hands in front of her on the table. "Holly was always so good about bringing the child to see us. Twice a year! All the way from Vermont."

"Sometimes I needed help to pay for the plane tickets, but we all chipped in," Holly said. "Over time, we became a family."

Byron smiled as he took a bite of his steak. "This is so good. I didn't realize how hungry I was."

Holly winked at him. "We all worked hard today . . . well, most of us," she couldn't help adding.

Sameera snorted.

Her cheeks were sucked in, giving her that haughty expression she was prone to wearing. "S-s-so that's it? He just left you behind? Pregnant? Alone? Were you alone the day you gave birth?"

"Oh . . . well . . . not alone. Sally and Toby Trombley were with me. Sally was my birth coach. And those two were better parents to me than my own ever were. My father left when I was small, and I never heard from him again."

Sanford and Coralyse stiffened. Oblivious to their discomfort, Sameera exchanged a long look with Montez. It was as hostile an expression as Holly had ever seen.

Holly put one elbow up on the table and leaned toward her. "It wasn't like what my father did to me; Montez didn't abandon us. He always found a way to stay in touch and be in our lives."

Sameera was not convinced—and it was clear she was speaking to Anthony and not to Holly when she went off on a rant in French. Considering the fact that Montez's parents were at the table, Holly was taken aback. She thought she caught the word *pitoyable*, meaning "pitiful" in English, and she flushed a deep scarlet. She was relieved the others couldn't see it in the dim candlelight—though even if they could have, everyone was focused on trying to decipher Sameera's private conversation with Anthony. Holly could understand little else they said, but she could hear the anger in Sameera's voice.

Finally, Anthony held up his hand for her to be silent and cleared his throat. "She's upset and English is not her first language. Sameera is saying that any *reasonable* man would understand the abandonment you had already experienced when your parents left you, and that *reasonable* man would be more careful with your feelings." He darted a look across the table. "Sorry, Montez. I am just translating. You should speak for yourself, Sameera."

"I'm too disgusted to say it out loud," she said.

Holly lifted her chin and scanned from Sameera to Anthony. "So, that's what you think you would have done in Montez's place? Been more reasonable? Although we adore our Byron, we were young. It was a shock that he was on the way."

Sameera did not meet her eyes—in fact, she deliberately avoided them, and also any further confrontation, by putting her focus on her plate of food. Though she did smile slyly when Holly said, "No one I know has ever called Anthony a *reasonable* man either."

As was intended, they all laughed.

Being the center of attention was not usually Holly's style, and she was suddenly extremely embarrassed she had confided so much to them.

"I think we're all a little drunk," she admitted.

The wind had picked up since she started telling her story. The later it got, the harder it was to hear each other over what was now a shrieking tempest. She thought she should get some sleep while she could. As a pointed gesture, she picked up the three plates that were nearest to her and carried them into the kitchen. She was relieved to see the clock on the stove was still glowing.

"It's nine forty," she called into the dining room. "Can we clean up in twenty minutes? We'll have to hand wash the dishes; there's not enough time to run the dishwasher."

"We will all help," Anthony said. "Byron is going to top off the oil lamps. At ten o'clock, we'll be helpless without them."

Holly went into the dining room to gather more plates. Montez started to sit down on the couch.

"I cooked this meal," Sameera snapped, glaring at him. "You can do the dishes, can't you? The least you can do."

He rose slowly and lumbered into the kitchen after Holly, where Anthony was already scrubbing away.

"Find a clean dish towel, man, and as you dry each piece put it in the cabinet where it belongs," Anthony said cheerfully.

Holly grabbed a towel, too, and helped Montez find the proper spots for all the kitchenware.

The cuckoo clock went off exactly at ten— *"C-coo, c-coo, c-oo!"*

With a great clunking sound, they were cast in total darkness.

Chapter 20

Holly went to bed. She tried to read, but it was hard to keep her eyes open thanks to the amount of wine she had consumed. There was nothing else to do so, she fell asleep—much more easily than she expected to.

She dreamed she was swimming back at the little island Anthony had taken her to earlier in the day. The wake was much rougher than it had been that morning, and some kind of errant current pushed her down toward the rays resting at the bottom in the sand. She tried to swim up toward the surface to take a breath of air, but the current held her. Caught between the poison sting rays and her fight to the surface, she panicked, her heart racing.

Her heart was pounding wildly when she sat up in bed, wide awake.

Her bedside oil light flickered; as she sat there, recovering from her dream, the cuckoo clock signaled midnight.

The roof groaned. The wind had become a deafening roar. She lay awake in a sweltering darkness, her mouth nearly glued shut from thirst. She had an ache in the back of her head.

A large piece of some kind of debris slammed against the house, shaking the walls. Holly nearly jumped out of her skin.

How big would something have to be to make solid stone tremble?

She tossed and turned. And sweated. Her bedroom was a one-story addition put on to the back of the main house. It had a metal roof. The pounding rain boomed. A great ripping sound in the rafters made her sure the roof would go flying off at any minute, right into the eye of the storm. She trembled uncontrollably.

Can my heart explode from fear? I've heard that happens to rabbits and mice all the time. If the storm hits hard enough, could my heart just give out?

She dove under her covers. Trying to hide. What was there to do but inhale and exhale slowly to calm the dread that consumed more and more of her as the minutes ticked by?

"Damn it," she called out from under the blankets.

As often happened to her in the middle of the night, she realized she had to pee. There was no position she could twist into to give herself relief from the urge; it simply couldn't be denied.

Earlier in the evening, Byron had been thoughtful enough to empty the dryer. She found her favorite cotton nighty and its matching robe folded on her bed. There were times she thought her son didn't notice a thing about her; this simple act made it obvious that wasn't true. She wished she had him in her spare bedroom instead of Anthony—that they could ride this out together. But he had his own private wing, and she didn't think he would have given that up.

The peignoir set fell just above her knees and she thanked God the crinkled white material could breathe in this oppressive heat.

She was also grateful Byron had supplied her with, quite literally, a hurricane lamp. She had been too afraid to blow it out before falling asleep, and it still glowed faintly now on the dresser across the room.

She looked in the bureau mirror. Although she was in her forties, the image she saw—petite, all dressed in white—looked like a far younger woman. She was fit and thin, and though she'd often thought she was much too old to consider love again, she suddenly realized she had been wrong. There was a wildness in her eyes she'd not noticed before.

I'm still sexy. I discover this about myself now? Terrific. We might not even make it through the night.

She tiptoed down the hallway, oil lamp in hand, past the ancient, dark wooden doors of the other bedroom. *Why am I being so careful—who could hear me above this din?*

Anthony had provided several large buckets full of water to fill up the toilet's tank, as the water pump was cut off when the power went out. He'd been very definitive when he said, "Only flush if you poo. I'm not sure if we'll be able to make it down to the cistern tomorrow."

He'd also put a case of bottled water on one of the shelves in the bathroom. She opened one and dug around in the medicine cabinet for an aspirin to go with it.

After relieving herself, she left everything as it was and tiptoed back out into the hall. Tiptoeing was a habit she couldn't seem to break tonight. The ripping sound in the rafters began again. Pops as loud as gunshots punctuated the wind's steady howl. Each time they blasted she stopped and put a hand against the plaster wall to steady herself. Even with the oil lamp, she was having trouble finding her way; the soft light dropped off quickly to extreme darkness that she found disorienting.

Holly's mind ran the same loop: *I hate this so much. I hate this so much.*

Cutting through the cacophony was a great sucking sound that chilled her to the bone. *It's right on top of us. It sounds just like Sanford said.* Her terror made her go numb, though she was still more than aware of the pounding in her ears.

I can't do this alone.

A stream of water squirted the right side of her face and saturated her hair. She madly swiped at the air, trying to find the source and stop it. She ran to Anthony's bedroom door. In one smooth endeavor, she pushed it open, put her light down on an end table, and jumped into his bed.

He sat up. "Holly?"

Her voice was as small and high as a child's. "Can I stay here?"

Anthony arranged some pillows so they could lounge back on them and put his arm around her. "Of course you can. It's been pretty terrifying, hasn't it?"

She trembled as she said, "That sucking sound." She could hear water streaming and dripping around her as she let out a single sob.

He pulled her closer and murmured in her ear, "This has to be the worst of it. If we can try to sleep, it will help us get through the night. It's sure to improve by morning."

He kissed her neck playfully and, although mere moments earlier she'd been too petrified to feel much at all, she tingled powerfully. She took in his masculine scent. The feel of the warm skin of his arms around her was a big improvement in her state of affairs.

She surprised herself when she snuggled into him. "This isn't so bad," she said.

"Hey, thanks." He laughed. "I've been thinking about you for hours. I'm so glad you're here."

Holly slid her hand under his T-shirt and played with the hair on his chest. "I could use a distraction."

"Oh?"

She gasped when he ran his lips from above her shoulder blade to her earlobe and then nibbled on it. She was thrilled in a way she hadn't felt in many years. It seemed his lips had made all the blood in her body rush to her lower half, creating a powerful, pulsating need.

When he turned her toward him, she didn't think to resist. "I would like to properly kiss you, Holly. What say you to that?"

A low moan of approval was her only response. The sound of it shocked her—but she didn't regret his reaction to it for a second. He moved his face toward hers and the instant their lips met, she was lost in another world—a world where the weather was perfect; where, in fact, *everything* was perfect. The sound of the whipping winds disappeared into the background, and Holly was in no hurry to get back to it.

Anthony wore a T-shirt that had been washed so many times it was exceptionally soft to the touch. Just below the collar band was a small hole from years of wear. Holly stretched the fabric a bit and managed to fit both of her index fingers inside it.

"What are you doing?" he asked.

She tore the shirt wide open, and he whooped. Smiling, she gently bit him near his collarbone and then down his chest.

The top of Holly's nightgown had a series of tiny buttons. He undid each one slowly, kissing the skin that was revealed as he went. He paused after the fourth button, and they took a moment to appreciate the vision of each other in the glowing light. His strong chest was exposed by the torn fabric, and he ran a finger over her tanned décolletage framed by the V of her partially open bodice.

Who knew? Holly thought. *I still got it.*

Anthony pulled what was left of his shirt over his head and threw it across the room.

In an excruciatingly patient manner, they began to explore each other. She savored the satin feel when she stroked his skin. The quivers she experienced when he did the same to her.

My God, it's been a long time.

By the time he cupped her breasts, she thought she would explode—but she was wrong. The easy dance they were doing ignited a tortuous desire in both of them.

Finally, she begged him to enter her. When he did, the sensation was euphoric.

Oh, hello old friend. I've missed you.

"Hello yourself," Anthony growled.

Good Lord, I'm talking to myself. Out loud.

And then the divine spasms took hold.

Yes, yes, yes.

Only a few minutes after they peaked, Holly and Anthony fell into a satisfied heap. But almost instantly they started up all over again.

Afterwards, she fell asleep in his arms.

Holly awoke to a greenish light that wasn't night but rather a strange-looking brand of daylight.

Anthony stirred. He slipped his boxer shorts on, stood up at the side of the bed, and stretched his back with a groan. He grinned at her. "Hurricane sex. It's a real thing, you know. Nothing better."

He padded toward the bathroom in his bare feet.

Huh. Apparently, that was all the discussion she was going to get for the time being about what had happened the night before.

She heard the sound of water gurgling and saw that the window drapes were saturated. Looking up, she found a slow drip coming out of the overhead light fixture; she made a mental note not to touch any switches or electrical outlets. The power may be out, but she didn't trust it.

Anthony had left the door wide open, but he swung it shut when he came back into the room. He gave her a quick kiss and started pulling clothes out of the black plastic garbage bag he had carried in with him.

Fishing around for her robe, she told him, "Fair warning: I'm going to use one of those buckets of water in the bathroom to wash up."

He chuckled—proudly, she thought—and, after pulling up his shorts, came back to her and gave her a long kiss. Looking directly in her eyes in a way that made her blush, he said, "You were marvelous last night," and stroked her face.

Perhaps he noticed the burning of her cheeks. It seemed to amuse him.

"Much too late for embarrassment, my love. Much too late for that."

Chapter 21

They were in the kitchen when Byron came downstairs. As she hugged him good morning, she held back a yawn as she said, "I snuck up to check things out; everything looks okay!"

"Not so bad, right?" he said. "It's depressing that everything is wet. Yuck. But we made it through. Some of the noises in the storm were crazy. But we're all safe and sound."

It was his turn to stifle a yawn, and Anthony did the same. They were all exhausted from the ferocious evening, but the general mood seemed jovial now that the worst of the storm had passed. Inconvenient as the lack of electricity was, they were prepared to live without it for a while. They were innovative people.

Anthony peeked out the back door and shouted, "Blast!"

"What is it?" Holly asked.

"After our celebration dinner last night, after we cleaned up, the grill was still hot and I foolishly decided not to go through the hassle of bringing it inside. I chained it to the porch railing with a padlock, thought that would be enough. Now it's nowhere to be found."

They all stared at the package of frozen hamburgers on the counter that they'd just taken out of the freezer.

Though there hadn't been time yet for strenuous activity, the three of them were already perspiring. No fan or air conditioner had run since the previous night at ten, and every window and door was shut tight. To say the air in the house was oppressive was a gross understatement.

Rather than light the burner on the stove, which would undoubtedly add more heat, Holly said, "The wind has calmed down enough; we might actually be able to get this old charcoal grill started on the back porch." She gestured toward the Weber on the ground in the corner of the kitchen.

Anthony nodded. "The grill will have a bit of shelter in the back corner. I think we can get it going."

Byron picked the grill up with both arms. That small exertion caused a big drop of perspiration to start streaming down his forehead toward his eye. He pushed his bottom lip out as he blew up at it. Holly grabbed a dishtowel and wiped it away.

She was sweltering, with no hope of a shower in sight. But the more important concern was how to feed a house full of people today. "Let's give it a go!"

Anthony held the door while Byron carried the Weber out.

Byron was barely through when a gust of wind coursed in and ripped the door out of Anthony's grasp, slamming it shut behind him. The force of it was so intense that, by rights, it should have broken the door into splinters and shattered the glass pane, but somehow everything held together.

Eyes wide, Anthony pulled the door back open and ushered Holly through.

The trio huddled around the grill in a tight circle, trying to create a windbreak.

The gusting! It's knocking me from side to side. If we get this fire going, I might fall right into it.

But she was still heartened about the state of the storm. It wasn't raining nearly as much as it had during the night.

Anthony reached for the charcoal, spread it out on top of some crumpled paper, and then doused it with a good squirt of lighter fluid. "I hate using this stuff," he said, "but the fire will never start without it."

It took many attempts to strike a match that didn't blow out right away. Getting the flame to the balls of paper was a whole other challenge. When they finally succeeded, a flare bellowed forth with a great whoosh, startling Holly into jumping back.

Anthony picked up the domed top of the grill to further shelter the fire as it took hold.

Abruptly, and seemingly out of the blue, the rained picked up and began to pelt them with enormous drops.

"Go back inside, Mom," Byron shouted. "I'll come to get you when the coals are hot enough to cook on." He scanned the sky. "On second thought—I'll cook the burgers myself. No need for us all to get wet."

She appreciated his protectiveness, but ignored his request just the same. Instead, she held up an index finger. "I've got an idea."

Before anyone could argue with her, she jumped down off the porch. *It's easier to ask forgiveness than it is to ask permission*, she thought, a little smile plastered on her face.

She had spotted a piece of corrugated metal roofing that had blown into the yard. Though Anthony called to her and warned her not to, she ran out and picked it up—and quickly realized her mistake. With the wind pushing against the piece's broad surface, she was blown in one direction and then another. She screamed when a gust lifted her several inches off the ground; then gravity prevailed, and she fell in a heap.

"Jesus Christ!" she shouted.

Anthony was already running her way. "Are you hurt?" he asked, brow furrowed, as he helped her up. He stood on the metal to keep it from blowing away.

She ran her hands down the length of her legs. "No. I think I'm fine."

They both shielded their eyes from the hammering of the rain. Anthony picked up one side of the roofing. "Can you take the other side?" he asked with a smile, though he winced when a raindrop hit him in one eye.

Together, they pushed until the section was bent in a V shape; then they carried it point first, slicing through the wind, until they reached the grill—where, to encourage the struggling fire, they stretched it out a bit and wrapped it around as a shield.

The piece was almost as wide as Holly's arm-span, and acted like a sail. Even with Anthony and Byron gripping a portion of it, holding it in place was a workout. She felt rewarded when their efforts to protect the flames worked.

The edges of the coals turned white as they all waited as calmly as they could. Worn down from lack of sleep, the humidity, and the physical effort of holding up their makeshift wind shield, Holly felt like she might topple over. But she was more than motivated by her hunger to stay put. She summoned an image of the smell and sizzle of their burgers when they hit the metal grate and began to salivate. She wondered if Anthony and Byron felt like she did.

A rumble as loud as a sonic blast sounded in the air, and all three of them dropped the roofing onto the porch decking with an earsplitting clang that rang out above all the other noise. Another great boom pierced the air, and Holly screamed.

"It sounds like an earthquake!"

Blind with panic, she grabbed on to Anthony's shirt with both fists. They faced the house and watched helplessly as pieces of the left exterior wall began to fall away. Holly pulled Byron into the huddle.

Holding them close, Anthony hollered, "We have to run!"

But where?

Holly was riveted by the sight of tumbling stone coming from high up on an exterior wall. With a sharp crack, a small piece of rock ricocheted toward her, barely missing her head. She heard it zoom past her right ear and terror made her reach out for one of the back belt loops of Anthony's shorts as he turned away. His momentum was what unfroze her and pulled her back toward the mansion with him. Byron was right behind.

Holly shouted over the roar, "We've got to get deep inside the house."

Getting the exterior door open was a struggle. It took all of them to do it. As scared as Holly was, she marveled at how well the three of them worked together.

Byron shut the door behind them with a crash and threw the deadbolts closed.

"Follow me to the back stairs," Holly screamed.

Montez was by the door to Coralyse and Sanford's room. "The walls in here are thicker," he said. "Come with me." He motioned to Byron emphatically.

"No, come with us!" Holly insisted. "We'll be safe in the basement."

Montez started screaming. He had lost his head.

Looking slightly panicked, Byron leaned over to Holly. "I should stay with Mami," he said quietly. "Dad isn't good under stress."

She knew that neither of Byron's grandparents should try to make it down the steep, rickety stairs to the basement. Especially under these conditions. There wasn't even a bulb working to light their way.

She could also feel Byron's resolve. He'd been set on making his own decisions lately. And this was no time to argue. Even if the bedroom *was* too small for all of them to be jammed in there.

"Go on," she consented, giving him a quick hug. "Go ahead. We're headed downstairs."

The Belonger

▶▶▶

As Holly descended the stairs to the basement, gripping the railing, she found herself face to face with an ancient mirror on an overhang, chipped and cloudy with time. She looked into her own eyes.

If we get out of this alive, I am living the life I want. No more caring about judgment and other people. I know I try. I try very hard to do the right thing. Always have. Many see it. Those who don't aren't going to mean a thing to me. Not anymore.

The howling of the wind was much louder than it had been when they'd started the charcoal. Her mind should be on the clear and present danger they were in. But it wandered. As if her brain couldn't take in any more information. Especially if what she saw was terrifying. She couldn't feel the tips of her fingers—in fact, she couldn't feel much of any part of her body.

More limestone collapsed from the walls outside in a series of three *boom, boom, booms*. She crouched down instinctively, looking for cover. Anthony and Byron had badly miscalculated when they told her they were sure Nestor was winding down. She was panting and sweat was rolling down her sides. She longed to surrender and lie down on the dirt floor. She shook violently as she tried to navigate the stairs in the dark.

Anthony was in front of her. She tripped and fell into him. Grabbed on to the stair rail for dear life.

"Where are we going?" he asked.

"There's a room at the bottom."

Holly hoped it would serve as a bunker for them.

Either that or the old house would collapse. And bury them alive.

Chapter 22

C oming down, Anthony missed the fifth step up from the bottom. Head over heels he went, tumbling, and hit the landing hard.

Holly ran to him. "Are you alright?"

He was sitting on the floor, shaking his head.

"Wait a minute. I'm seeing stars. Whoo!" But he was laughing, so Holly relaxed.

She helped him up and, holding him tightly, said the same thing three times: "We will get through this. We will get through this. We will get through this."

They both had tears streaming down their faces when she pulled away.

"Deep breaths," she said. "Deep breaths."

Though her heart still raced she knew they had to act quickly. Reaching out in front of her, she found the door. It seemed to burst open for her. She was rewarded with a dim light coming from transom windows.

It did seem quieter down here. Still loud, but not earsplitting.

She raked her fingers through her hair. "Let's see what we've got to work with." She looked around the small room, made of stone and plaster walls. An antique kitchen used for storage now.

With a loud crack, one of the exterior door's shutters flew open. The sight of an exposed paned glass transom window above the door made Holly anxious. Fragile, old glass, completely exposed to the elements. The elements being Hurricane Nestor.

Within seconds, branches from a tree crashed through the almost two-hundred-year-old panes, sending glass flying.

Holly and Anthony crouched and shielded their faces.

I have tempted the universe. And the universe wins every time.

The rain was coming down sideways, which meant water was blowing in through the broken window with the velocity of a fire hose. She motioned to Anthony. They moved an old table toward an iron cook stove. They took the two heavy panels of cement board that had been leaned up against a wall behind the table and laid them across the top, bridging the space between the stove and the tabletop.

"Holly," Anthony said urgently, "quick."

She dove underneath the flimsy protection.

Nothing had been done to prepare for Nestor's force down here. Wherever there was a gap in the limestone foundation, thick streams of water shot in. As hot as it had been upstairs, Holly was now soaked through and freezing, lying on a dirt floor that was getting muddier and muddier by the second.

Anthony produced a length of rope, seemingly out of nowhere. He looped it around his and Holly's waists, literally tying them together, and then secured the ends to the leg of the iron stove.

Another earthquake-like rumble shook the house. Holly let out an uncontrolled scream, but then, so did Anthony. *Some small comfort that a strong man like him is as traumatized as I am.*

She was rigidly afraid something huge was going to break loose inside the building and land on top of them. The tumbling stones. Anthony had already proved to her he was the kind of man who was genetically hard-wired to protect, so she was not at all surprised when he held her and tried to cover her body with his. They were as close as two people could possibly be.

Even to her own ears, her terrified weeping was pitiful to hear. For Anthony's sake, she needed to do something to quiet down. She needed something to transport her mind to another time and place, as last night's activity had done for her.

Above the shriek of the torrent, she began to sing, as loudly as she could:

Will the circle be unbroken,
By and by, Lord, by and by
There's a better home a-waitin?
In the sky, Lord, in the sky

The chorus was all Holly could remember of the old Christian hymn, and she sang it through twice. Her eyes widened when Anthony responded in a powerful baritone the second time around. She quickly understood that he meant to fill in the verses, and she laughed out loud.

For the few minutes they sang together, she was filled with joy, despite the danger and the hammering of her heart inside her chest.

The wailing banshee wasn't in charge when Holly sang. With music, she and Anthony took back a small measure of control of their lives.

Anthony sang all five verses twice. When he was done, without a beat to spare, he exclaimed, "No woman . . ."

Holly giggled and finished, "No cry!"

In unison, they belted out the Bob Marley song. After that, she found that she knew the Beatles' "Twist and Shout" by heart. When she got to the "Ah, ah, ah, wow" line, she gave it all she had.

As huddled and miserable as they were, they delivered each other to a better place with their singing, and it was refreshing . . . even restful.

Anthony yelled into Holly's ear, "I adore you, girl. Don't you ever forget it."

Somehow, with the bedlam whipping around them, his statement seemed natural to her. Her tense muscles got looser. She placed her head on his shoulder, and the pandemonium faded long enough for her to close her eyes.

She must have fallen asleep, because she awakened with a jerk and cried out loud, "Byron! Byron! Where is my son? Byron!"

Anthony wrapped himself tight around her and held her tenderly, whispering soothing sounds in her ear, even though she fought against him. In her mind, she was desperately trying to find her boy. She couldn't hear anything above the crashes echoing off the old stone walls, and she felt convinced that Byron was outside in the storm. She kept trying to stand up to reach him, not understanding what was holding her down. *I don't care at all about getting hurt. I'd take on much more to know for certain that he is safe.*

Cracking noises sounded, making her feel as if the other three walls, or perhaps even the roof, of Roseate House could collapse at any moment. *Take me, Lord, not my child.* The pops and cracks of the old building straining against 160-mile-per-hour winds were torturous.

When Anthony started screaming, she came out of her hallucination about Byron. It was time for her to be the lucid one.

If they somehow survived this, she would erase the unhinged monologue currently bursting forth from her companion from her memory. If they survived, she decided, they should go to their graves with what was said.

It was pitch black. If she moved a limb, the mud sucked at it, making her feel as if they were being pulled down to hell. Anthony, meanwhile, had lost his mind. As he ranted, she felt utterly alone and abandoned. A feeling she had known as a girl.

As irritating as the sound of a broken shutter flap, flap, flapping against the house was, the relative quiet when it broke away and left another window exposed was worse. In this agonizing fashion, time crept along. Anthony exhausted himself and stopped his crazed shouting. They dozed in and out against the great roar around them. Their alternating sobs reduced down to a single word that was repeated over and over again:

"Noooooo."

Chapter 23

Holly lurched awake when Anthony shot up to a standing position next to their makeshift shelter. Holly looked down; the rope he had tied them together with lay in a pile around her.

"Damn I have to pee," he said before taking off in a run.

Holly barreled quickly behind him as he headed toward the murky daylight coming through the broken transom window.

Wind was still gusting and it was cloudy, but the weather had nowhere near the severity of the previous day or night. As Anthony threw open the doors, he shouted, "I'll take the corner to the left."

Holly hollered to him, though he was already gone, "I've been holding it so long I don't know if I'll be *able* to go!"

As she squatted, she saw Byron come stumbling out the front door to relieve himself as well. It was only when nature's call was answered that they had time to take in their decrepit state.

Anthony and Holly were coated in wet mud. Their hair was matted, and their clothes had hardened onto their bodies. Holly thought Anthony looked like a brown papier-mâché doll—then realized, with a grimace, that she likely looked the same.

The battered landscape caused another wrenching jolt to Holly's gut. Of the trees left standing, not a single leaf remained. Two dead flamingos floated in one of the deep ponds that had formed during the storm. The hurricane had snapped a utility pole in half and shot the top part, like some grotesque arrow, into the neighbor's roof. Bizarrely, no other damage to the shuttered dwelling was evident. But Holly could see that many of the other poles on the main road had come down in the wind.

The three of them went for a short walk down the road to check out the businesses nearby. At least half the buildings had sustained serious damage to their roofs.

Montez, Coralyse, and Sanford stood on the front porch together. Where was Sameera?

The rain hurt her face as she ran back toward them.

"God is good," Coralyse said. "He is good to us today."

Holly squeezed her hand and nodded. "Sameera?" she asked, looking at Montez.

He spat on the ground. "Oh, don't worry about her. If there's one thing she knows how to do, it's take care of herself."

Holly returned to the group after doing a full circle around the house to check out the damage.

"Thank God it's low season and we didn't have any guests," she told them. "It looks bad out here. But I can't tell exactly how bad. I want to check upstairs of the house—see what's still standing after the pieces that cracked off. Byron? Anthony?"

The front door opened with the loudest and longest creak Holly had ever heard. It gave her the kind of goose bumps that made her shimmy, trying to shake them off.

She was sure their earlier preparations to keep the water out and fabric goods dry had helped to some extent. But it was immediately obvious that there were places in the building that had leaked. Tabletops and kitchen counters had a layer of standing water on top of them, and everything in the house felt damp to the touch.

They stood together, paralyzed; no one seemed to know where to begin.

The Belonger

This is overwhelming to the point of depressing.

Though her shoulders remained slumped, Holly eventually broke the spell she was under. She found a broom and began to sweep the inch of water on the floors toward the front doorway. Anthony opened it for her, after which he rolled up the sopping Persian carpet in the living room and dragged it outside with Byron's help. The sky was already clearing.

It took Holly hours to make any difference at all, but she was obsessed and kept at it. Byron found a second broom, albeit a battered and beaten up one, down in the Bermuda kitchen. When he came back up, he went to the end of the house opposite from Holly and began sweeping as well.

Each time she pushed the bristles along, a little wave swelled and moved toward the open doorway, splashing over the worn middle of the threshold where countless feet had stepped over the centuries.

There was no way to know when the sun would fully shine again. *But when it does, we are going to drag the mattresses and couches outside to dry. I can't believe the clotheslines survived, but thank goodness they did. We'll hang the sheets and towels out, too. Until then, we'll have to be grateful for what we have and make do.*

The pieces they had seen falling off the exterior wall turned out to be the carved stone rain gutter. They really couldn't see it till they got up onto the roof. Nearly the entire length of it had fallen, but the sub-roofing underneath it had held.

"I could never imagine how they set that limestone trough up there to begin with," Anthony said. "There's no telling how you are going to repair it."

Holly shrugged. "Given the power of this storm—how destructive it was, its sheer force—I think Byron and I were lucky. We lost a few shutters and panes of glass as well, but that's about it."

▶▶▶

While Holly, Anthony, and Byron got the floor as dry as was possible in the circumstances, Coralyse and Sanford went to lie down; they looked worse for the wear. She didn't know where Montez had gotten off to.

After hours of work, Holly went to look for her personal things.

Even damp clothing is better than fabric that's sweat-soaked, muddy, and saturated with rainwater.

Her gratitude quickly dissolved when she discovered the kitchen stove wasn't working. The idea of a gas line malfunctioning made her ill. There obviously had been no propane on Grand Turk when The Roseate was built, so when they had installed the new stove, they'd built a small storage cabinet to house a tank against the back wall on the porch.

If I survived a massive hurricane only to be blown up by a propane leak, I'll . . .

She let the remainder of that thought go. In a fit of cursing, she rummaged around in drawers for tools, including the white Teflon tape plumbers use.

Anthony bounced in, freshly changed. "What on earth is the matter? I could hear your shouting all the way on the other side of the house."

"Do you smell propane? It's going to poison us—if it doesn't explode first." Her arms were filled with an array of items and her breathing was becoming more and more jagged by the second.

Anthony leaned toward her and examined the items in her arms. There was a distinct tinge of awe in his voice. "Do you know what you are doing?"

Holly glowered at him. "I was a single mother for over twenty years. I *had* to fix *and* build a great many things. The stove in my first house was left over from the sixties. I installed a new one myself." She snapped her fingers in the air and rushed past Anthony, headed for the tank outside.

He followed, and appeared uncertain, as if he wasn't sure if he should offer to help or not. In the end, he hovered nearby and watched her stick her head into the damaged storage shed.

"The wind shifted the tank around and it stripped out some of the threads on the connector," she called out to him. "Don't worry; I turned it off. Looks like we have escaped death twice in the last twenty-four hours."

For the hour that followed, she ran back and forth between the kitchen and the tiny shed, cramming herself into uncomfortable spots, clanking and cursing away.

For a while, Anthony simply sat back and watched. Holly knew from experience that men hated feeling helpless, but she thought, *I don't have time to babysit him right now.*

Anthony got the hint. As the rain abated, he came up with a different project for himself: he started a burn pile, as well as a second pile of items that would need to be bagged up and dragged off to the dump . . . if and when the dump reopened.

One more crawl out of the shed and Holly headed toward the stove. She lit a match on a striker box and held it to one of the front gas burners, then slowly turned the knob . . .

The whoosh of ignition made her smile.

She danced back and forth, singing, "I did it, I did it, I really, really did it!"

She plunked a pan down on the stove and started cooking immediately.

Both Byron and Anthony suddenly appeared at her side. The simmering aroma of garlic was almost agonizing, and set all their stomachs to growling.

"You two can't stand around here underfoot while I'm trying

to cook," she scolded them. "I'll come get you when the food's ready."

She stirred some red pepper flakes into the sauce she was simmering. *Just the way Byron likes it.*

While vegetables sizzled in a pan, she stole away and stabbed a meat thermometer into the precooked pork roast she'd left packed in ice in a small cooler she'd stuck inside the refrigerator before the storm hit. It had stayed cool enough that she was certain it could be safely eaten.

"That's dinner," she announced to no one in particular.

She felt powerful when she cooked—and as Anthony had pointed out when they arrived, there was food here that would spoil if it weren't prepared soon. She quickly surveyed the contents of the two freezers, trying not to let too much of the still-cold air escape, and grabbed out the veal she had stockpiled some months back. She decided to make piccata, which she sliced thin and marinated in lemon juice. She would finish the meat by sautéing it with butter, minced garlic, and spices just before everyone sat down.

In a wide wooden bowl, she made a huge salad. They'd bought bread from the bakery before Nestor and stored it in the freezer; she cut it into chunks, smeared a dollop of garlic butter on each one, and tossed them into the oven to warm.

Anthony was outside on the porch, picking shards of broken glass out of a window frame. As she cooked, she could still hear Byron sweep, sweep, sweeping. She dried her hands with the dishtowel she'd tucked into her waistband as a makeshift apron and went to talk to him.

Byron seemed as if he was lost in the motion of the broom. She wondered if it was serving as a sort of mantra, helping him concentrate on quiet meditation. Perhaps it was helping him regain some sense of calm in a world that had so recently been pandemonium.

Chaos wasn't healthy. That much she knew for sure. She decided to leave him in peace for now, and turned her attention to the table—used her towel to dry it, and then put out a paper plate for each person and seven paper cups she had filled with bottled water.

She furrowed her brows, thinking of everything they'd been put through.

"To hell with it," she said out loud, and put a large bottle of rum in the middle of the table.

She cupped her hand to the side of her mouth. "Come and get it!" she called out before scurrying back to the kitchen to finish off the veal.

Chapter 24

Holly's muscles ached as she slid into her bed early that night. She was tormented by dampness too. Her sweaty hair stuck to her head. Even though she'd hung her sheets out that day, they were still dank. With every little move she got a whiff of mildew coming off the fabric of her nightgown.

She hadn't bothered bringing her pillows inside. They would take days and days to dry. But this bed was the only place she had to sleep.

And I am lucky to have it. I bet there's plenty who are sleeping on the floor. Maybe without a roof over their heads.

There was no food to be wasted, so it worried her that all the boxed goods in the pantry were sagging with moisture. There were only a few stores here. Replacement articles would have to be shipped in from Miami. That would take many months. Even years.

For someone like her, who liked the old saying, "A place for everything and everything in its place," the visual chaos brought her to tears. Cleaning up the garbage and tattered plastic shreds caught in every branch and crevice outside felt impossible. It would take forever to pick up the debris and rake the shattered glass out of the sand.

Though she was heavy with fatigue, she still couldn't begin to think about sleep. She was agitated. Discouraged beyond anything she'd known before. It was a sinking feeling that sucked the energy out of her. How could she find the will to go on? As much as she wanted to, how would it be possible?

When she had come to bed, she'd found her son had surprised her, once again, by slipping two novels onto her bedside table. She knew them well; they were her favorites. Now, hoping to quell her restlessness, she opened *To Kill a Mockingbird* and leaned over toward the flickering lamplight as far as she could without falling out of bed.

God—please, please, keep all of our friends safe tonight. If you just let everyone live, it can be a new day. A new start. If we can get through this, our priorities will change for the better. After Nestor—how could they not?

She practically knew the words of the book by heart, so really, her reading was another form of prayer. *The message of this book is that human beings can choose to stand up in the face of catastrophe. But the author makes it clear that both courage and bravery are needed to get through the most difficult times.* It made her sad. She didn't think she had fight left in her. Her head collapsed into the pages of the book and she started to cry.

Although she'd left her door open, she had no intention of seeking Anthony out. Having sex with him had been a form of insanity. Perhaps it had been no more than a desperate bonding over the small matter called *survival*. Maybe the fight over life and death had simply been too intoxicating to resist. If this was not true—if she meant something more to Anthony—she knew he would come to her on his own.

A difficult lesson I learned from the years I tried to win Montez over. No matter the outcome, Anthony showing up tonight or not, I intend to sleep soundly. Tomorrow will be another hard day. In fact, all I see ahead of me is an unending series of hard days. She remembered a time not long ago when she'd thought about planning a vacation. It made her laugh. A vacation indeed.

A light knock on the doorjamb caught her attention.

"You are a vision, Miss Walker." Anthony smiled appreciatively.

"Ha! I don't feel like a vision. I feel hot and sticky."

He held two glasses full of amber liquid aloft. "I thought you might like a nightcap."

Despite the low light, he smiled at her in a way that lit up the room. "Also, since I've been through hurricanes before, I hope you don't mind a piece of advice."

"I'll take anything that might make me feel better. I just want to sob. My home, my businesses, my inventory . . ."

He handed her a glass. "But you and your son are still alive." He held up one finger. "That is all that matters in the end."

Holly nodded but her eyes skittered away from his. *Can it really be that simple? Am I supposed to sing "Whistle While You Work" and skip down the street collecting the garbage?*

"You will quickly find that we have been incredibly fortunate," he said gently. "We're unhurt. We still have some food. Tomorrow you will feel much better. You'll see." He patted her leg.

It had a ring of truth to it—and Holly heard it. "You're so thoughtful, Lord Bascombe. You may be a lesser one, but I kind of like you. You're growing on me."

He took her hand and pulled her up from the bed. "Come."

He wrapped his arm around her and kissed the top of her head as they walked to the bathroom. It was lit by an oil lamp. Four five-gallon water bottles sat next to the bathtub.

Holly gaped. "What's all this?"

"I filled them and had them sitting in the sun all day. Not hot, but warm enough. Get in and I'll pour it over you. We can wash your hair. You'll feel so much better when you're clean."

"For heaven's sake. I'm so grateful."

This guy is full of surprises.

Chapter 25

By midday the sky was a brilliant blue and a gentle trade breeze fanned the island. Holly's front and back porch were strewn with upholstered furniture and linens and pillows baking in the sun.

Montez informed Holly that he was going to try to navigate Coralyse and Sanford through the flooded streets to their house. Byron was insistent that he join them.

This thing of his lately—wanting independence from me, making his own choices—I feel like I can't open my mouth anymore. I'd love for him to stay here and help with the cleanup. But if I say so, he will fight me on it. If I say the sky is blue, he will argue the point.

"Once we assess the damage and get them situated, we'll move on to Aunt Rosie and Uncle Harold's," Byron told her. "Since there's no Internet, power, or cell service—can we agree to operate under the assumption that no news is good news? Just take on the next task in front of us and do the best we can?"

"I can try. But I'd like you to keep in mind that your mother is going to worry until you make it back home. That's what mothers do."

Holly tried to push Byron out of her mind as she and Anthony readied themselves to check on the older folks who lived closer to Roseate.

It turned out Mrs. James, Anthony's childhood nanny, lived

just around the corner. Matius showed up at her front gate just as Holly and Anthony arrived—Mrs. James had taken care of him when he was young as well—and they all hugged as if they hadn't seen each other in a decade. It certainly felt that long.

Matius raised his hands to the blue sky. "Hurricane gone."

"And good riddance!" Holly said, smiling.

Anthony broke the spirit of the moment when he started pounding on the door. "Mrs. James!"

"There's no need to scream," Holly insisted. She pretended to plug her ears as she stood next to him on the stoop of the old stone cottage, which had seen better days.

He shot Holly a glance. "I'm not screaming. I'm shouting. Mrs. James lost most of her hearing years ago."

Holly fell back a step. *Once again, I have underestimated the man.*

The door eased open and a frail old woman blinked into the sunlight where they stood. She took one look at Anthony and clapped her hands together. She then shook them back and forth above her head in celebration. "Oh, Ant'ny! My boy. I know you was comin ta look fa me. You done fall down and get up wit' me ova de years and now ve make it through one more time. Praise de Lord! Tank ya Jesus!"

He reached out and held her tight. "We sure did, Mrs. James. We sure did." As he rocked her, he wiped away a tear from his eye. "This is my friend Holly."

Mrs. James then hugged her with gusto . . . apparently, any friend of Anthony's was immediately okay with her.

Anthony's face fell from relief to confusion as he searched for Matius. He was just saying, "What the hell?" when Matius came back around the corner from the back of the house.

"Two of her windows blew out," the younger man reported. "The good news is I found a piece of plywood I can use to mostly cover them."

Mrs. James let go of Holly and threw herself around Matius. "Tank yinna fa comin' 'gain ta help de old woman. Yinna is good, science boys." She patted him on the back with both of her hands.

"Of course, madame," Matius said. "It's how we do, isn't it? We take care of each other. Just as you did when I was a baby."

Mrs. James searched his eyes and briefly laid her forehead on his chest. After a few moments, she laughed and pushed him away. Then she took both of Anthony's hands in hers, saying, "My boy, my boy, my boy."

A lump of emotion grew in Holly's throat, nearly choking her.

Looking at Holly over Mrs. James's shoulder, Anthony explained. "She was our caregiver. From the time we were born, really. I can't remember my life without her in it. Nor do I want to."

When he pulled away from Mrs. James, he turned and leaned on the front gate and stared out into the street. He seemed overcome.

Something I can totally understand. It's been happening often. I guess this is a normal part of the process. The last few days had been a heaving series of dramas.

"Mrs. James," Holly said, "I own The Roseate House. As you know, it's not far, and we've got some extra supplies. Do you need anything in particular? Towels? Sheets?"

A slow smile spread across her face. "Towels? Oh yes, tank ya! Dis vedder muck up e'ryting I own. I sure wud feel good if I cud wipe off my skin."

"They'll be clean but a little damp from the air. We'll hang them out in your backyard in the sun. I'll go get some. Back in a few minutes and I'll help with . . ." She gestured to the chaos around them. "All this."

Holly waved to Anthony as he ducked back into the alley-way and turned the corner onto Duke Street. Though town was a disaster zone, she wasn't afraid. She had made a decision.

Never again will I count on someone to save me. Or wait around for a man. From now on I am in charge of my own life—I am running the show. If someone wants to come aboard and enjoy my company, fine. But I am steering my ship from this point forward.

Holding on to one of her "welcoming arm" stair railings, Holly made her way up into The Roseate. Though she felt like skipping, it was hot already. She looked forward to a few long drinks of water and washing her face again.

The front door wasn't locked. She didn't even know where the key to the house was. The previous owner had told her when she bought the place that in all the many years he'd lived there, he'd never needed one.

As she wandered through the living room, she thought she heard a noise. She stopped short, listening hard. Her heart raced like mad in her chest.

Is it my imagination? The walls of the house could still be shifting, maybe that's it. Or smaller pieces of stone falling from the roof. There had been so many noises over the last few days. *Let's face it, we're all in shock. I'm jumping at every little thing. That's what trauma does. It makes you . . . what do they call it? Hypervigilant.*

The need for water was greater than her fear. She went back toward the kitchen, though the hair on the back of her neck was standing on end in warning.

Three young men stood in the dim light. Spotting them, a surge of stress hormones flowed through Holly so powerfully that she thought she might pass out.

A strong smell of hard alcohol wafted into her nose, making her snort. When one of the boys saw her, he leered, "Ve come lookin' fa food, and ve find rum. Oh yeah! Now see wa else ve find?"

The two other teens shushed him.

The Belonger

"Charles, don't," one said. He was the boy who worked in their dive shop. Robert.

Holly stared at him. "Robert, what are you doing?"

"I tried to stop them," he said weakly.

Charles sneered at him. "You drank your share of rum, though."

He moved quickly toward her and her instinct took over. There was no time to waste. She knew exactly where the knife rack was; she leaned into the counter and grabbed a short, and very sharp, paring knife. Her choice was deliberate: she thought using a short knife instead of a long one might spare the young man's life.

He pushed her so hard her head crashed into the hanging cabinet behind her. Then he asked in his slurred voice, "Wa you think you gon' to do with dat?"

"I'm going to cut you, you little shit."

He laughed as he lunged at her.

Having survived a massive hurricane and so much else over the last forty-three years, Holly had no intention of letting herself be attacked. In some corner of her brain, she hoped Charles would survive. However, her father had told her years before that if you knock a man down, you better make sure he can't get back up. Though he was little more than a kid, he was more than old enough to hurt her badly—so, with all the strength she could summon, she stabbed him in the side of his neck just as Robert grabbed him from behind, trying to pull him back.

Amazingly, the blade only went in half of the way. Charles was stunned silent for a moment, breathing hard. She stared over his shoulder into Robert's eyes as he wrestled with him, her hand still on the blade handle.

Charles had shoved her up onto the countertop, which was fortunate for her. She released the knife, reached behind her into a canister she kept there, and drew out her Glock 43. She always kept the 9mm pistol loaded, just in case. Once again, the choice of weapon was deliberate. The small bullets it used were meant to stop an intruder but hopefully not kill them.

"Stop where you are, boys," Holly said in her best teacher voice. "Do not move one inch. I already stabbed Charles. I'm sure you can see that I wouldn't think twice about shooting any of you—and I am an excellent shot. You have to be when you grow up out in the country like I did. Charles, you have made a terrible mistake picking on me. I have been through too much to put up with anyone's bad behavior."

She reached out and pulled the knife out of the boy's neck in one quick movement. Between the gun she held and the sight of blood spurting, the three teens did as they were told, though Charles did raise one hand to put pressure on his wound.

"Back up," Holly demanded. "Give me some room to get down."

He did.

"You alright?"

He nodded, backing away.

With one eye on the trio, she pulled a flashlight out of a drawer. From another she pulled out a pile of dishtowels; she took one off the top and handed it to the injured boy.

"Let me see that wound," she ordered him.

When he didn't move, she made an impatient gesture and he removed his hand from his neck. She shone her flashlight on his neck, scrutinized the cut carefully.

"I didn't get the jugular vein," she said. "I tried not to, though all I know about physiology I learned from dissecting a baby pig in college. Turns out we're both lucky. You won't die today. It will be sore as hell for a while, but it won't kill you."

She ducked down under the kitchen sink and produced some

peroxide. She handed it to Charles, and looked each boy in the eye as she said their names. "Robert. Charles. Bradlio. I know all of your parents. I know *you* from church. If you leave now and don't bother us again, we won't talk about any of this for now. But if I hear of a whiff of trouble involving any of you in the coming days, I'm going right to your family. Because I think the police are a little busy right now, I don't want to bother them. But I will if you force me to."

The young men had their hands in the air and were backing up toward the front door.

She followed them—shouting now, finally feeling her rage. "It's up to you, boys. My friends will be back shortly, and we are more than capable of defending this house. I promise you. If you decide to report me when the army gets here, I doubt you'll get much sympathy. Trespassing was a bad decision . . . but I don't really want any of you to go to jail. You're still so young. Do you want another chance?"

In unison they said, "Yes, ma'am!"—and promptly scrambled out the door.

She'd never seen anyone move so fast.

Chapter 26

Holly had a small stack of folded towels in her arms and her pistol stuck into the back of her waistband. She honestly didn't know what she would encounter on the way back to Ms. James's house, or when they returned to Roseate later in the day. Best to be prepared. But she didn't plan on telling her friends about what happened. Not yet. She had handled the situation for the moment.

They were still outside clearing debris when Holly approached Mrs. James's house.

As Holly handed her the towels, the old woman pointed to the two men in her yard and whispered, as if telling her a secret, "Ant'ny is my heart string. I love him timmich. He always been a sensitive chile, but so loyal. You caan find a more loyal man. He aint no raft fa sure. His poor heart always been tender." She pointed at Holly with great humor. "You, now. You take good care of it. I can see he fallin' fa you."

Holly put the palm of her hand to her face. "Me?"

"Oh yes," Mrs. James said. "You full his eye."

When Anthony returned to them, Mrs. James wiped her eyes with one hand as she held on to his arm with the other. "He duz take good care of his nanny. The roof strong, my boy. It hold tight."

"For what I paid for it, it better have." Anthony winked at her, and it seemed to melt her.

She giggled uproariously and made a gesture like she was shooing a fly.

Mrs. James told them, "De noise was somethin' though. I was 'fraid, but not like when Ike came. Dis time, I didn't think I would kick de bucket. I even sleep fa part of it. Holly, how tings by de Roseate?"

She shrugged. "A bit battered, I'm afraid."

Mrs. James's face fell. "Oh no."

"We'll fix her up. We will. Don't you worry. We will manage somehow."

Mrs. James clapped her hands together again. "Yinna come out de hot sun. Only ting I ga here is water. Yinna wan' some water?" She motioned for them to enter through the front door.

Inside, she pointed toward two chairs in her sitting area. Holly promptly sat down, as if she were there on a regular visit—like any other day—but the men set about exploring the other three rooms for damage.

"Nanny's getting old," Anthony said quietly to Holly after he'd done some recon. "I'm going to clear off the walkways for her. Don't want her to get tripped up on anything."

It will take months before insurance claims are processed and paid out, building materials are ordered, and workmen make the rounds repairing buildings. For now, I am grateful to be alive. And relatively unharmed by that boy. She was thrilled that Mrs. James had made it through the storm without any injury at all too.

In a half hour, they had her house and yard as secure as it was going to get for a while.

"Nanny, we have to see about some of the others, but I'll come back and see you soon."

Holly thought the old woman was extraordinarily brave as she cheerily waved goodbye to them from the other side of her gate.

Holly's heart sank as she, Anthony, and Matius reached the Lightbourne family's home a quarter of a mile down the road—most of the roof was gone.

They began calling to the elderly couple as they hurried their steps.

It turned out the Lightbournes were sitting outside on what was left of their back deck, unharmed, although both were wide-eyed and shaking their heads as if they were seriously confused. While Anthony and Matius took a tour of the building, Holly stayed with them, explaining what she knew about the state of the island—which wasn't very much.

"I only have one blue plastic tarp with me," Matius told them, "but I can tack it up on the roof to create a temporary cover."

All five of them had a long discussion. The kitchen was the largest room in the house and a constant trade breeze blew through the large windows at either end of it; the Lightbournes called it "the wind tunnel." By consensus it was decided since this was the room that had sustained the least amount of damage, they would move their large table out and replace it with the couple's double bed.

Holly worked on securing hinges and fasteners that had come loose from the wind while the men moved the furniture. When they were done and Holly saw that the Lightbournes were seated on two of the kitchen chairs, looking a bit lost, she told them, "You'll still have room in here for a small table. I've got one in storage. Anthony?"

"We'll bring it over this afternoon."

The couple nodded by way of response but still seemed dazed. As if they didn't understand what had happened.

Holly went outside and hollered up the ladder to Matius, "I'm going back to The Roseate to start lunch. When you're done here, come over to take a break and eat."

She ran inside to Anthony, who was now helping the Lightbournes clear out some debris.

"I'm going to start food," she told him. "Come home when you can."

His eyes fixed on hers with such intensity that something stirred inside of her—and that something was quite torrid. *Hmm. Later we can see about that.*

Anthony swept off his hat and bowed to her. "Will do. And I thank you, fair lady."

Holly let out a delighted laugh. "You are such a dork."

"Perhaps. But I'm a gallant one . . . and you are a ravishing woman. Simply ravishing."

She casually waved away his compliment, but as she walked out the front gate and toward The Roseate, she couldn't stop smiling.

Even so, she reached toward the back of her waist band and felt for her revolver before continuing on.

Although it lay upside down, her picnic table had survived the storm. Holly thought it would be wonderful to have a meal *al fresco* after the many hours they had been closed up inside. She was so pleased by the idea that a burst of adrenaline surged through her, enabling her to hoist the table up onto one end and then drop it onto the ground right side up.

One of the boards on the top was cracked, but other than that it was in perfect condition. Pivoting it to one side and then the other, she moved it closer to the house and into the shade.

She went inside, selected two packages of thin-sliced pork chops from the freezer, and set them in the sun to defrost. Everything else in the deep chest freezer was still pretty cold but finally showing signs of thawing. She wondered how much longer it could last. They should make a plan during lunch for giving some of the meat away.

Now, how to cook these pork chops?

The Weber grill was nowhere to be found, gone the same way of the gas grill that preceded it.

I need something fireproof to hold the coals, she thought. As a memory flashed, she jumped up in the air with excitement. There was a huge terracotta planter under the house. In the past, she'd seen chimineas made of terracotta that held outdoor fires; like those, the planter would probably contain the heat.

Some distance from the house, she spotted a mesh grill on top of a pile of debris; she ran over to grab it. *Perfect, I can just lay that over the top.*

Now the real challenge: moving the giant pot out from under the house.

It took some time for her to dig out the potting soil still caked at the bottom of the planter. She hadn't been overestimating the weight—it *was* heavy. She was drenched in sweat by the time she rolled it outside along its bottom edge, this way and that, in many small steps. It was an unexpected, but exciting, victory when the grate capped the planter perfectly—as if it had been custom made for it.

Holly got the fire going, then dusted off her hands and bobbed her head in satisfaction.

It was nearly three o'clock by the time Anthony and Matius straggled in. They told her they'd gone from the Lightbournes' to check on the Inghams and the Rigbys. Although they were ravenous, they told Holly they couldn't bear to sit down and eat without cleaning up first.

She fully understood the need. "Grab a towel off the clothes-line," she told them. Luckily, the smell of the great outdoors had tamped down the musky odor the hurricane had left behind in the linens.

There was a gravity-fed hose from the cistern and the water was air temperature, so it was lukewarm. In turn, Anthony and Matius went in and sprayed themselves down. As they cleaned up and changed, Holly finished setting the table.

With glowing skin and wet hair, they sat down to a feast for their early dinner. Besides the pork chops Holly had grilled, she had made hash browns using the onions and canned potatoes in the pantry. Determined to use up the last of the fresh vegetables before they turned bad, she also served a cold salad and a hot sauté.

No one said a word while they wolfed down what was on their plate; only the scraping sounds of knife and fork filled the air.

Matius finally joked, "It must be terrible. No one is talking."

Holly laughed. "You know, I could live with the quiet for a good long while. After all that ruckus, there's something to be said for silence."

Chapter 27

After lunch they brought the small table to the Lightbournes' house, as promised. The old couple greeted them like they hadn't seen them in ages, but the trio couldn't linger.

"We still have a long way to go before nightfall," Anthony told them with a sigh.

As she was leaving, Holly looked over her shoulder. The old folks were preparing to enjoy a cup of tea together in the kitchen—on the very table they'd brought them. What a sweet vignette they made together, holding hands.

She unlatched the gate to let herself out of the yard. *Get ready. It's going to be a long walk in the hot sun.*

Anthony wanted to check on the wife of a close friend—Joab, someone Holly knew only peripherally.

"Many years ago, we became fishing buddies," Anthony explained, "but we got on so well it grew into a friendship. We're one another's confidants. I'd trust him with my life." He pinched the bridge of his nose. "Joab has been away in the Dominican Republic on some business. Goods there are so much less expensive. He and his wife live toward the west side of the island, in Macaya Point. It's pretty isolated, even by Grand Turk standards. I fear it's likely, in the aftermath of the storm, that Joab will be stuck off-island for some time. I must check on his wife. Theresa is her name."

The Belonger

Holly went through her backpack. She had stripped down its contents to what she considered bare essentials. As nails, screws, staples, and other fasteners had turned out to be what was needed most often, they'd split the weight of the hardware and the tools required to install them between the three of them—though Holly suspected the men had weighted their rucksacks more heavily than hers, in addition to the tarps, new and old, they were lugging with them.

I've got three medium-size bottles of water. One to keep me hydrated during the trip; the other two to leave behind for whoever might need them. My medical kit and some dried goods, too. Will I need anything else?

"It may take many months for the power to be turned back on for the whole island," Anthony said. "I certainly hope the governor will airdrop supplies in soon, but even that may take days to happen. We have no way of knowing what's going on here, let alone the outer islands. For now, we are completely on our own and must be cautious."

A chill ran down Holly's spine and she prayed he was exaggerating. But one look at him revealed that a deep crease had formed between his eyebrows.

"I know from a very difficult experience that people are capable of most anything when they get desperate," he said grimly.

As they started walking, Holly turned Anthony's words over in her mind. She was certain his biggest concern was anyone in his care getting hurt—namely, her. In fact, given the way he was now clenching his jaw and grinding his teeth as they marched along, she guessed that was all he could think about. She pushed her recent attack to the back of her mind. Someone had to keep a level head. She was sure it could be her.

Anthony stopped abruptly and spun to face both Holly and Matius. "Keep your eyes wide open. If anybody stops us on the way, stay together and listen carefully to what they are saying.

Matius, I'm quite serious now . . . take care of Holly. No matter what else is going on. And, if I may be so bold . . . I hope I don't sound like an arse . . . please let me do the talking."

The view as they climbed was spectacular, eventually giving way to an ocean view on all four sides of them. Holly was sweating dreadfully under her wide-brimmed straw hat, but with her fair skin, she dared not take it off. She couldn't be of help to anyone if she got burnt to a crisp. Mercifully, the higher they got, the stronger the trade breeze blew.

They stopped to take a rest under the shade of a large palm tree, Holly removed her hat for a moment and put her face toward the wind with her eyes closed.

"Not far now," Matius said. "Just there." He pointed up the road to the right.

The second he said it, a man on a bicycle turned the corner. Holly's breath caught and she glanced over at Anthony, whose face seemed set in stone. She wondered if they were all thinking the same thing.

Where could he possibly be going? As far as she knew, no businesses were open; everyone was still busy digging their shops out from under rubble.

The rider waved as he zoomed past them, then flew off down the hill, zigzagging around potholes as he went. They all turned to watch him and waited until he was out of sight before resuming walking. After scanning the empty streets around them, Holly felt they were safe to continue.

Anthony must have come to exactly the same conclusion, for he said, "All right. Let's move along."

The exterior of Joab's house had bare patches that looked like raw wounds. Its once-white masonry walls and aqua shutters, still tightly closed, had been blasted by the high winds and the sand it carried with it. Much of the paint, even sections of the stucco layers, were gone. Here and there the stone underneath was exposed.

The house's enclosed yard was filled with more of the random trash and rubble present everywhere they went. What branches were left on their shrubs and trees were strewn with shreds of plastic.

The group stood together by the unopened front gate.

"I've suddenly got that overwhelmed feeling again," Holly whispered. She was sure the sight of all the garbage everywhere was what caused her sinking sensation; something about it left her feeling defeated before they'd even begun. Standing there in the baking late-afternoon sun, she couldn't imagine how it could ever be cleaned up.

They all stood perfectly still, as if mesmerized by the mess, until the front door quietly opened and a hugely pregnant young woman in a gauzy pink cotton dress stepped out.

Well, this must be Theresa.

Her skin shone like seasoned cherry wood and her long braids were perfectly groomed. She shaded her eyes from the sun with one hand and scanned the group with a slight frown—but when she recognized Anthony and Matius, her face flew open in a huge smile. "Have you come all this way?"

Holly watched as Theresa picked her steps carefully over to Anthony. She seemed to be moving more slowly than caution required. *Is she limping?*

Meanwhile, Anthony pushed the gate open little by little, reaching over it and clearing the garbage blocking the arc of its swing as he forced it inward.

When it was fully clear, Theresa threw herself into his arms. "I have never been happier to see anyone in my life," she cried.

Holly knew it was unusual that Theresa, a married woman in this particular culture, allowed herself to be held by a man who was not her husband. But hug each other she and Anthony did—with palpable intensity. One squeeze he gave her was so tight it forced a moan from her.

He pulled back and stared at her.

"Are you hurt?"

Theresa lifted her skirt up to show her knee, which was colored with deep shades of black and blue.

Holly's eyes widened. Something about the color seemed much worse than a bruise. It was the color Byron's skin had been when he broke his arm. "How far up does the discoloration go?" she asked.

"Here." Theresa touched her hip and winced. "A window gave way and blew in on me. Even one of the shutters bashed in."

"Did the impact hurt the baby?" Anthony sounded woeful. "Holly, please take a look at those scrapes."

Theresa's mouth hung open as she held her belly and gasped. Holly began to step forward, but Theresa held up her hand and held Holly's eyes in a silent cry of anguish. She gasped loudly, but the moment eventually passed.

"It . . . seems I'm in labor, Anthony. Rotten timing, don't you think?" Theresa asked with a laugh.

Her dark humor made Anthony chuckle as well, despite the seriousness of the situation.

These two are longtime friends—close friends, you can tell. I have to do everything I can to help her. A fellow mother.

With his hand under her arm, Anthony braced Theresa against him. "Do you think you can walk with us, dear? I want to take you to The Roseate."

Theresa didn't get a chance to answer because Holly jumped into the conversation.

"No. She can't walk it. It's not safe. I know what to do. I'll run back to Front Street and see if I can find a motor scooter.

Byron has one around sometimes. If not, I'll go door to door." She paused a moment to catch her breath. "I'm a fast runner. I was a long-distance champion when I was young." She placed her hands on her hips, as if inviting anyone to argue with her.

Anthony slowly blinked his eyes twice. "Alllll . . . right. I'll assume you know how to ride it. I hope there's gas in the thing. We'll do what we can here until you return. But just to be clear, *I* will be the one driving Theresa back. These roads are so rutted they are perilous."

Despite the somewhat dodgy transportation she was proposing, Holly knew Theresa would be better off at Roseate House, and the sooner the better. She was alone out here on Macaya Point, and as Anthony had stated so clearly earlier in the day, in this state of emergency, things could become dangerous, fast. The need for food and water was a primal concern.

Rumor had it the medical clinic had sustained extensive damage and wasn't functional. Extraordinary times called for extraordinary measures; they would have to try to deliver this baby themselves. There was a retired nurse who lived downtown who might be able to help if Theresa's labor went awry. Holly wondered if they could find her should they need to. Equally important was something else Anthony had said earlier—that at some point in the not-too-distant future, the government of Turks and Caicos would send a chopper out to assess the damage, and the beach in front of The Roseate was one place where they would surely land. Perhaps they'd be willing to take Theresa back to the hospital in Provo when they did.

Anthony left Theresa with Matius for a moment and leaned in close to Holly. "I don't want you to be alone," he whispered. "Let Matius come with you. I feel the need to stay with Theresa because it's all I can do right now to hang on to some shred of confidence this birth will turn out all right in the end." As if he was giving himself a pep talk, he pointed out that Theresa was a healthy young woman. "Most births happen quite naturally. If it comes down to it, this will be the third baby I've helped bring into the world."

Holly's eyes widened. "Why? I mean—what happened?"

Anthony shrugged. "Another story for another time, luv. Actually, two stories."

Holly didn't mind Matius coming along but she didn't wait for him, either; she took off running down the hill at breakneck speed, thinking about what Anthony had just told her.

Mother of God, where hasn't that man been? What hasn't he done? More importantly, is he full of it? Or can he really deliver that baby?

Chapter 28

The tropical sun could be a cruel taskmaster even when it started dipping toward the horizon. Holly had left her backpack behind and had taken off in such a hurry that she'd forgotten to bring any drinking water. Within minutes, her legs felt heavy—but she pushed on because she had seen the look in Theresa's eyes. As coolly as the young woman had tried to handle the situation, Holly was sure she must be beside herself with worry.

Holly had had a difficult labor with Byron—thirty-four excruciating hours. In the end, she'd been so exhausted that she'd fallen asleep between her contractions, which felt like a cruel joke when she jolted awake only moments later in horrible pain. They'd had to make a cut to get the baby out, and then call in a special surgeon to stitch her up again. It had been months before she could walk normally again. The idea of Theresa having her baby without a hospital to care for her made Holly shudder.

The best they could do was to get her to the mansion, where she would be safe and where they had water that could be boiled and used to sterilize.

Sterilize what? she asked herself.

All she really knew was that germs would die in high heat, but she actually knew very little about birthing a baby. The panic this realization made her feel helped propel her forward, and soon, running at full force, she saw the coral-pink Roseate in the distance.

Inside The Roseate, Holly pulled her gun out of her waistband, put a not very cold pack on the knot on the back of her head, and took an aspirin. She did not linger for long. But she did drink an entire bottle of water before heading back.

The last few days had been like a war zone. In war, you keep going because you have to. Holly had never known she was so strong.

Byron had left his scooter out in the shed; it was flooded, but only with a foot of water. She backed the scooter out and started it with a roar. *The roads are in rough shape, but I think I can pick my way along the shoulders until I reach the rise of the hill.*

Time dragged as she bumped along, getting drenched by the muddy water of the deep puddles she wasn't able to avoid. It felt like an eternity until she saw Joab's house.

I did it. And there is Anthony, anxiously waiting for me. I bet he never doubted I could do it.

She wasn't surprised when he loaded Theresa on the bike and headed downhill toward The Roseate without much discussion. He had boxed up some of Theresa's things, and he paused only long enough to ask Matius and Holly to carry them home before zooming off.

Holly surveyed the contents of the box. *This won't do at all.* She ran inside to gather up more of Theresa's clothes.

When she came back out the front door, she could see Anthony and Theresa weren't making much headway. Anthony was trying to ease the bike over the large bumps and down into the unavoidable ruts. She imagined Theresa moaned as he did so, and Anthony silently cursed the rough landscape.

Although she and Matius couldn't quite catch up to them on foot, she was able to see them as they reached the house in the distance. Step by slowly rising step, Anthony helped Theresa until she reached the top of the long stairway.

By the time Holly and Matius arrived at Roseate, Anthony had installed Theresa in the cream-colored armchair in Holly's bedroom. Matius ducked away to the kitchen in search of food to prepare for the group while Holly dug around in her closet and found a waterproof mattress pad, a thick natural fiber second pad to put over it, a fresh set of sheets, and a stack of smaller quilted pads.

Holly was grateful that she was a pack rat. The previous owner of the inn had told her, "I won't lie to you, darlin.' My mother was sick for a long time and even died in this room. Thought this stuff might come in handy one day, but you do what you want. You know how it is out on Grand Turk—we save everything for a rainy day." And look what had happened. They now had what they needed to get through this crisis.

The baby's birth will bring everything around full circle from losing the old woman in this room. This will be good karma. Good juju. There will be joy here from this day forward instead of sorrow.

Once the bed was made, Anthony told Theresa, "Get as comfortable as you can. I'm going to start hauling water from the cistern up to the bathtub." He said to Holly, "She'll want to be clean before she lies down. It must be 90 degrees outside today. The water will be warm."

"When did anyone last clean the tub?" Holly asked.

He gave her a sheepish look. "I didn't even think of that."

"There's a stack of white buckets under the house," Holly said briskly. "Bring me a full bucket and I'll use it for scrubbing. I'll come down and help you haul water as soon as I'm done."

She made short work of cleaning the tub, and soon she was filling the buckets and bringing them up to the bathroom alongside Anthony. He nearly sprinted the stairs as Holly followed behind more slowly. Every once in a while, she put the bucket she was carrying down and rested before starting again.

She called to Anthony, "You're doing twice the work I am."

"You're still a help. Take your time," he said with a wink.

Holly had already noticed how in sync she and Anthony were when an important job needed to be done. Preparing for Theresa's labor, she found their natural teamwork was impossible to mistake.

When the bath was ready, Anthony took Holly's hand and walked her over to the chair where Theresa was reclined. His touch was warm and tender and, though she felt silly about it, her heart fluttered.

Jeez. This is no time for mushy stuff. I'm like a teenager around him lately.

"Theresa, I want you to know I've attended a baby's birth before," Anthony said.

The look on Theresa's face was beyond shocked.

He held up the palm of his hand as if to stop any questions she may be formulating. "Chalk it up to a long and—shall we just say 'richly lived' life."

He gestured toward Holly. "Holly's a mother, too. None of what is about to happen is new to us. You will start off the labor with your usual modesty, but as time passes, and the time to push grows near, you will forget all about that. Being embarrassed is counterproductive, so please try very hard to put your faith in us. I think we can all agree that our goal, in the end, is a healthy baby."

Holly wasn't sure if she should share her most humiliating moment of childbirth with them, but Anthony's eyes were pleading with her to agree with him. She pushed her lips together and stared at the ground.

"Yes. Ah . . ." She felt her face burning red, but she started to laugh, hoping to lighten the moment. "I pushed so hard when

Byron was born that . . . well . . . I pushed something out besides my son." Holly screwed up her face. "If you know what I mean."

Theresa squealed like a young girl. "I would be humiliated!"

Holly laughed hard. "I know, it sounds awful, but at the time I didn't care. You get *that* engrossed, believe me."

Theresa's face began to contort with pain. The twitching of her cheeks seemed beyond her control. After her contraction reached its peak, she told Holly softly, "I've heard that can happen."

Her tone was so sweet Holly shrugged comically. "Like the old saying goes . . . accidents will happen." She held on to Theresa's hand as she shifted around and tried to get comfortable.

Holly felt sorry that the linens, like everything else inside the house, were still clammy, but she was at least confident they were relatively clean.

They heard banging coming from the kitchen.

"That would be Matius," Anthony said. "We can call him when we need something. Holly and I will stay right here with you."

"Ready for a bath?" Holly asked.

Theresa nodded tentatively.

Together, Anthony and Holly helped her up, and Holly brought her into the bathroom. When she was pretty sure the labor pains had calmed down for the time being and Theresa was able to be on her own for a few minutes, she went back in the bedroom and rifled through the clothes she'd brought from Theresa's house.

She found just what she was looking for.

Cotton nightgown in hand, she knocked on the bathroom door. "Yes?" Theresa called out.

Holly cracked the door, slid the nightgown inside, and quietly shut the door.

About ten minutes later, Theresa emerged, appearing incandescent. "I feel so much more refreshed. Though this leg is aching. Can I take some Advil, do you think?"

She barely made it to the bed before she groaned again and grabbed her belly. Anthony appeared immediately, and he and Holly each took one of her elbows and helped her to lie down.

Holly was desperately trying to remember what the nurses had done to help her during her labor with Byron. "Maybe we should walk around for a while," she suggested. "They made me do that when Byron was coming."

The memory of his birth made Holly's throat constrict. It didn't seem that long ago that she'd held him as an infant in her arms. *Where is he now? We all agreed to assume that no news is good news, but . . .*

Theresa's eyes rolled back in her head as another contraction took hold. "I think it's too late for walking."

Holly was surprised another contraction had come on so quickly. "When did your pains begin?"

She grabbed Holly's hand hard and tried hard to speak. "Last night . . . oh, Lord . . ." There was silence, but the grimacing expression on her face spoke volumes. "About dinner time."

Dinner time? Holly spun around to Anthony, though her knees were trembling. "Can you find out what time it is now, please?"

Chapter 29

Though Holly was focused on Theresa, she couldn't help but hear the door open and close. She was sure Anthony had gone to the living room to check the old grandfather clock.

When he came back, his gaze shot to Holly, then Theresa, and back again. He wiped his face with one hand and pushed his hair up out of his eyes. A sigh escaped him. "We all know it often takes time for a first child to come, but it's already been over twenty-five hours."

Holly was shocked. She stammered, "But . . . but . . . Theresa . . . you've hardly made a sound."

A careful examination of the prone woman was revealing. Her limbs were stiff and the muscles in her face were jumping.

"I didn't want to be a bother," she whispered. "Actually, my back hurts so badly, I could cry." At that, she reached up and wiped tears from her eyes.

"Do you want to try some breathing exercises?" Anthony asked her. "I took Lamaze classes when I was younger."

Holly cocked her head to one side. Out of the corner of her eye, she could see Theresa doing exactly the same thing. She thought they must make a funny sight. "*Really?*" she asked, toying with him.

He didn't take her bait, but he did have a self-satisfied smile on his face. "This is neither the time nor the place to tell that story.

Maybe when this is over and mother and child are well and happy I can describe what happened."

Holly squinted at him. "At least tell me this: I thought you'd never been married. You make quite a joke out of it, as I recall."

"No. No, I never have. I was a birth coach . . . Nothing more. I've told you this already. Theresa, can I try something for your back pain?"

He motioned for her to sit up and he eased himself onto the bed so he was sitting behind her. Holly saw he was careful not to put any pressure on her injured leg. He had one of his feet on the floor to keep his balance. He began to massage Theresa's lower back, which immediately brought out an "ahhhh" of pleasure from her.

"Holly, can you please see if there's any ice left in the freezers or the coolers? Break it down into chips, if you can, and bring it for Theresa. She'll have to focus on her deep breathing soon."

"Right . . . right," Holly said, still standing in the same place.

"The breathing will, no doubt, make her thirsty," Anthony explained. "But we can't have her gulping water. That won't do. It will be much better to have bits of ice to suck on."

Theresa let out a yelp of pain and held her breath to the point that she turned red in the face.

Anthony quietly reminded her to inhale deeply and exhale slowly. "And try your best to relax, dear."

It was all so intimate. So miraculous. So beautiful. Holly ran her hands down her sides. *Am I intruding? Do I even belong here? Should I give them some time alone?* She started to leave the room, but Anthony stopped her with a jerk of his head. She stepped toward him and lowered her ear near his mouth to listen.

"Can you see if Matius has made us any food? See if you can bring in a plate in for each of us—"

"For you and Theresa," she muttered, feeling dismissed.

Anthony chuckled. "No, Theresa can't eat right now . . . the food is for you and me. We've got to keep up our strength, too. Do find something light for Theresa. Maybe just bring in some saltines. We don't want her to get nauseous."

Reassured that she was actually needed, Holly took off for the kitchen wearing a smile.

When Holly slipped back into the room, ice and crackers in hand, she whispered to Anthony, "Matius says dinner will take a while."

He nodded to her.

While he continued his massage, he and Theresa talked quietly. The pains were coming closer and closer together now.

"We couldn't afford to fly over to Provo week after week to attend childbirth classes," she said. "My doctor on Grand Turk gave me two books and a video to watch that showed the techniques for each stage of labor."

"Will you allow me to coach your breathing?" Anthony asked.

"If Joab can't be here, you are the perfect substitute," she said regally. "And I thank you for doing it."

He was visibly moved by her response.

A powerful contraction hit Theresa, and she went rigid.

"Slowly take the air in . . . eight, nine, ten," Anthony said softly. "Now release . . . slowly . . . slowly. I am glowing with happiness for Joab. His woman is a goddess."

"Oh, sure." Theresa chuckled between gulps. "I'm sure I look a fright."

"You are gorgeous," Anthony told her, and he was right.

An idea struck Holly; she found her purse and fumbled around for her phone.

"What are you doing?" Anthony asked.

"I want to take some video for Joab. I still have some charge left."

Anthony's expression softened. "That's incredibly thoughtful."

To an outsider looking in, with Anthony's body wrapped around Theresa's, it might seem like they were lovers.

What a testament to the strength of their friendship. Anthony must be so relieved to have found Teresa alive and relatively unharmed. I think I even heard him say a heartfelt prayer of thanks on their behalf when we first saw her.

As she filmed them, Anthony spoke to the camera. "Joab, my friend, you mean the world to me. You've been a good friend for many years. It may look like I'm moving in on your lady, but, in fact, I am applying counter pressure to Theresa's back. You can thank me later."

Holly hit the red button to save the life of the battery for another shot later on.

Anthony squeezed his eyes together and sat back, looking exhausted.

"Are you okay?" Holly asked him.

He didn't open his lids, but he said softly, "With my sixth sense, I am willing a message to Joab across the 230 ocean miles to the Dominican Republic. He must be beside himself that he can't come home. In my mind, I'm saying, 'I've got your darlings, buddy. Until we see you again, I will do everything I can for them.'" He opened his eyes and gazed up at Holly. "God save us all."

Holly gave him a halfhearted smile and patted him on the shoulder. He shook out his hands and stretched them.

"You need a break," Holly told him in no uncertain terms.

"You're right. If I stay here too long, I might seize up."

Theresa reached back and squeezed one of his arms. "Of course. I will be fine."

With that, he carefully eased his buttocks back toward the foot he already had on the floor. Holly watched as he struggled to slide his other leg out from behind Theresa and off the bed. She jumped to help him, but it was still an awkward maneuver.

"I am ancient," he groaned, grabbing at the back of his elevated calf. "Muscle cramp. Careful, Theresa. I don't want to kick you."

Once Holly got him on his feet, she said, "Stand on it. No, put your foot flat on the ground and let the cramp settle down. Bend your knees some."

Anthony let out an exaggerated whine. "You are incredibly bossy."

They all burst out laughing—even Theresa, who was having a momentary break from her labor pains.

Holly stroked Anthony's back as he grunted and did as she said. As soon as he seemed more comfortable, she said, "I'm going to check on dinner. I'm suddenly starving."

# Chapter 30

H olly was at the kitchen counter when Anthony came in. "Needed a short break," he said.

Holly nodded. "Matius says it will be ready soon."

Matius sat at the table with a chopping board in front of him. With his usual smile, he said, "You two take a few minutes. I'll leave this on simmer and go sit with her awhile."

Holly was happy for the respite.

Anthony went in the pantry and Holly could hear rustling sounds. "I'm just collecting a few things," he called to her.

She assumed he would return with some rum, so she got two glasses down from a cabinet. She also nabbed a small block of cheese from the cooler she'd filled earlier with refrigerator staples. She was sure he noticed the mess in the pantry from the boys who had broken in, but when he came out with an armful of items, he pointed toward the front of the house without a word about it.

They sat down on the decking of the front porch and let their legs and bare feet dangle off the side like children. She made figure eight designs in the air with her feet.

Anthony said quietly, "Matius told me there was a scuffle in the kitchen."

"How did he . . . ?"

"He's an incredibly observant man. Do you want to tell me what happened?"

She ignored the question. Since it happened, she'd tried not to think about it. She stretched her feet out in front of her and announced, "After all we've been through, my pedicure still looks fantastic."

When he put his arms around her, she jolted a bit and studied his face.

"I get it. You're not ready to talk about it." He patted her back.

She shrugged. "I guess you should know the basics. In case the police or the army show up asking questions."

"I suppose I should."

"When I got back to the house looking for towels for Mrs. James, there were three young men in the kitchen pantry. They'd already had a lot of rum. One of the kids, Charles, was clearly drunk. He pushed me—hard."

"Charles? I think I know him." He didn't look happy.

She reached up to the knot on the back of her head and winced. Anthony reached out too, for her hand. He took in his and waited quietly.

"The other boys didn't do anything wrong besides trespassing. In fact, Robert tried to stop him. But it all happened so fast. Charles had me pinned up on the counter. Based on the things he said, I knew what he planned on doing. I stopped him."

"How did you do that?"

"Stabbed him in the neck. With a short blade, though. I didn't want to kill him, just make him stop before it got out of hand."

"My Lord." He pulled her closer.

"Then I got lucky. Because Robert was holding him back, I could reach my pistol. I suppose if someone were to be critical about it, I held them all at gunpoint. But just long enough to get him fixed up with peroxide and a clean cloth for pressure. I hope they don't come back."

He snorted out a bitter laugh. "Oh, I don't think they will be back. You should prepare yourself to be something of a legend after this, though. I don't think you need to worry about anyone breaking into your house again, but you may not get many dinner invitations on this island."

"I didn't have time to think. I just did it."

He squeezed her thigh. "Of course you did. My poor girl. All that's happened here will take time to come to terms with."

Holly didn't answer. With her eyes shut, she lifted her face to the balmy breeze; it felt like a loving touch. Anthony laid a plate between them. It was filled with crackers, a variety of olives, and Holly's cheese. Ever so smoothly, he uncorked the rum and poured Holly two fingers' worth. She giggled when he, with a dramatic flourish, doubled that amount in his own.

"Don't be a cheapskate." Holly took the bottle away from him and put another splash in hers. When she took a sip, she again closed her eyes. The alcohol burned as it went down, but it had a delicious, toasted caramel finish.

Anthony lit up a cigarette and offered the pack to her. Instead of taking a new one for herself, she reached over and took Anthony's cigarette from his fingers. Pressing it between her lips, she inhaled a deep drag from it and then let it out.

She groaned with happiness. "I haven't had a cigarette in years."

Anthony chortled. "Every once in a while won't kill you."

"Well, don't tell Montez. He was after me to give it up."

Anthony grimaced. "Montez? What's he got to do with this?" There was a clear note of jealousy in his tone. She was honestly surprised.

She handed the cigarette back to him, and he took a drag.

"He scolded me more than once—'You are the mother of my child. You need to stay healthy.' He was right." Holly shrugged. "You have to admit, smoking is never a good idea." Yet after he took a drag, she reached for it again and took another hit—and she enjoyed it tremendously.

A noted harrumph escaped Anthony. "He sure as hell is busy leading his own life; I don't see why he gets to have a say in yours. As hard as this day has been, let's face it, this night will be a long one. We deserve a little *pleasure*."

The way he said "pleasure," accentuated by the manner in which he locked eyes with her, sent a rushing sensation coursing through her stomach. Once again, she was overpowered by her attraction to him, and she found it was a draw that seemed to have a mind of its own. When she handed the cigarette back, he leaned in and kissed her playfully on the lips three times. He must have decided that he liked it, for he took her face in his hands tenderly, being careful with his cigarette, and kissed her again—this time deeply.

Inside of Holly, something powerful burst open. She discovered she didn't look forward to the feeling ending.

He pulled away a bit, bringing them nose to nose. They traded stares.

"You, my darling, are a beauty. *And* you have a heart as big as the great outdoors."

Holly sat back and blew a smoke ring at him. Anthony guffawed.

"That's my only comment on the matter," she said.

"You see? That's my girl."

He put his arm around her while he continued to laugh into her hair. She informed him coolly, "I'm too old to be anybody's girl, sir." But she smiled when she said it.

Where is all this headed? Are we a thing now?

Without letting go, he sat up straight and sipped his drink. It was a bit of a reach with the plate between them, so he picked it up and moved it to Holly's other side. "Slide over here. Snuggle up."

She wiggled over and leaned into him.

"You know," he said, "one thing that surprised me about you . . . I always thought beautiful girls couldn't cook."

She laughed out loud. "Where did you hear that?"

"I suppose I thought they didn't have to work hard in general. But you, my sweet—you are a trooper. If I was in a tough spot and Matius was unavailable, you would definitely be my second choice."

She convulsed with laughter. "Oh, oh *thanks* . . . I've always wanted to be second fiddle." Chortling, she laid her head against his shoulder.

Overcome with silliness, having lost any pretense of control, they both snorted and heaved and wiped at the tears that were leaking from their eyes. Truth be told, Holly was giddy from fatigue and dehydration following a day's labor in the hot sun, not to mention the energy required to stab someone—in the neck, no less.

Much to her bewilderment, her laughter turned to sobbing in a heartbeat.

Anthony squeezed her gently. Another calm sip of his rum was rapidly followed by an inhalation off his cigarette. He blew the smoke forward and stared straight ahead. "I wondered how long it would take for you to start worrying about Byron. I'm not going to try to placate you by saying he's fine. We have no idea where he is at this point. As close as you two are, it must add to an already terrible day."

"It's more frightening than a drunken Charles. And that was pretty bad."

Anthony's face went dark. "You've no need to worry yourself about them anymore. We have a system here. It will be dealt with."

Holly gulped. It was only the one kid who'd meant her harm; she hoped the others didn't get in too much trouble. But the thought was fleeting. She had a one-track mind at the moment.

"My fear about Byron comes and goes, but right now my stomach is twisted into knots. I guess because we are having a quiet moment, I'm going wild with the horrible possibilities. I can't tell you how much I appreciate your understanding."

"We do understand each other, don't we? You know what I mean. You see what we can do together. I don't know your parents, but they must be so proud of you." He gave her a gentle kiss on her forehead.

He gave the cigarette back to her, which she contentedly inhaled with her head still on his shoulder. A few moments later, she said huskily, "I hope you won't be shocked when I tell you this: My parents hardly know me. Or knew me. My mother is dead." Her voice broke when she added, "And I doubt I'll ever see my father again."

He caressed her face. "That is their loss, my love, as you have turned out to be a formidable woman. Formidable. If it means anything at all . . . I, for one, am proud to know you."

A few precious moments passed where she felt suspended, alone with Anthony in a moment of complete tranquility. Their breathing synchronized as they stared together up into the night sky. When a shooting star exploded into a long arc, they both let out a sigh. A lavender cloud was swept across the very faint glow of the horizon. It was like a bubble of splendor had surrounded them—one which burst wide open the second Matius popped his head out the front door and called out, "A little help in here, please."

Holly slowly stood and brushed herself off. She downed her rum and Anthony did the same. He lowered his chin and locked eyes with her. "I love a woman who can handle her liquor," he said appreciatively.

Like the hellion she could sometimes be, she smiled boldly. "You love a woman under any circumstances."

He cracked up again. "True enough. True enough. Until you came along, Holly, dear. Until now."

Holly took Anthony's hand in hers.

It didn't even occur to her that he might be exaggerating his feelings for her. What he said rang true. For the last few days, his adoration had radiated from him constantly, washed over her and made her feel warm and safe. Their time together was, perhaps, the safest place she'd ever known—today's fracas in the kitchen notwithstanding. With Anthony, it never occurred to her to be anything but herself.

He stubbed out his cigarette on the bottom of his shoe and Holly picked up the plate from the porch deck. He was behind her as she started back into the house, but he stopped her and wrapped his arms around her one more time. As he nuzzled her neck from behind, he ran his lips up the length of it, making her quiver from head to toe. "I dig your ass. It's perfect."

Holly's eyes flew open. "Dig?" she asked as she whirled around to confront him. "If you tell me that, in yet another previous phase of your life, you were a jazz musician, I think I'll lose my mind."

He raised both of his hands up and out. "What can I say?"

She pounded on his chest with her index finger, demanding to know the story. "What instrument do you play?"

"My darling, in the end, I'm really such a cliché. Can't you guess?"

"The bad-boy drummer. I see."

"Precisely." He seemed happy with her for figuring it out so quickly.

She shook her head and muttered a few curses. By contrast, her life seemed dull as dirt.

I'm going to make him tell me all his stories. Including about those babies he helped deliver.

Chapter 31

Matius had been right to call them back inside when he did. Once they reentered the bedroom, they realized Theresa's baby was ready to come out.

Holly watched Anthony coach Theresa through the last stages of labor as if he had been born to the task. When Theresa's lips grew chapped from deep breathing, he rubbed them with balm; when she complained of thirst, he fed her ice chips.

"My dearest hope is that I can convince Theresa I know what I'm doing," he whispered to Holly at one point. "She doesn't need to have uncertainty loaded up on top of her suffering."

As she cried out in pain, he told her with great authority, "It's normal, my dear. I'm sure it's bloody excruciating, but it's totally normal. We are so fortunate you are progressing the way you are."

I hope he really does know what he's talking about, Holly thought.

Only minutes later, she asked Theresa, "Do you think it will help to change positions?"

She did, and within seconds Anthony hollered out, "Is that a push? Are you ready to push?" He sounded thrilled to his core.

"Yes," Theresa said definitively.

Holly helped Theresa bear down and relax on the pillow after the first push. Suddenly, Theresa started thrashing her arms and legs and scanning the room blankly. Holly had no idea what she was searching for.

"I have to," Theresa wailed. "I can't help it." Her body heaved up and she made a grunting noise that sounded something like, "Hunh, hunh, hunh."

When she lowered back down to the bed, she seemed mortified that she hadn't been able to control the thrusting. "I feel like an animal!" she screamed.

She pulled her legs up and Holly crouched down, calmly searching for signs of the baby's head emerging.

"We *are* animals," Anthony told Theresa gently. In a whisper only Holly heard, he added, "A wonderful thing to remember. Despite the fact that we often feel superior to the rest of them."

He suddenly jumped to his feet, startling Holly.

"Holly! What do you have at the ready?"

For a second, she was uncertain about the question. But she realized he was talking about what they were going to do with the baby. She nervously glanced around the room, taking inventory.

"Oh. Oh! I've got a clean sheet to wrap the baby in, and a cotton towel as well. A water basin, kitchen twine . . . and scissors. Clean beach towels if we need them, and a box of large garbage bags. I sent Matius on a scavenger hunt to find clean bedding. We can strip everything down and put on fresh linens once the baby is born."

"Excellent . . . because . . . here it comes." He reached down in preparation to cup and support the baby's head as Theresa pushed it out. "Theresa! Breathe! Pant, pant, pant. Ha, ha, ha, ha . . . that's right."

The panting seemed to slow down Theresa's urge to push for the few seconds needed for Anthony to run his fingers around the infant's neck. Because she'd worked in a school, Holly had a little emergency training. She was certain he was feeling around to make sure the umbilical cord wasn't wrapped around the child's throat.

He let out a sigh of relief. "All clear, luv. Push."

With a great swoosh, the child's shoulders were out, and then its entire body followed.

Anthony roared with joy, "You have a son, Miss Theresa. A boy." He quickly fell silent and gingerly put the infant down on the foot of the bed. It was completely limp, and the bluish color of his skin made Holly's pulse race. She used her pinky finger to feel inside its mouth. It was warm and there didn't appear to be any obstruction.

She swiveled to Anthony. "Can you come look at him? My close-up vision isn't great anymore. Check and see if his nostrils are clear."

Anthony bent over next to her. Theresa let out an anguished cry.

Holly wiped the baby's face with her towel and put one hand on the base of his skull to make his head pull back. Theresa and Anthony both gasped when she made a seal with her lips around the child's nose and mouth. She puffed for three seconds and his tiny chest rose. Holly pulled away to inhale deeply and then performed the mouth-to-mouth again.

By the fourth breath, she was near tears and Theresa was hysterical.

Holly studied the child for a split second. *Lord, please. Don't take him.* She decided if one more breath didn't revive him, she would try CPR. She leaned down and puffed in again—and was rewarded when she heard a strangled, gurgling sound.

Suddenly animated, the baby began to cough spasmodically. Holly picked him up and flipped him over on his stomach across her arms. She knew if anything was blocking his breathing tube it, was more likely to clear in that position. As she bounced him a little, he let out a furious cry. Holly cheered, then turned him to cradle him in her arms. The relief of finding his skin turning pink hit her like a brick wall; she sat down hard on the edge of the bed as her legs gave way.

The wailing made her think of her own baby boy.

Where the hell is he? Not a word. You can take me, Lord, just not the children.

The baby looked a bit better to her—but not robust the way Byron had been when he was born. He seemed tiny and vulnerable. How long would it be before they could get him to a doctor? So many of the roads had been washed away or were still flooded.

She wondered who of all her friends had survived. *I know it's wrong to be so selfish, but if there have been injuries and deaths, I pray the ones I love are not among them. It is the one thing I know I can't live beyond.*

She gave the baby to Theresa, who was still sobbing . . . only now with happiness. "Oh, my Lord. Lord. Holly. Thank you."

Unable to form words, Holly simply patted her cheek and went into the bathroom to wash her hands and face.

When Holly reentered the bedroom a few minutes later, she went over to the armchair and sank down into it with her head in her hands. A wavy haziness covered her eyes momentarily. Confusion and terror clouded everything. Every. Single. Thing. Her ears rang, echoing her deep-seated misery. She missed the delivery of the placenta, although she could hear Anthony's enthusiasm as he cut the cord.

Though she was spent, she rallied. Resilience was a talent she had, and she knew it. Holding the white towel in her hands, she walked over and wrapped the baby in it.

"Give him to me," he said.

He held the infant to his chest and then offered him up to the heavens, weeping. "Save this child, Lord. Save him, I beg you."

Still weeping, he gave the child back to Holly. She wrapped him up in another layer and put him on Theresa's stomach, then covered Theresa from the waist down with one beach towel and wrapped the second one around her like a shawl. Satisfied that the new mother was comfortable, she went to Anthony, whose shoulders were still heaving, and tenderly rocked him back and forth.

"The worst is over," she whispered. "The baby is fine, I think. It's all going to be fine." Holly wondered if she were truly as calm as she sounded or if she had returned to the numbness she'd felt so often over the last few days. The baby may or may not be fine. She wasn't a doctor, and she didn't know when they would have access to one. *If* they would have access.

Within moments, Anthony broke away from her. Clearly, he was embarrassed. "I don't know what came over me," he said.

Wanting to give Anthony some sense of privacy while he wiped the last of his tears away, Holly went down the hall to the bathroom.

Standing at the sink, she met her own eyes in the mirror.

I told him everything is fine. Is it, Holly Walker? Is it really?

Chapter 32

They were gathered in the kitchen making breakfast when they heard the unmistakable *swoop-swoop-swoop* of helicopter blades. They all ran outside to watch it as it grew closer.

The noise soon became overpowering; Holly cowered against it. It didn't take long for the pilot to lower the aircraft onto the wide stone pier out front that jutted into the ocean. Despite the racket, and the fact Holly had to plug her ears, she ran toward it.

A side door slid open and a single person launched himself out of it. His posture was a familiar one. She froze in place and, with a sinking feeling in her stomach, blinked hard to make sure she was really seeing Montez.

It never once crossed her mind that he was there to help her. No. He was here to deliver bad news. Her mind screamed the same question over and over again:

Where is my son? Where is my son? Where is my son?

Holly hurled herself toward Montez with a violent expression on her face. With the strength of a she-devil, wild with fear, she pounded on his chest with both of her fists.

He captured both her hands in his own and held them tight.

"What? What!" she screamed out. "What's wrong?"

"Shush. Shush. Shush. Holly! Byron is alive. He's alive."

She quieted as the words sunk in, and then slumped with relief. Thankfully, Montez held her up; if he hadn't, she was sure, she'd have fainted dead away. Gasping for breath, she glared into his eyes and jutted out her chin, even though it trembled.

"Where is he, then?" she asked pointedly.

Montez continued to hold her hands with both of his. "He's in hospital in Providenciales. He was up on Auntie's roof, trying to patch it, and . . ."

She freed her hands and they flew up to her face. "And *what?*"

Montez took a sharp breath. "Both of his arms are broken. He's going to need surgery, but he's all right. Rather, he will be all right after they fix him up."

Relief once again cascaded over Holly, making her knees buckle. Montez gripped her and her head dropped to his broad chest. For just a moment, she rested there. Until she heard a man calling to her in the distance.

"Holly!" Anthony approached with the deepest concern etched into his face. It was as if he'd aged ten years in the last few minutes. She brightened at the sight of him and waved him over.

Montez shouted, "Byron's alive. He's badly hurt, but he's alive."

Holly wondered if she imagined Anthony staggering backward a bit as he received the news. He hustled over and reached for her. She twisted away from Montez and fell into Anthony's embrace.

"When I saw it was Montez, I gathered what things I could find," he said in her ear. He held a strange duffel bag up for her to see. "You've got to hand it to him. Somehow he commandeered one of the few helicopters in Turks and Caicos."

"Where's my suitcase?" she asked.

"God only knows." He gently pinched her cheek. "Darling," he said with some urgency, "take this and put it in your pocket." He pressed an impressive roll of bills into her hand.

"What on earth . . . ?" She tried to give it back.

"No. No. This is not the time to fight me," he said firmly. "Not on this. I feel bad enough about sending you off." He pulled her in tightly and, though he remained silent, she knew he was trying to communicate something important. It dawned on her how good Anthony was at nonverbal communication. She tried hard to interpret his meaning, but she was distracted by the sight of the front door of the mansion bursting open.

Matius had an arm around Theresa as they walked, and he had a bag in his other hand. You couldn't make out the baby, who was swaddled and tucked into Theresa's bosom. Holly thought Roseate House, grand old empress that she was, had maybe lost a part of her crown—the ornamental stone rain gutter—but she was still glorious as she framed the background.

The pilot turned the engine off. Although the blades continued in a slow twirl until they came to a stop, it was suddenly quiet. When the others grew close, Montez told Holly and Anthony in no uncertain terms, "We're headed for Provo. Only the Lord knows what we'll find when we get there. Most of the buildings are damaged. The hospital there is in bad shape, too, although I don't know how badly. You're better off where you are right now—at least you have water and food and some safety. I only came for Holly because . . ." He paused, then burst out laughing so hard he bent over at the waist. "Well, she'd surely kill me if I didn't bring her to her injured son."

Holly laughed too, because what he said was true.

Theresa approached and Holly could see the confusion in Montez's eyes. "What is *this?*"

"*This* is a brand-new mother," Holly told him, motioning between the two of them. "Theresa, Montez . . . Montez, Theresa . . . she gave birth last night. She needs to go to the hospital too. The baby had a hard time."

He sucked in his breath. But, as Holly had always known

him to be, Montez proved to be a decisive leader. "There is just enough space. I'm sure our pilot will agree. I will speak to him immediately."

Holly gave Anthony one more hug and kissed him on the lips. She was anxious to get going and see about Byron. When she released him, he and Theresa embraced around the sleeping infant, carefully and tenderly.

Holly saw the look Montez gave them. "It's not Anthony's child," she hissed.

Montez raised his eyebrow at her and shrugged.

"I'll thank you properly when we return," Theresa said to Anthony. "When Joab is home as well."

Montez's eyes revealed an animated skepticism. "*You* are Joab's wife?" When she gave him a curt nod, he let out a low whistle. "He is a lucky man," he muttered.

Ignoring Montez, Anthony said to Theresa, "We'll look forward to better times, my dear friend." He lightly clapped her on the shoulders and added, "When Joab returns, we'll have a party. Hell, we'll invite the whole town."

Holly couldn't help herself. She threw her arms around Anthony and kissed him with her whole soul—and then, before he could say anything, blurted out, "I have to run," and took off for the helicopter.

Montez was already strapped into his seat when Holly climbed inside. He attempted to stare her down; she just rolled her eyes and sat down.

As the helicopter ascended, she peered out the window and watched the white sand beach grow smaller. Though she longed to see Byron, she had a bittersweet ache in her chest over leaving the island . . . or, more precisely, Anthony. Even this far above him, she remained powerfully connected to the man.

Holly slipped her hands under her thighs and fidgeted. Montez gave her another look that she ignored. The flight would take less than an hour, but it already seemed like an eternity to her. She'd always believed men had a way of understating pain and suffering, so she didn't actually trust that what Montez had told her about Byron's injuries was entirely true.

Next to her, Montez massaged the hinges of his jaw with the outstretched thumb and forefinger of his right hand and stared out the window. She thought he looked a bit crazed. She was perplexed by the phrase he muttered several times: "*My* family."

She assumed he was thinking about his parents. *What the hell is he talking about?* "Coralyse and Sanford? What happened to them?"

"No. Not them. Their house was damaged somewhat, but they came through everything just fine." His eyes looked dead as he continued to stare out the glass panel.

Holly knew him well. "Montez. You keep saying, 'My family.' You're scaring me."

He still did not turn toward her; he simply whispered, "I'm sorry."

She thought she saw his lips tremble—a rare occurrence for the ever-stoic Montez Curry. Her head pounded. She reached over and pinched his arm, which made him turn toward her. He scrutinized Holly. Like shadows, a myriad of emotions crossed his face. Confused, she furrowed her brow. *Why doesn't he just come out with it?*

He opened his mouth to speak, and she leaned in closer. He sputtered, "It took this tragedy for me to realize . . . you and Byron . . . *you* are my family."

He reached for her hand and looked at her in such a loving way she felt painfully awkward. She was sure her cheeks were colored a deep red.

He waited. Though she felt compelled to respond to his disclosure, she had no idea what the correct response would be.

Finally, in a falsely calm voice, she said, "You're like family to me, too, Montez. Of course you are. You're Byron's father."

His expression turned to brooding and he let out a sigh. "You misunderstand me, Holly. I don't blame you. I have been a lagga head—you know, stupid—in the past. Let me explain the best I can. I have figured out that *you* and Byron are my family. I didn't see it before. It took the mighty Hurricane Nestor to make it clear to me. To bring me to my knees. Sameera? I'm ashamed to think I told you I was in love with her. Called her my girlfriend. The way she treated my parents during the storm?"

"Okay . . ." Holly shook. Physically trembled. She had waited many years for Montez to turn around his feelings for her; many nights, she had longed to hear him say these very words. But at this moment, she found she was baffled. Her mind tried to make sense out of the situation.

Is this because I slept with Anthony? Does Montez somehow know what happened?

He went on talking about Sameera: "From the start, she complained there wasn't enough room for all of us at Roseate." He tilted his hand back and forth as he described her reactions. "My mother and father got on her nerves. She wanted more attention from me. Mami never said the right thing." Montez threw his hands up in the air. "Poor Papi was in horrible pain. You saw him—the air pressure made his arthritis worse—but only *she* could have the most comfortable chair in the room."

Holly was surprised by this. She'd been so busy taking care of everyone, she'd missed the nuances of what was going on.

He went on with his story. "The entire experience was made to be all about her. When the storm was finally over, I dropped her off at a friend's house. A *male* friend. I hope I never see her again."

Holly gulped and she found it was hard to exhale. Woodenly, she was able to muster, "Oh. You must be very disappointed. You thought she was the one." Her anger spiked. "It had to be *my chef* that you chose? I just have to point that out. You tell me you're smitten for the first time in your life, and it's with a woman in my employ?"

His eyes bored into hers with a fierce purpose. His nostrils flared. "What I have finally discovered after all these years . . . is that *you* are the one." He pounded on both his armrests in frustration.

Holly glanced over at Theresa. Thankfully, she was fast asleep.

She, meanwhile, felt rooted to her seat. *This has been the most unreal few days of my life.* She considered the idea that she was asleep and would wake up any time now. Like some bad old movie. But despite everything, her heart went out to Montez when she saw his cheek muscles flexing.

"Montez!" She reached out to try to soothe him.

Witnessing his vulnerable state, she couldn't help but acknowledge the sheer exquisiteness of the man. When they were younger, she'd felt she was the luckiest girl on earth to be seeing him. He'd been as gorgeous as a bronze statue. He still was. Time had been kind to him. But back then, she would have given anything to hear Montez Curry say he loved her.

Decades of waiting had formed a thick layer of insulation against his allure. A callus that ran so deep that she really had no idea how to handle his revelation now. If anything, she felt trapped.

When he was able to collect himself, he went on, "I was a fool for not seeing it until now." He choked a bit on his words, and he swallowed before finding the composure to continue. "Sameera doesn't compare to you. You took care of everyone during Nestor. That's how you are. When my mother cried, you put your arms around her—didn't become annoyed and pout like a child. I don't know what I was thinking, falling for that girl. At the most difficult times in life, no one needs a self-centered diva."

Once again consumed by her worry for Byron, Holly was only half listening to Montez. Her son was the one who mattered. She was also anxious for Theresa and her fragile newborn. Yet there was a part of her brain where Montez's words registered.

This is interesting. Now that Anthony was crazy about her, Montez was too. It had been her experience that men often professed their love at the most inconvenient of times. And they often wanted what they suddenly couldn't have.

Her lips pursed. She was suspect of Montez's grand announcement. It grated on her. Now was not the time for any nonsense about who was and who was not "the one." Although Montez held her hand and she continued to allow him to do so, it was only because she didn't want to put energy into finding a way to extricate it without hurting his feelings. She went from an out-of-body experience to a crash. She was physically and emotionally drained.

One finger at a time, she pulled away from him and concentrated on her prayers. As many do in such moments, she bargained with God. She thought of all the good she could do in the world if only He would grant her Byron back, whole and happy once again.

Although her mother had not been a woman of faith, she'd sent Holly to vacation bible school because it was free daycare. Holly had always loved the Hail Mary prayer. She recited it silently now . . . *pray for us sinners, now and at the hour of our death . . .*

Her mind was stuck on that final word.

Death was not what she had in mind at all.

Chapter 33

Without fanfare, they landed on a circular helicopter pad at the airport. Holy looked around outside the chopper's windows and questioned the reality of what she saw. The Providenciales International Airport appeared to be completely shut down. It was eerie, even otherworldly.

I've been stuck at an airport overnight before, but there were still people there. Where is everyone?

The pilots she'd flown with before hadn't hugged their passengers goodbye. Today, however, in this extraordinary circumstance, hug them he did. He embraced all of them and wished them a heartfelt safe travel.

Theresa, in particular, made sure to express her gratitude. The pilot, a father himself, seemed very emotional as he bade her goodbye.

Montez shook the captain's hand before he turned to Holly and Theresa, clearly intent on taking charge. "The Medical Center is only three kilometers down the road, but we'll have to cross the Leeward Highway. We don't know what kind of shape the roads are in or who is out traveling on them. If we run into anyone . . ." He paused for a moment, and his tense expression said it all. "Theresa, I'm sure any doctor worth his salt wouldn't want you out hiking right now, but we have no choice. I know you'll do the best you can. We may run into someone who has a vehicle and can help us. Someone safe. This is what I hope for. Give me the baby and I'll carry him for you."

The blade on the helicopter began to turn. They were forced to move on.

Holly steeled herself. *Here we go.*

The first part of their trek was inhabited by a long series of rental-car businesses and gas stations. The buildings were modern cement structures and had fared the hurricane pretty well. Their large metal business signs were another story. Most were badly mangled, if not completely blown away.

The road had flooded, so they had to pick their way around the high spots in order to make any progress at all.

Just as on Grand Turk, the arbitrary piles of debris were a curiosity as they walked. Holly saw pieces of furniture, part of a window, a child's doll missing both its legs and one eye, a broken tennis racket, and, sadly, many dead birds jumbled together. The carcass of a horse lay by the side of the road under a portion of a utility pole; a cloud of flies was already buzzing around its bloated torso and feasting on its eyes. A dog ran across the road in the distance and she heard others, obviously in a pack, barking. From time to time, they let out a high-pitched squeal that, to her, sounded both hungry and desperate. It was a reverie of noise that made her blood run cold.

She heard the roar of an engine and tires sluicing through inches of water on the pavement, and stood tall. Theresa grabbed at her hand; her ears began to roar. She actually saw stars start to swirl around her.

Montez pulled her out of her state when he sternly ordered, "Stay behind me."

It was a police vehicle, the words "Turks and Caicos" painted on its side panel, that pulled over—*Thank God*, Holly thought.

"My son is at the hospital," Montez told the officer. "And this young lady here has just given birth to a beautiful baby boy."

The next few minutes of driving were a blur to Holly. She didn't remember a thing until she stood in the doorway of her son's room.

Byron was covered in white. He had on a white neck brace, his head was bandaged, both of his arms were casted, and his sheets were pulled up high on his chest. The only color in evidence was the purple around his two blackened eyes.

He was asleep. When he opened his black-and-blue lids, she could see his unique blue-green irises focusing and refocusing and finally recognizing her. The biggest teardrop Holly had ever seen rolled down his cheek.

He said a single word: "Mom."

She patted his cheek. "There's my boy."

She carefully sat down on the edge of his bed, all the while surveying the damage. Though she was horrified by what she saw, she forced herself to remain quiet.

Holly heard Montez come into the room, and she watched Byron's face brighten when he saw him. His voice was hoarse and gravelly as he joked, "Haven't you two heard we're in the middle of a state of emergency?" Then he barked out a rumbling cough that set Holly on high alert.

He held up one finger, indicating she should wait a minute. When he stopped hacking, she handed him a wad of tissues and he spat into it.

Eventually, he was able to ask the question that seemed to be weighing on his mind: "How did you get to Provo?"

"Don't ask me how, but your father got us a helicopter," Holly told him.

Montez flashed his most brilliant smile. "Don't ask me how either. I promise you none of it was legal, so be quiet about it."

The Belonger

It was obvious laughing was painful for Byron, yet he couldn't seem to help himself. He held his face in both his hands, apparently applying pressure to it.

Concerned, Holly jumped up.

"None of the bones in my head are broken, Mom," he quickly assured her. "I'm just bruised up." He turned a little to address his father. "Was it the same guy who brought us over here?"

"His brother," Montez answered with a wink.

Holly had assumed that Byron had been airlifted off Grand Turk on a government aircraft. She was grateful Montez had handled the transport and returned to Grand Turk to get her.

She could tell Byron was embarrassed about his accident. He explained why he went up on the roof.

"There was a big tear over Auntie's beloved green bedroom— you know, her guest room? Not much of a climb up the ladder. So, I brought a staple gun and a tarp up to the roof, and right when I got up there the wind started gusting like a mother . . . not my mother, of course." They all laughed. "I lost my balance and fell off; there was nothing graceful about it. I landed with my arms out in front of me and smacked my face into her back fence."

Montez sat back in a hard chair, casually chewing on a toothpick. Holly could still sometimes see exactly why women were so dazzled by him. His sheer physicality was breathtaking. And never had she met anyone else who was as comfortable in their own skin.

He chuckled. "The ignorance of youth. He thought nothing could possibly hurt him. He told me he was going up and I knew nothing could stop him."

Holly grew quiet. She stared hostilely at Montez. He stopped talking.

Byron noticed immediately. "Mom! It's not Dad's fault."

Anger coursed through her veins. "You know perfectly well

I would have stopped you. How long was it before your father came to check on you?" Though she was shaking, she tried to remember Byron was already hurt. It wasn't going to help his overall misery for her to get mad at him. "I bet he was having a beer next door with Fabienne's father."

Neither one of them denied it. She'd hit the nail on the head.

She tried to make her voice gentle again. "Was it awful?"

"I'm not going to lie to you: it wasn't great. But at least none of the bones broke through the skin. The doctors said if they'd been compound fractures things would have been a lot more complicated. Fabienne came over and she took care of me the best she could."

"Really?"

"Yeah, she was great. She made makeshift splints to keep me stable. The smartest thing she did was assembling icepacks that she put on top of and under my forearms. It helped with the pain and swelling."

"And how long, exactly, did it take for your father to find you?"

"A . . . while," Byron admitted. "And when he did, it took him time to figure out what to do with me. I'm not sure what you could have done either," he added hastily. "Even if you were there."

Holly stiffened. "For starters, I would have stopped you from ever getting up on the roof in the first place." She jerked herself into a standing position and walked over to the window. She figured with her back turned toward the bed, he couldn't see the fury on her face.

"I went to help the old folks," he said. "You can't do that by being a scared little kid. I knew I was taking a risk. And it's me who's paying the price. Not you."

A nurse walked in, interrupting their conversation and prompting an awkward silence. She introduced herself as Audrey.

"Are you Byron's parents? I am so happy you could come to him. He's been pretty lonely stuck in bed."

"I'm sorry," Holly said, cutting her off, "I'd like to speak to Byron's doctor as soon as possible. I want to know the full extent of his injuries and his short-term and long-term prognosis."

Audrey regrouped. "Sure, I'll call down right away. I can tell you they've scheduled the surgery for his arms for tomorrow morning."

Holly needed rest before she could face the reality of multiple metal plates being screwed into her son's ulna and radius bones. The only thing that could be worse than the situation at hand would be for her to also fall into a fit of vertigo. Tomorrow would be another long day. She had to take care of herself in addition to Byron.

"I have a question for you, if you don't mind, Audrey. Now that we made it to Provo, it occurs to me we don't have a place to stay. Do you have any ideas?"

"Normally," the nurse said. "But then, there's nothing normal on island right now. We have a list of places that give a special rate for families who are here for a patient, but I'm not sure which ones are open. We're lucky to have our generators going here at the hospital; not many others have power. The phone lines are down, too. I wouldn't know how to get in touch with anybody."

Montez again handled the situation with an authority Holly admired, even though she was currently livid with him. "If you could give me a copy of the list, I'll find us a place. I saw a cab in front of the hospital when we came in. I'll get him to drive me around."

Holly was grateful he was willing to take the investigation on.

"Thank you," she said. "No matter what, I'm not going to leave Bryon right now."

"I never thought you would. Now that you're here, wild horses couldn't drag you off. Don't I know it?" He chuckled—just oozing charm. "Besides, even a grown man needs his mother when he's feeling terrible."

Montez laughed again, seemingly oblivious to his culpability in all that had happened.

Holly's eyes narrowed into slits of resentment.

Montez took Holly's suitcase and his leather duffel bag with him when he followed Audrey out into the hallway. He looked back over his shoulder before he disappeared and gave Byron a two-fingered salute and an encouraging smile.

The room fell silent after his departure, and it didn't take long before Byron looked like he might fall asleep. As his eyelids drooped, he shook himself awake.

"It's the pain medication," Holly said. "Go ahead and rest, honey. I'll go look around for something to read."

"No. Please, Mom. That's what I did yesterday, and I don't think I slept all night. Hey, one of the other nurses brought me a deck of cards. Can you unwrap them? They're in that drawer."

Holly retrieved them and then peeled off the plastic wrapper. She took the cards out and squared the deck across the sides and the ends on the tabletop. In a well-practiced move, she pulled with both hands in opposite directions and split the deck precisely in two. Then, she tightly shuffled one corner of the piles with just her thumbs and started the process again. She repeated it eight times before she said to Byron, "Name your poison."

"Omaha Hold 'Em."

She almost split her sides with her amusement at his choice. "That's pretty daring for a kid who can barely keep his eyes open."

It was such a relief to laugh. The past days had been a roller coaster ride of tension; now, even with her son about to go into surgery, it felt like things were looking up.

She dealt them four cards each, their "hole" cards, and then laid down five community cards in a row on his rolling meal table. Their goal was to make their best five-card hand from two of their own cards and three from the common row. As Byron couldn't actually hold anything, Holly positioned the rolling table across his lap and laid his cards down on the bed where they were hidden from her but he could see them.

"I won't peek," she promised him.

He stared down his hand and the muscles of his face started working. "Dad flew back to Grand Turk to get you?"

"Yes, he did."

"Wow. You've gotta admire that kind of commitment. He must have all the pilots around here on some kind of retainer."

She could tell Byron was proud of his father. Even she had to admit he had every right to be. Byron always knew how to soften her up.

"We brought another woman with us on the trip over. Her name is Theresa. She had a baby the day after Nestor. Only yesterday, I guess it was. It seems like so long ago."

Like an apparition that had been called from beyond, Theresa appeared in the doorway with the baby in her arms. She was wearing a hospital gown and robe and a huge ace bandage that wound around her injured leg.

"There you are," Theresa said, a friendly grin on her face.

"I was just talking about you," Holly exclaimed. She jumped up and went over to hug Theresa, as if they hadn't just seen each other, before leading her into the room and introducing her to Byron.

Theresa's eyes skittered over Byron's many dressings and her face became grave.

He did what he could to assure her. "It looks much worse than it is. They're going to take the neck brace off soon. I don't know why I have this huge bandage on my head when I only got five stitches." He shrugged—and immediately winced at the effort and pain it caused him.

Theresa held up a hand. "You rest yourself, young man. You will give your poor mother a heart attack."

"I know, I know," he said. "My mother tends to overreact."

Oh really? I haven't had a chance to get used to the sight of him like this; that's an "overreaction"? He's brushing me off.

She could tell Byron was extremely curious about Theresa—and thought she was pretty. *Doesn't he know that nothing he says is going to make him seem cool to her right now? Look at him. He's a mess.*

But he gave it his best try. A huge smile lit his bruised face. "So, is your baby a boy or a girl?"

"A boy," Theresa said proudly as she pulled the swaddling blanket away from his face and stroked his cheek. The infant pushed out his lips and made cooing sounds while Theresa glowed like a Madonna. "I am here to tell you that your mother saved this child's life. I was sure you would be proud of her; I wanted to tell you myself." She hugged the sleeping child tight and watched him quietly.

Byron's face fell in a deliberately dramatic fashion. He stared at Holly with huge eyes, waiting for an explanation. "You don't lead with this information?"

She raised both hands in the air and then dropped them into her lap with a smacking sound. "We haven't had a chance to talk about anything. So, brace yourself—a lot has happened since you left me to bring your grandparents home."

She seesawed her raised hands like an old-fashioned balance scale. "Yes, I saved a baby's life. Then again, I was also put in a position where I felt compelled to stab someone in the neck."

Byron snorted. "You *what?* Who was it?"

"I'm not going to tell you. Not yet. When we get back home, you'll be in no position to go off halfcocked. It's going to take weeks to catch you up on all that's happened. And I bet you've got some stories of your own to tell."

"A few . . . but nothing like that." She didn't want to talk about her travails right now.

Her son understood her well. He steered the conversation in a different direction. "What's your baby's name, Theresa?"

"My husband is in the Dominican Republic. I have to wait to confirm my choice with him." She held the baby up so they could both see his little face. "But I think we will call him Hollin. Hollin Anthony Moore."

Chapter 34

By the time Montez returned to the hospital, Nurse Audrey had already come in and said Byron should try to nap before dinner. The flaming redness in his eyes was a dead giveaway that he was exhausted. The contrast of the color against his white dressing and attire made it look even more dramatic.

Holly hated that she couldn't help him more. Looking back, it had been easier when he was a small child and she could take him in her arms and dry his tears. Now, she felt awkward and ill equipped to comfort him. He got angry with her when she over-stepped. She would have loved to sleep overnight in the chair by his bedside. But she knew he would never allow it now that he was grown. He would have to be fully unconscious to let it happen. So there was nothing to do but get through the night and get back to him as soon as the sun came up.

Before she and Montez left, Montez gently put his hand on Byron's shoulder and locked eyes with his boy. "I promise you, my son . . . if it takes every penny I have left in this world, I will be here before they take you into surgery," he said solemnly.

Byron nodded and cast his gaze down. "I cost you a lot already. I'm sorry, Dad."

Byron choked up, which made Holly choke up too.

She put on a fake-cheerful voice to try to smooth over the moment. "Try to get some sleep tonight, honey. We'll see you in the morning." She paraded out of the room before she could change her mind or started to bawl.

Outside the room, she gasped. How had this happened? How had they gotten here?

And is he going to be okay?

The two flights of stairs down were unbearably stuffy. Getting to the lobby was a huge relief. Holly pulled at the fabric of her shirt under her arms and fanned herself.

Waiting outside the glass-paned main entrance was a cab.

Holly pointed to it. "Is that for us?"

Montez nodded and led the way to the car.

It was clear he'd kept the same driver, whose name turned out to be Charlie, all afternoon, because as soon as they got in, the two men started talking about all the information they had gathered during their exploration that day.

Charlie looked in the rearview mirror at Holly and pointed to Montez with his thumb. "This is the guy you want during an emergency," he said. "He knows how to get things done."

Montez puffed up his chest, a smug smile on his face. He looked ridiculous.

Holly stubbornly stared Montez square in the eye and said, "I really wouldn't know. I've never been with him in an emergency. After the fact, yes. But I usually manage the difficult moments of my life on my own."

Montez's inflated posture collapsed and he let out a long exhale.

Holly felt profoundly satisfied. She knew she was being a bit mean, but at the moment she didn't care.

They remained uncomfortably quiet until the cab pulled up under the massive portico of the luxurious Many Stars Beach Resort. Holly was certain Montez's choice was meant to impress her, and she raised her eyebrows at him pointedly.

"I-it's rated for a category five hurricane," he stammered. "They are doing some things by lamplight right now, but they have backup generators. The bar and restaurant are up and running."

They thanked Charles and headed inside.

They made straight for the elevators once they entered the lobby, but the concierge spotted them and stepped forward.

"Mr. Curry, I'm glad to see you made it back in one piece." He nodded his head in Holly's direction. "Mrs. Curry."

"My name is *Miss* Walker." She was taken aback by the edge of her voice. *I am just so sick of this. I am a Ms. or Miss, never a Mrs.* But what she was feeling toward Montez wasn't this concierge's fault. She put her hand out and smiled as she shook his. "Holly Walker."

He seemed very concerned. "How is your son?"

She was surprised he knew about Byron. Montez must have talked to him about it. "We think he'll be fine. We still have to get through surgery tomorrow."

He nodded solemnly. "I see. Well, I am so sorry about the accident. I wish you the best and I hope you enjoy your room. Welcome to Many Stars."

Hmmm. He'd gestured to both of them when he said, "Your room." Singular. Holly contemplated the meaning of it.

As Holly had suspected, Montez had only reserved one bedroom—albeit a quite large room with its own, separate living room.

It was at the exact moment she entered it that she understood why Anthony had given her five hundred dollars when she left. They hadn't been able find her wallet or her passport anywhere after the storm, which meant she didn't have any identification with her. She supposed she was lucky to have the few clothes she did in her bag, but without a way to prove her identity, she was dependent on Montez right now for almost everything–an uncomfortable feeling.

Thankfully, there were two queen-size beds. One was piled high with women's clothing, including two cruise-style dresses of a light gauzy fabric and five sets of exquisite bras and panties. Holly frowned.

Montez caught her reaction. "I may have gone overboard on the lingerie," he admitted.

She continued her inspection of the bed's contents. There were capris pants and shorts with coordinating tops, and three sleep sets that looked so comfortable she wanted to get into one now and fall into a deep slumber immediately.

A uniformed woman appeared at the door of what turned out to be a bathroom and Jacuzzi suite. "Madame," she said. "When you're ready." Without another word, she disappeared again.

Argh.

Holly was dumbfounded by the whole scene. Montez went to the door the attendant had just retreated from and said, "Give us a minute." He then opened the glass terrace door and motioned her outside.

The view was spectacular. She couldn't help but appreciate that they were going to have quite the sunset.

He took both of her hands in his, bent his head, and gazed at her through his lush lashes. "I was wrong. I never should have let Byron up on the roof. It's a decision I will live with the rest of my life."

Holly nodded. Though she held her chin up, her eyes were downcast. She listened.

"He is a man now and he looks to me to teach him how to be a good one. I respected that he wanted to help my aunt and uncle. But letting him take a risk like that is not something I would do again."

"All right." Her body relaxed into a position that was more at ease.

"What I question . . . looking back . . . is whether I did it because it was more fun visiting Fabienne's family"—he waved one hand around in the air and shook his head—"or because Byron wanted me to agree with him that he should climb up there. I'll just say it. I'm ashamed. You can say many things about me, Holly, but you know I love my son."

She nodded. "I know you do, Montez. It's the only reason I didn't kick your ass a long time ago."

He sighed. "Or stab me in the throat."

She honestly didn't know how to respond. "How on earth do you know about that?" She chewed on the cuticle of one of her index fingers.

"Byron told me when you went to use the ladies' room. You should never have been put in that position. It's another reason I feel ashamed. I know I let you down. We should have stuck together. As a family. I'm just trying to make up for it now."

Holly went over to the railing and surveyed the yard and the patio. The trees were pretty beaten up. A full crew was out clearing the debris and garbage in the heat and humidity. Any beach and patio furniture they might have had was gone, although Holly didn't know if it had been blown away or simply put in storage. Nestor had dredged the beach, too. It wasn't nearly as wide as it had been. The drop-off down to the white sand was now quite steep.

"What's the maid for?" she asked him with a resigned sigh.

"Her name is Laurette. She's a masseuse and hairstylist. I thought it would be a nice treat for you to have a massage, take a bath, and get your hair done before dinner."

Holly sat down on the end of one of the chaise lounges. She was still stewing. "Wow. I don't know whether to say thank you or screw you." She stroked the fabric of the cushion she was now reclining on. It was cool to the touch, though the texture was rich.

"You can decide afterward." He chuckled. "We have dinner reservations at six forty-five, so you better get started." He winked at her and went back inside.

"Madame is ready to begin," he called out to Laurette.

Again, with the "madame." Pretty presumptuous, Montez.

Chapter 35

With Laurette's help, Holly looked so flawless that evening she could have walked a red-carpet event and blended right in. She wore one of the long dresses Montez had purchased for her—a pale lavender number. Though the cut of it was elegant, its gauzy fabric made it seem more casual. This was some comfort, as she doubted anyone else would (or could) be dressed to the nines right after the storm.

When Laurette brought her three pairs of shoes to choose from, she was astonished to find they were a perfect fit. *How on earth?* Laurette convinced her to wear the pair of heeled, but not-too-high-heeled, sandals. She also strung a long, slinky silver necklace around Holly's neck and handed her a matching set of earrings to put in her ears. The woven chains on the studs swung low and danced every time she moved her head. Laurette tucked a final blond tendril into Holly's upswept hair and said, "*Exquis.*"

They heard a knock at the door. Laurette answered as Holly fussed with her makeup in the mirror, and came back in with a sealed envelope.

Holly broke the seal on the hotel stationery with one finger and read the note inside:

Meet me in the bar. I've gotten a head start.

At this, she smiled; she was very much looking forward to a drink.

Holly offered Laurette a twenty-dollar bill as a tip, but she shooed the money away. With a confident smile, she said, "It has all been taken care of, madame."

Holly began to correct her: "Mademois—oh, never mind."

They exited together and rode the elevator down to the ground floor. Laurette hung back at the archway that led from the foyer to the bar; she told Holly she wanted to see Montez's reaction.

Holly couldn't help but notice that he immediately stood up as she entered the room. He was absolutely stunning in his slim-cut black European suit. Then again, she realized, all decked out like this she was a bit of a head-turner herself.

She was annoyed to see that Montez was scanning everyone else in the room but her—observing other men's reactions to her entrance instead of appreciating her himself. And the men were indeed looking.

When she was a much younger woman, this kind of attention would have made her feel uncomfortable, but when a man in the corner called out, "Hey beautiful—after this nightmare, you sure are a sight for sore eyes," she turned to him and smiled from ear-to-ear.

The maître d' appeared at Montez's side carrying two menus. As Holly approached, he swept his arm out to indicate he was leading them to their table.

They were seated on the ocean side edge of the main deck of the outdoor restaurant. The pounding waves immediately put her into a relaxed state of mind. Before the hurricane savaged it, the once lush landscaping had probably provided the feeling of sitting down in a garden. At this point, she was just grateful the sky was clear and the resort had been able to clear enough windblown sand out of the way to set some tables out.

Fluffy clouds streamed across the sky. Holly knew they would soon catch the changing light and colors would shift from oranges to pinks to purples, every hue melding as time passed and the breeze blew. It would be quite a show.

After their waiter pushed in her chair, he told Montez, "I will bring the champagne immediately."

When it was just the two of them, Montez scanned her up and down. "I knew lavender was your color the minute I laid eyes on that dress. You look wonderful." He lifted one of her hands and brought it to his lips. She hated to admit that he could still make her tingle all the way down to her toes.

She cocked her head to one side, "Yeah . . . well . . . you really went all out. Anyone would look glamorous after the treatment I got today. I'm not keeping this jewelry, by the way. It's too much. I wouldn't want to feel indebted."

Montez waved her comment away as if none of it mattered. "You deserve it and more," he told her in a sincere voice.

A tall wineglass was set before her and the maître d' poured the cold sparkling wine.

Montez raised his glass to her. "To better times ahead."

As she clinked the rim of her stemware against his, she joked, "I don't see how things could get any better than this." She let out a feminine titter that was unlike her. "Remember when we were young and had to make picnics to go out on a date? We couldn't afford to go out to eat. Now look at us."

"Yes. God is good. We've done very well . . . very well . . . and, more importantly, our son lived through his fall. In fact . . ." He raised his glass to her again and stood. He caught the attention of the diners at the other three tables outside, and they all held their glasses up. "We should give praise tonight that we lived through the historic Hurricane Nestor!" he shouted.

It was clear the crowd agreed with him as they quietly toasted.

Holly and Montez sipped their drink and watched the giant

orange ball that was the sun sink quickly into the sea. Not a single voice interrupted its last light as it dipped over the horizon. A flutter of activity began immediately, however, the second it fully dropped: a three-piece band started to play a soft instrumental song and staff ran to light torches.

Montez smiled the way only he could, so blinding Holly thought it would melt anyone's heart.

"*You* made the picnics back then," he reminded her, "and I thank you for it. I merely came along for the ride. You were always a great cook."

The waiter brought them a delicately flavored appetizer of shrimp ceviche; it had been marinated in exactly enough lime juice and spice. By the time they'd finished their second course of Niçoise salads, the bottle of champagne was empty. Montez asked for the wine list and ordered without consulting her.

"I don't get a say?" Holly objected.

"If I don't know what you like by now," he said, "I never will."

Holly had to admit, when the food came, that the grapefruit hints in her Sauvignon blanc paired perfectly with her seafood entrée.

The music the band was playing had picked up in tempo. They were now doing soft swing ballads and two other musicians, a sax player and a female vocalist, were setting up to join them.

By the time the waiter came to take away their dinner plates, Holly was more than content.

"Shall I put the charges on your room, sir?"

Montez, watching the band, didn't bother to look up at him as he said, "That would be wonderful."

A big bear of a man approached their table. "*Bon soir, monsieur et madame.*"

Holly's face winced ever so slightly.

"I am the master mixologist, Henri." He let out a jolly laugh. "I understand you are celebrating tonight?"

Mary Kathleen Mehuron

Are we?

"Yes, we are," Montez said with certainty.

"In that spirit, may I make you one of my signature cocktails? The dancing is about to begin."

Holly widened her questioning eyes at Montez. She knew the following day would be hard and she didn't want to risk a hangover, yet she was enjoying cutting loose from all the fear and worry they had been living with for the last few days.

Montez nodded; with a flourish, Henri produced two lists of drinks and put one in front of each of them.

"Let the dancing commence and the party begin," the singer said into her microphone. "What shall we say about tonight? Nestor didn't win! We are down, but not out, Mr. Hurricane. We made it—and now we are going to switch things up and play some more contemporary songs. If you'd like to make a request, we have paper and pencils at the foot of the stage. We love a challenge! A couple of times during each set of music, we will try to do one of your suggestions. It may not wind up perfect, but it's always fun."

The drummer banged his drumsticks together four times and they took off in a terrific rendition of The Eurythmics' "Sweet Dreams."

The next song they played was Dion's early sixties classic "Runaround Sue." A group of white-haired tourists got up to jitterbug and the other patrons applauded them when the song ended.

As the ensemble seamlessly started a lively cover that got many more people out on the floor, Montez yelled into Holly's ear, "Let's go."

Holly didn't have to be asked twice. She was already out on the floor when Montez was barely up from the table. She turned to watch him. Just the way he moved his shoulders was a marvel— but it made her remember the night she'd danced with Anthony.

The Belonger

He didn't have great rhythm, but his full attention had been on her. Anthony made it into a high form of communication, whereas Montez seemed to revel in being in the spotlight.

After a couple of songs, Holly told Montez, "I need a sip of water."

She went over to their table and did drink some water—but she also tasted her cocktail. *Delicious.*

The band hardly wasted a minute; they appeared to be having a great time, and the audience was clearly in a mood to have some fun. A chord progression from the iconic album *Thriller* began. She'd long forgotten she and Montez both knew how to moon-walk to "Billie Jean."

They brought the house down—and as soon as the next song began, two younger girls pulled Montez away from Holly to dance with him. Apparently, they were impressed.

She didn't have a moment to be resentful, as a man her age cut in to be her partner. Within the hour, the group on the dance floor reminded her of Friday nights on Grand Turk at Salinas. As an audience, they were all in it together. Everyone rotated around the space, trying to mingle and to dance with everybody. Perhaps the best moment of the night was when Holly ended up with a female partner in her eighties. The old lady was dolled up in a pink spangly mini dress, and she shook those bangles around like someone half her age.

By the time Holly and Montez stumbled up to their room later that night, she was giddy. She'd made new friends, and she'd felt like a celebrity on the dance floor—pretty and funny.

I don't know when I've had so much fun.

She walked into their hotel room on unsteady legs. She found that someone had cleared the clothing off what she considered to be her bed and also turned it down, and was grateful for it.

"Montez," she announced, "I am going to sleep." Without any hesitation, she grabbed a nightgown and went into the bathroom to take her hair down and wash her face. When she crawled into the crisp white sheets, Anthony's was the face she saw before she drifted off.

Chapter 36

A bout three o'clock in the morning, Holly woke up parched. Although the drapes were closed, moonlight streamed in around the edges and every time the breeze gusted and blew them up, it lit the room. She reached around to find her water bottle on the bedside table and unscrewed the top.

Out of the darkness a voice said, "I'm already awake."

"Hey," she said in a groan.

"There's some aspirin in the bathroom. Do you want me to get it for you?"

"Thanks, I'm okay . . . just thirsty."

"I can't sleep," Montez said. "I've been lying here thinking about the surgery. It sounds like it will be awful. You want to go out on the terrace with me and sit?"

Holly thought about it. Although the bed was extremely comfortable, there wasn't enough power from the hotel generators to run the air conditioners in the bedrooms—and since their room only had windows across one wall, the cross-breeze wasn't strong either. Inside the room, they were stuck with the heat and humidity.

"That sounds like a good idea," she said.

She grabbed the light throw folded on the end of her bed and draped it over herself as she settled into one of the cushioned chaise lounges outside. Montez did the same; he even brought a pillow out with him.

"What time is it?" she asked.

"Three fifteen."

"Well, that's it for us then. We'll never fall back asleep before daybreak." Holly pulled the throw up around her neck, for, thankfully, the trade winds were strong outside. The feel of the knit fabric against her skin was luxurious. "Is this cashmere? It has to be. How much did this room cost, anyway?"

"I'd be too embarrassed to say. Even with the storm, it's not cheap." Though it was still pretty dark, she could make out his wide smile.

Holly giggled. "The room, the clothes, the *jewelry*."

"After all we've been through—and I don't just mean Nestor, we've come a long way in this life—we deserve it. *You* deserve it."

Holly was silent for a time. When she opened her mouth again, she couldn't help saying, "I've thought since you landed in that helicopter to get me that you were trying to impress me—to seduce me, if you want to know the truth."

He laughed out loud and clapped his hands. "Of course I was! What man wouldn't try?"

Holly was relieved they were chatting honestly.

"I told you on the plane that I've made a terrible mistake all these years. I don't know what I was thinking, Holly. Maybe many young men think someone better is bound to come along. I don't know if you can, but I hope you will forgive me."

That doesn't change what happened. Still, she was grateful to hear him say it. "I was bitter for many years. But so much time has passed. I forgive you."

They reached out from their chairs and clasped hands for several seconds. Holly gave his hand a squeeze and was the one to let go. "I had a wonderful time last night, thank you. Let's hang out here for a while. It's cool. Then we can both shower and get ready to head to the hospital. I can't wait to see Byron again." She rolled over on her side, enjoying the sensation of the knit cover sliding against her legs.

Montez took a swig from his water bottle. "The surgery's scheduled for eight. I don't think going at six is too early. He's probably nervous."

"I know I am," Holly said. "They screw metal plates into the bones and then we have to bring him back to have them taken out? It sounds painful." She cocked an ear in Montez's direction. Although she couldn't see him clearly in the moonlight, she knew he was crying.

"What is it?" she whispered.

She could make out him wiping his eyes with his expensive throw and she heard him sniffling. "Byron getting hurt . . . I feel like God is punishing me."

Holly drew her knees up to her chest and wrapped her arms around them. "For what?"

"For leaving you two. For acting like a part-time father was as good as a full-time one. I should have been there for the two of you all along."

Holly didn't say anything. Her mind spiraled through the history of their relationship. She remembered well that back then Montez hadn't thought she was good enough for him. It still hurt her deeply. She'd known she wasn't like the girls he'd grown up with. But in the beginning, he'd seemed to really like her. They'd had a whirlwind of a sexual affair that had sent her head over heels—only to be quickly followed by persistent judgment and criticism.

It wasn't long before he decided he didn't approve of how she drank and smoked. He pressed her to join a church with him, though she'd never had much religious affiliation and felt uncomfortable about the idea. More than anything, he said he was mystified that she was on her own when she was still so young.

He never came out and said so, but he seemed to blame her for the estrangement from her parents, which was outright abandonment. This was especially painful, for while Holly was sure that being an emancipated minor had led her to make some bad decisions, she was proud of herself for working her way through the last few years of high school. And getting through college had been a real challenge as well, what with the baby and all.

When she'd unexpectedly conceived Byron, Montez had been clear they would never be together as a nuclear family. He'd always pledged his help, as had Coralyse and Sanford. Yet the truth was, except for two weeks at Christmas and in the summer and the small but steady check that came in the mail, Holly had raised Byron Curry on her own.

And that was the crux of the matter.

Toby and Sally Trombley had done as much as they could to help. Especially with babysitting. But for the most part the burdens had sat squarely on her shoulders because Montez had lived an ocean away.

Day was just dawning when Holly stood and told Montez, "I'm going first. I've got to wash all this hairspray out of my hair."

The surgeon walked in wearing blue scrubs. He pulled off his face mask and told them, "He did great, but his recovery is going to take time. Really bad breaks. We've got to keep the pain under control for a few days and then you can bring him home."

Holly broke out in a cold sweat. She wondered how on earth she would get him back home in this condition. "Byron and I have The Roseate House on Grand Turk."

The doctor's eyes crinkled warmly. "And the Sand Dollar, too? You buy it from Teddy?"

"*We* did," she said. "Byron and I did. And we were there when Nestor hit. It's in pretty rough shape."

Montez fiddled with his cell phone, although he knew as well as anyone there wouldn't be any reception for many weeks. "He can come stay with me," he said. "I'll rent something."

"Montez!" Holly brayed.

His eyes shot up to hers, and she held his gaze for longer than seemed possible. She was not about to entrust her son to anyone else.

"All right, little mami. I get it." He stood and came over to give her a hug. As he held her, he said, "You stay here with Byron. I'll fly to Grand Turk and see if I can't get a couple of rooms at your place habitable. Then we'll fly you both over."

Holly's relief was so profound she could hardly breathe.

Chapter 37

B yron and Holly's helicopter landed at the JAGS McCartney
Airport on Grand Turk Island four days later. Though it was
totally shut down and most of the roof was torn off the building,
the pilot was able to set the chopper down on a runway.

Montez's truck was already parked and waiting when they
opened the helicopter door. Fabienne and Sameera were there
with him, the two of them huddled together out of the range of
the blast of air the propeller was sending out.

Since Byron couldn't use his arms to hang on to the doorjamb
as he got out, both Holly and Montez helped him with the long
step down.

The pilot didn't bother to cut his engine, and it was deafening.
Montez reached into the chopper to grab their bags, and the three
of them ducked as they got out from under the blades as quickly
as possible.

As soon as they were clear, Fabienne came running toward
them. Holly was mystified when she tried to hand her an old
green beer bottle whose label had peeled off.

Fabienne repeatedly pointed to the neck of the bottle, so Holly
took it from her and looked inside. She discovered a note that
had been rolled up and inserted. She pulled it out with her pinky
finger and read it on the spot.

The Belonger

My dearest Holly,

If you are reading this, you have found your way home to Cock-burn Town, and I thank God for it. I would also assume Byron must be well enough to travel; I, for one, will be anxious to hear that good news for certain.

I was out fishing to try to help feed our neighborhood, here on Queen's Cay, when I coincidentally ran into our friend, Kel, doing the same for his own friends on Grand Turk. I asked if he would bring this note back to you; a bottle was all we could find to keep it dry. Although the choice was born of necessity, I think a message in a bottle is a good seaworthy image—don't you?

I miss you terribly, but I fear it will be some days before I can consider making the trip over to see you. The first issue is we are still patching up buildings simply to keep the weather out and people safe from falling rubble. Water for bathing and cooking will continue to be an issue until we can fix some of the cisterns. The army brought in limited quantities of canned and dried foods after you left for Provo but people here on Queen's Cay still need the fish we are harvesting for fresh protein. There is a serious shortage of gasoline that inhibits my ability to travel as well, though the gov-ernment may help me on that count because I'm out doing official work foraging for food.

My life is very primal these days. I feel like it's me against the sea and when I'm on land, the elements. Mighty foes indeed. Thank God for Matius, who sends his regards, by the way.

To be completely truthful, the only thing that keeps me going these days is the many memories of you I keep carefully stored away in a corner of my mind and the anticipation I may once again hold you in my arms. Please don't give up on us, Holly, my beautiful girl.

I wish you a dry place to stay and food on your table. We can't hope for more than that right now, can we?

Mary Kathleen Mehuron

Until I see you again,
My love always,
Anthony

Holly flattened the letter, folded it in half and slid it inside her shirt, where it remained next to her heart.

It was over two weeks later when Holly spotted Anthony's fishing boat in the distance and even—just barely—made Matius and him out on deck. She jumped up and ran into the kitchen, where she reached for a clean napkin off the top of the linen pile and buried her face in it, wiping her eyes. It was barely three o'clock in the afternoon. She waited for him on pins and needles. The minutes found her bouncing from the ball of one foot to the other.

When *The Angelfish* was anchored and the men got into their kayaks to head for shore, she ran down to the beach to greet them, waving her arms high over her head.

It only took one look at Anthony as he staggered in dragging his kayak up onto the beach to assess the situation. "You're drunk?" she scolded him.

"Of course I'm drunk," he shouted back to her. "I started drinking the second we got on board." As he drew closer, he added with a laugh, "How else could I find the courage to come to your place of business and declare my everlasting love for you?"

She threw her hands up. This wasn't at all how she'd planned for their reunion to go. For one thing, Byron and Montez were leaning over the railing of The Roseate, watching and listening to everything they were saying. With a jerk of her thumb, she pointed toward them to indicate that him saying such things in their proximity embarrassed her—but she couldn't help but shake her head and smile.

As was their custom, she felt compelled to give him a hard time.

She mugged at him. "Maybe you should come back when you've had a chance to sober up and think things over, Lord Bascombe."

Shorts dripping, one hand clasping each of her shoulders, he held her at arm's length in front of him. His appreciative once-over made her feel like a ripe piece of fruit he was dying to bite into.

"I've had forty-eight years to think things over," he said. "You can see for yourself all the good it's done me." His eyes were soulful, though puffy, and his face covered with a salt-and-pepper stubble.

Holly hugged him tightly, even though he was sticky with sweat. "I've missed you, you old scallywag."

She let go of him and called over to Matius, "I've missed you as well!" before turning on her heels and heading back toward the Sand Dollar. Celebratory cocktails to mark their unexpected arrival were in order.

When the drinks were made and poured, Holly raised her own glass to Matius and Anthony in a toast.

"Welcome back," she said. "I will never forget your courage during and after Hurricane Nestor. Here's to a calm and tranquil future."

"Here, here," they chorused, including Byron and Montez, although they were all fully aware that two more months of hurricane season, not to mention a massive cleanup, stretched before them.

In many ways, the Sand Dollar was the heart of old Cockburn Town, even when it wasn't serving food. It remained a handy gathering spot for the community, and that warmed Holly's heart.

The restaurant still wasn't officially open, and wouldn't be until the town's power and water were restored. Holly figured it would be months and months before that happened. The damage, at least, wasn't overly bad; though the restaurant floor was fairly open to the elements, she'd spent the extra money early on to install secured hurricane doors for the kitchen and bar, and that foresight had spared the contents inside from destruction during the storm.

Like many of the buildings on Grand Turk, most of their exterior paint job had been sandblasted off in irregular patterns and taken off chunks of the wall stucco. It gave the Sand Dollar the look of a run-down, inner-city tenement building. When Holly and Byron had first arrived back from the hospital on Provo, the outdoor floor of the restaurant had been covered with over a foot of sand and one corner of the roof of the seating area had been pushed up by the howling forces into a shape resembling a ski jump.

Since then, Holly and her staff had cleared off the cement floor, first shoveling the heavy sand—her arms had ached for days after that effort—and then sweeping in endless rounds. It was as if fine particles were still falling out of the sky. Holly would think they were done with the cleaning, only to find another fine layer of grit to deal with when she came back fifteen minutes later.

It was still possible to cook on the built-in oil-drum barbecue, as it had survived relatively unscathed and she had numerous bags of Haitian charcoal stashed away that had, fortunately, stayed dry. She could also use the propane range in the kitchen if she lit it by hand. Water to flush toilets was hauled from the two cisterns on The Roseate's property to the bathrooms. She was vigilant about this area of maintenance. She was fine with the idea of sharing her facilities, but she was not about to clean up after other adults—and she wasn't going to ask her staff to do so, either, not when there was so much other work to be done.

Every corner she walked past was filled with garbage. Every minute of every day was needed to return the street to some kind of order. She firmly believed if each person worked toward it, they could establish a new sense of normal for their island in good time.

Holly encouraged locals to gather on her property around lunchtime, dinnertime, and even long into the night, as she and Byron had plenty of fuel to fill their tiki lights after the sunset. The mere thought of going home to blackness was daunting for many, and people often stayed on until late in the evening and visited.

She dragged two coolers out and left them at the restaurant for others to use. Those first weeks after the storm, someone would get the charcoal going about ten in the morning; folks would stop in throughout the day and into the dinner hour with a piece of meat to cook and a drink to sip. She also set up a folding table for the dishes friends brought to share. Her supply of paper plates was dwindling; fortunately, people were polite enough to wash their used ceramic plates in water from a bucket. For the most part, Holly's open-door policy was working well.

The harmony of these unspoken agreements with her neighbors seemed to stem from one simple fact: no one in Turks and Caicos had been killed by the massive Hurricane Nestor. This was a miracle. A true miracle. God had been good to Grand Turk.

Chapter 38

Byron's arms were crossed in front of him by a system of slings that Holly helped him put on every morning. Because he couldn't hold a glass up, he was forced by necessity to drink liquids through a straw. Even that was an interesting process to watch, as he was only able to move his index and middle fingers.

Right now, the beverage in question was a beer.

"Is this experience supposed to teach me something?" he demanded from his seat at a low table near the bar. "You know I hate feeling helpless."

"Who doesn't?" Holly said. "The idea of getting old terrifies me. That you will have to do things for me. How do you think your grandparents feel that they can't even change a lightbulb anymore? Maybe the lesson is simple. You give me a hard time because you think I don't see you as a grown man. Okay. You're grown. You've still got two broken limbs. It's temporary. I'll be hands off when you're a bit better."

Fabienne stood by him now and helped him by guiding the straw to his lips. Byron, looking taken by her kindness, beckoned her closer and kissed her on the cheek. An entire universe couldn't have contained the smile she gave him in return. He stroked her cheek with one of his working fingers and she glowed down at him.

Montez cracked open a beer and took a sip. Holly could tell

by the look on his face that he was disgusted by its nearly warm temperature. But he didn't dare complain to her.

As the days passed without electricity, ice was harder to come by on the island. Holly and Byron had had the foresight to install a small gasoline generator for their chest freezer. It was saving much of their inventory, and they were happy for it. Every evening, Holly snuck in a few trays of ice to use for the following day—but the truth was, clean bottled drinking water on island was running out, too.

Rumor was her only news source, as there was no television, radio, Internet, or cell service. There was gossip that another boat full of supplies was coming over from Provo. Until she saw it pull into the cruise center with her own eyes, Holly would keep a conservative eye on her reserves of drinking water and even the runoff reserves in the cistern. If that meant less-than-ice-cold beer, so be it.

She stood behind the bar wiping it down and feeling the grit as she cleaned. She would only serve hard alcohol if a customer had cash, but even then she felt uneasy unlocking the grates that protected their rows of liquor bottles. Since no one knew how long the isolation on Grand Turk would last, she didn't want to flaunt the fact she had a full inventory of booze when there were only a few police to keep order.

At the moment, the police officers have many more important demands on their time. My alcohol is far from the top priority. Two strong men with crowbars could easily break into this locked system. Then I'd have to repair that, too—and who knows how long it would take to get new parts in from Miami?

Nevertheless, Anthony had cash—an unending supply of it, or so it seemed to Holly—and he stood before her now, wanting another rum punch.

She smiled as she filled his order. "Only two pieces of ice," she said in a bossy tone. "That's all I'm giving you."

He scratched his chin and spoke in a low voice, "That's fine, my lovely. I understand." His collared shirt was rumpled, his face flushed. "You should probably give me a bottle of water, too."

Byron rose from his table and came over. "I can't believe our boats survived. It's unbelievable."

Anthony raised his glass to Byron. "A little worse for wear. But considering. I know yours was damaged, but it's still afloat and serviceable. We can't ask for more, can we?"

Byron nodded his head in agreement, and they clinked glasses.

"Crazy," Byron said. "Then again, I've always heard Deep Creek's a good refuge for boats."

"It proved to be this time. What a stroke of good luck."

Holly noticed when Montez turned toward Anthony with a curled lip. Her heart skittered with concern. Montez had already told her he'd decided his priorities in his life as it stood right now. He said he needed to help his son navigate the physical demands of life with two casted arms, and patiently show Holly she could trust him in the way she had over two decades earlier. He had three times now explained to her in great detail how he'd made a terrible mistake and it turned out he loved her after all.

She didn't argue with him when he said it, but she stopped the conversation each time with a fairly quiet, "People have all kinds of reactions to devastating events, Montez. In this hurricane, we've all been through trauma, so it isn't the time to make an important decision. We need to heal . . . and there's so much work to be done."

After the third of those uncomfortable moments, she'd finally realized he was interpreting this to mean she was much too busy to be thinking about *him*—and she knew Montez well enough to know that must be making him crazy. He was not a man to be kept waiting.

He always assumed if he ever came around to my way of thinking, I would be right there waiting. And I would have been. I always thought he would go out and sow his oats but, in the end, come back to me and Byron. What has changed? It can't just be that I had sex with Anthony. Granted, it was good; but it wasn't good enough to change everything—was it?

Holly wasn't trying to play games with Montez, but it seemed her reticence made her all the more attractive to him. He said he didn't take Anthony as any kind of serious threat, but he had wondered aloud more than once about what happened between them during the storm. She felt she could read his mind: *I have money and prestige in our community. He's nothing but a clown. A bit of a madman, even. What possible competition could he be?*

To add to her confusion and distraction, Anthony had already declared his love for her twice today since arriving back on island. She'd smacked him the second time, though not terribly hard. She had rolled her eyes too. She was simply too worn out to make the effort considering her future with any man would require. Being pushed to decide between these two during these especially difficult times was ridiculous.

Anthony was planted at the edge of the floor now—waiting for her, she knew—but he must have gotten bored, for he had turned around to face the waves. It made her laugh when every now and again she saw some ocean spray shoot up and spray him in the face, though it also made her nervous that he was standing where the only section of the railing was missing. They'd had to remove it because the storm had bent it so badly it had blocked the flow of traffic in and out of the kitchen.

As Holly saw it, the big problem with Anthony's position was the five-foot drop-off in front of him. Luckily, there was a deep swimming hole below, so it would be hard to hurt yourself in a fall—unless you didn't know how to swim, or, as in Anthony's case, you were drunk. Some of the local children had discovered it after Nestor and begged her the last few days to let them jump off. They now called it "The Big Splash."

Anthony had admitted to drinking on the way over on the boat and he now had the second tall tumbler in his hand that she'd poured for him. They had all lost too much in recent days for her to want to risk any further injury, but neither did she have time to watch over the man. She had to run inside and find some serving spoons.

As she passed him, she said, "Anthony, go save us some seats. All the food will be hot soon."

Much to her relief, he did as she asked, and she saw Byron sit down across the table from him. The breeze carried their conversation straight to her.

Byron's bright green eyes lit up. "How ya doin', Anthony?"

"Never better, Byron. The better question is, how you are doing? Is it terribly painful?"

"It's not the best time I've ever had. But they took good care of me in the hospital and it was awesome that Mom and Dad got over to be with me."

Holly was so grateful to Montez in that moment. She couldn't keep a satisfied little smile off her face.

Anthony looked somber. "Let's hope the worst of times are behind us for a while."

Montez slid into the chair next to his son and Holly brought over four white dinner plates and four table settings wrapped up in paper napkins.

As she laid out the place settings, she told them, "Go up and serve yourselves, but be mindful of your portions. Who knows how many people we'll need to feed here tonight?"

Chapter 39

Holly drifted to the front door and watched the street for signs of more guests coming down the road. She thought to wait an hour or so to make a plate for her own supper, allowing others a chance first. She changed her mind when she ran her hands down her sides and thought about all the weight she'd lost over the last few weeks.

You need to eat something, Holly Walker. You can't take care of others if you don't take care of yourself.

She saw Byron had found some friends while waiting in the line. As she stood with her plate, she watched him horse around as best he could, given his limitations.

She was at the end of the queue, not far from where Anthony and Montez were still seated. She heard Anthony say, "Shall we wait for them to start?"

"That could take ages," Montez said. "You know how the two of them like to talk."

Anthony laughed in response.

"Anthony—I want you to know I have proposed to Holly a future," Montez said slowly. "One we would share together."

Holly took in a sharp breath. *This can't be happening right now.*

Anthony was clearly astounded. He carefully enunciated, "You proposed?"

Montez raised his brows. "Well, I didn't buy a ring if that's what you're asking."

"So . . . let's be forthright," Anthony said. "It's just us two men sitting here. You don't want to lose Holly, but you don't want to marry her either?"

Holly surreptitiously looked over her shoulder, wanting to see their faces.

Montez gave a shrug. "What are formalities to people at our age?"

Anthony pushed his plate away and put his forearms on the table. He shook his head and stared into Montez's eyes and, in a deep and rumbling voice, said, "It's *everything*. Celebrating falling in love, for probably the last time in our lives, is *everything*. You are an idiot, Montez. Though we've been friends for years, you are as wrong as wrong can be."

He shot up out of his seat and ran over to Holly, who had just reached the food table. The look on his face told her he had a desperate need to talk to her. He offered her his help holding her plate while she spooned the various dishes onto it. He kept a running dialogue going concerning his opinion on the different covered dishes that made up the buffet.

She laughed when she and Anthony finally sat down. "Honestly, I'm more than capable of carrying a plate of food across the room," she told him.

"No matter," Anthony said. "It's a chance for us to steal a moment. I must confess, I am happy to see Montez has moved on from the table."

Holly stopped short of teasing him any further because of the hangdog expression he continued to wear.

He gently took one of her hands in his. "My darling, I need to tell you something. Something that can't wait."

Since it was obvious he was serious, she released a silent sigh and pushed her plate away. "Okay."

He began to talk a mile a minute and set to painting a picture. "When I was young—a boy, really, just eighteen—I fathered a child."

Holly noticed Anthony was watching her carefully, so she tried not to show a strong reaction to this disclosure.

"The mother was a girl who came to Queen's Cay, as so many do, for work."

"She was from another country?" Holly asked.

"Yes, and a few years younger than me. It was as if I couldn't resist her beauty . . . not that she encouraged me." He shook his head. "I was persistent, and I won her over. And when she gave herself to me, it was with her whole heart. My parents were furious—not because she wasn't one of us, but because she was poor. And callow fellow I was, her Catholicism proved to be an inconvenience to me. You see, I couldn't see any reason for her not to be rid of the baby. I confess this to you freely, because I want you to understand who I was back then—and, perhaps, better understand the man I am now."

The story was a shock. Holly's face reddened. She met his eyes but then lowered them down to the table, somehow knowing he needed this to continue.

He let out a quivering sigh. "Cheeky bastard I was, I started dating an American girl whose name I can't even recall now. I made a show of it so my child's mother would understand I was done with her. Quite simply—I don't think I'm exaggerating at all when I say this—it broke her heart. I'm overcome with shame when I think about it." Anthony's voice shook with emotion. "I can't believe I was capable of such a thing. She went home to Haiti in disgrace."

The admission made Holly clasp her hands together and bow her head as if in prayer.

Before she had a chance to ask, Anthony cleared his throat and said, barely above a whisper, "I never met my son." He closed his eyes and took a moment.

Holly sat perfectly still, anxious for him to finish.

Finally: "I heard through friends that they both died years ago in the earthquake. Since I had disappointed her in such a spectacular fashion, I didn't believe I deserved love. And that"—he reached across the table and pulled one of her hands to his mouth and kissed it—"my dear, dear Holly . . ."

When he paused again, Holly's entire being mourned from the suffering of the situation. One she could easily understand.

Anthony drew in another firm breath, seemingly so he'd have the strength to continue, and said in almost a whisper, "That is the reason I have never married."

Holly wiped her lips with her napkin. "Until me?"

She shook her head. *I go forty-three years without an offer and now the two of them are fighting over me. Unbelievable.*

He stroked her hand with his thumb. "You always understand me. Intuitively. It's a gift, really." He wore his affection for her with the open face of someone far younger than he actually was.

Holly fought the desire to nervously laugh the moment off—it was just too intense to bear.

She was startled to see Montez suddenly appear over Anthony's left shoulder and stare at her with a frown and his arms crossed. She removed her hand from Anthony's and nervously took a bite from her supper plate. *I am starving.*

Montez appeared impatient as he shifted in place. With a glare that was almost comical, he said, "I wish to speak with you."

"I'm eating," Holly said, and waved her hand in the air to

dismiss him. "Sit down and speak if you want to speak. I don't have time for a big drama right now."

"I want to speak to you alone," Montez insisted.

She grinned up at him with what she knew was an impish expression. "That's not possible, Montez. As soon as I'm done eating, I've got to get back to work."

Is this really about their respective love for me or is it a male competition? Just two studs staking their claim?

Anthony stood and asked, "Would you like me to refill your water glass?"

She was happy he had broken the tension. "Please."

When he walked away, Montez followed him. Holly was horrified to hear Montez yell, "She is not for you, Anthony!"

Everyone froze. She was embarrassed that all their friends and their son were now listening.

Anthony was rooted to the ground, his feet planted wide apart. "You had your chance, Montez. Be a gentleman and let Holly and me explore this time in our lives."

If looks could kill, Montez's dark gaze would have done so. He said, "*We* are a family."

Anthony spit on the ground near Montez's feet. "Only last week you didn't think so."

Holly began quaking that this altercation might come to blows. *Honestly, do men ever really grow up?*

"Why would she choose you?" Montez asked tersely.

"I know you think I'm just an old beach bum, Montez. Perhaps that was true in the past. But that woman makes me want to be a better man, and so I shall be. Besides, let us face the facts . . . I'm just more fun than you are."

That last statement caught Holly off guard. She laughed so hard she put her forehead down on the table for a few seconds. *Truer words have never been spoken.*

After composing herself, Holly rose from the table. Both men turned and watched her when she stood up and walked toward the kitchen carrying all their plates. By this time, Coralyse had arrived with four volunteers from her church; thankfully, she had just missed the confrontation. Although Byron could be of no real help to the church ladies, he went over and stood next to his grandmother and teased her playfully as she stood in line, which gave Holly some comfort.

No matter what those two old fools think is going to happen next, this is my world, here at the Sand Dollar with Byron.

She watched as Fabienne fed her son a special treat she had brought with her and Holly noticed how he nearly doubled over at something she whispered into his ear.

Hmmmmm. What's going on with those two?

Coralyse swatted at Holly with a towel when she attempted to enter the kitchen to clean. "You've done quite enough work for one day, missy. Shoo!"

She opened her mouth to argue, but she was loudly overruled by Coralyse and her friends. She knew better than to disagree with Byron's grandmother, so she wandered back outside.

Recent days had been a flurry of crucial activity, making it impossible to relax; she remained the same bundle of nervous energy she'd been since the day she learned Nestor was coming. Uncertain where to turn next.

Anthony brought her glass of water to where she stood by The Big Splash, feeling wistful.

"A penny for your thoughts?" he asked.

Holly knitted her brows and flung one side of her hair back over her shoulder. "I was thinking about the kids who were jumping into the water here today. They were so thrilled. Nothing could make them happier than the simple joy of bounding in . . .

I would give anything to feel that way. I didn't have much of a childhood, as you know, and I'm afraid it's too late for me. Maybe I don't have the capacity for feeling that kind of thrill. Or even happiness. Maybe I don't have the aptitude for it. I know how to work. That's all I know how to do." She stared at her feet and held her breath.

I don't want to disappoint Anthony, but I've only fallen head-over-heels in love once in my life. If it hadn't been for Byron, I would say it was a big mistake. It's not like I'm going to become someone else overnight. I've been on my own for so long.

Anthony put his arm around her and kissed her on the top of her head. "When things settle down here, what say I rent us a sailboat? I know this ocean like the back of my hand. Oh, Holly, the places I can show you will take your breath away."

She thought it was a wonderful idea—the perfect opportunity to get to know each other better without making any kind of long-term commitment—but she didn't get the chance to answer him because just then, Byron came over with a glass of rum balanced between his casts. "Mom, this is for you."

Three sips of lip-loosening rum and she growled out, "Byron, what am I going to do about your father?"

Seeming surprised by the question, he said, "Jeez," and looked away.

Anthony nudged him.

Looking back at Holly, Byron released a soft laugh. "You mean the whole 'We need to be a real family' thing?"

She was grateful she wasn't the only one who'd been listening to this. "Yeeeees. What is that all about?" She had an unintended whine in her voice.

"I'm not sure . . ." Byron shrugged. "We've all been through hell. A lot of people are saying crazy things lately. Dad's not alone."

As the rum warmed her thoughts, she steadied her blue-eyed

stare into his green one. "How do *you* feel about what he's saying, honey?"

Anthony held up a finger. "Would you two like some privacy?"

Byron put his hand on Anthony's shoulder. "No, it's fine. Don't leave. Mom probably needs us both right now." He met his mother's eyes again and she nodded. "When I was young, I used to dream you and Dad would get together," he admitted. "Isn't that every kid's dream if their parents are apart? But Mom . . . I'm a grown man now. As I have been telling you so often lately. You've done so much for me. And you did *everything* yourself. If I have a say, then I say it's all about you. This is *your* time."

I could not be prouder of him, Holly thought. *I did at least one thing right with my life.*

"Thank you, honey." She reached up and gave his shoulder a gentle squeeze.

When Byron walked away, Anthony continued on about his idea of taking a trip. "We'll have a wonderful time sailing. Surely Byron will give you a few weeks away—after the cleanup, of course. He's more than capable of taking care of things here. In the meantime, my dear . . ." He took her hand and pulled her toward the edge of patio to behold the aqua swimming hole below. "When I feel foolish about trying something that's fun, I think of your American poet, Robert Frost: *'So was I once myself a swinger of birches. And so I dream of going back to be.'* What do you think, Holly? Shall we give it a go?"

She appreciated his sentiment more than he could possibly know.

"Can you please wait one minute?" She handed him her glass.

Holly slipped the bottoms of her shorts down. She unbuttoned the blue-checked shirt she wore over her bikini and took it off. After stowing the shirt and shorts in the kitchen, she watched Byron and Montez from inside. They were now together at the bar, sipping their beers, unaware of her presence.

After some reflection, she walked back outside and headed straight toward them. But once she was behind them, she discovered she was unable to find her voice.

With sudden resolve, she managed to squeeze in between them and say, "I've got to talk to your dad. Can you give us a minute?"

Holly thought Byron must have a sense of what was going on. He shrugged and moved away.

Though she felt clumsy, she placed a hand on Montez's forearm and got his full attention.

"You're a good man, Montez Curry," she said slowly. "I'm so glad we had our Byron, but that was a long time ago."

He flinched, blinking his eyes rapidly. Upon recovering from her statement, the expression he wore was blazing–determined. "Long ago, but not too late," he said firmly. "I am sure of it."

Holly shook her head. "There are other things left for me to do and I'm sorry, but . . . they have nothing to do with you. So I'm going to say 'no' to your offer. But thank you, Montez."

"Holly . . ."

She put her hand on his and shook her head again, stopping him. She really didn't want to spend any more time on this fantasy of his. With a relieved smile on her face, she realized she considered his proposal a trivial matter. *Who would have thunk it? I trust my ability to create a beautiful life for myself more than I trust this man to give me one.*

"The truth is, Montez . . . I'm sure you'll get over it quickly. Let's just leave it at that."

She spun away and headed for The Big Splash. As she approached, Anthony bowed deeply at the waist. She found she was getting used to his swashbuckling ways. He gestured toward the aqua pool, and everything was perfectly clear; no further words needed to be spoken.

Holly ran forward and jumped with her knees and arms high in the air. She let out an extended whoop of delight that lasted until she landed on her behind in the water. Though she took in a mouthful of salty ocean as she went under, she laughed with joy upon surfacing. As she wiped the saltwater from her eyes, she heard another splash close to her and allowed herself to float back toward the noise she knew was Anthony.

They treaded water as they watched the sun setting. It would be any second.

It seemed right when the rim flashed green with the true color of hope just as the last of the sun sank below the horizon. A great cheer went up from those assembled.

"Somehow you make magic wherever you go!" Anthony shouted to her.

For the first time in my life, I actually believe it.

Epilogue

Three weeks after Hurricane Nestor moved away from Turks and Caicos and on to decimate part of the coast of Florida, a few flights were landing on Grand Turk Island. As they later told the story, Toby and Sally Trombley were two of twelve passengers onboard their Air Caribbean flight who were dying to see their loved ones. They anxiously deplaned and searched for a method of transportation to get to The Roseate House.

Although tools would not normally be allowed through a security checkpoint, Toby managed to bring in a suitcase full of them, along with solar chargers for the batteries that powered them.

The way he told it, the woman who was completing their visas at customs asked, "Anything to declare?"

His response was a decisive, "No."

She unzipped the suitcase and stared at him defiantly. "You sure?"

"It's a state of emergency, miss," he said—and she let him through.

Holly was down the street, visiting with her friend Deb in the shade of a stucco wall, when she saw Cabman Jack pull his van in front of the inn. When she saw the Trombleys climb out, without a word to Deb in parting, she took off sprinting.

She didn't know she was making a sound, but they later told her she was screaming, "Ahh!" for the length of the two short blocks it took to reach them.

Both of the new arrivals had their arms outstretched in antic-ipation of her embrace, but it was Toby who absorbed the impact of Holly's one hundred and twenty pounds as she hurled herself into his arms.

He was much taller than she, and her legs dangled as he rocked her back and forth. Sally moved closer to pat her on the back as he did. When Toby set her on the ground, the three of them stood together in a group hug.

Sally whispered hoarsely, "We have been worried sick," but it wasn't until Byron emerged and she saw his crossed arms bound up in slings and his still blackened eyes that she burst into tears.

In addition to having the daily communal meals still going on, Holly now had a full house.

School was canceled indefinitely. Town garbage trucks combed the roads, back and forth, up and down. Every inhabitant who was old enough to walk and young enough to pull the garbage out of the trees and bushes and off the rooftops that were left intact did so. Oversize garbage bags were distributed, filled, and picked up by the drivers manning the trucks within hours. Despite the efficiency, the cleanup seemed a Sisyphean task. Days turned into weeks, which turned into months. Still, the hard work continued, and at the end of every long day, there were some who needed to be fed.

Thanksgiving was approaching when Toby and Sally told Holly they simply had to get back to the farm. By then they had singlehandedly torn the damaged roof off the section of the inn that was Holly's bedroom and replaced it with new plywood and blue corrugated metal roofing.

"It's better than the old one," Holly told them as they were saying goodbye at the airport, which now had a few flights a day regularly going to and from Providenciales, although the main building was still boarded up.

The Belonger

When Sally turned away from Holly with tears in her eyes, Toby stepped in. "Just remember, the Trombley clan—all of us—is coming for the week of Thanksgiving next year. And no discounts. You need to make a living like everyone else."

"That's a lot of money. You'll fill the place." Holly flushed.

Toby grabbed Sally and put his arm around her. "It's our thirtieth anniversary right around then too. It's what we want. All those rug rats of ours are coming with us."

Holly stood transfixed, trying to think of ways to make the week special for them.

Byron, as if reading her mind, said, "We'll borrow a bunch of kayaks and take them all the way up North Creek. It'll be fun."

"All right, then," she agreed. "A year from now we should be ready for company."

Food donations from the churches and local government were piled high in the kitchen of the Sand Dollar. A water truck came regularly to fill Holly's tanks, and a local provider dropped off a steady supply of propane. There were volunteers to help, but it fell primarily to Holly to make something out of the resources. After all, how many ways were there to turn beans and rice into a hot meal for a crowd?

Ten months passed while Grand Turk islanders worked to salvage their homes and businesses, to rebuild the seawall that bordered Front Street, and to raise money for the library and the hospital, both of which had suffered serious damage from Nestor. Holly and Byron fully participated in those fundraising efforts, and when the opening days for the facilities arrived, they were filled with satisfaction.

A renewed sense of order came when utilities were finally restored from one end of the island to the other. The obvious choice to host a gathering of celebration was, of course, the Sand Dollar.

Over time, as people slowly recovered from their traumas, they began telling, and retelling, tales of the great storm. It became clear to townspeople that there were several citizens who had acted heroically during Nestor and its aftermath. It was not an exaggeration to say they had saved lives and, certainly, helped the town to rebound after the direct hit of the eye of the storm. An idea was born to have a ceremony to celebrate these people at Dillon Hall, which had the largest capacity for a seated audience in town.

It was a historic building that belonged to and sat behind the Anglican Church on Front Street. Like the church itself, its stucco was painted white and it had glossy, bright red exterior shutters. Inside the hall, the soaring ceiling with its ancient, exposed wood beams was awe-inspiring. Along one wall was a stage with a sound system. The floor was made of the same dark wood as the beams, though it had a shiny patina from thousands of feet walking across it through the years.

Holly was humbled and honored to even be invited to the event, let alone chosen to receive a plaque.

Theresa was composed and regal as she stood before the microphone in a long red dress that evening. Her husband, Joab, was behind her wearing a suit and tie and holding their baby, Hollin. He also sported a proud look on his face.

Theresa spoke at length, though Holly's ears roared so loudly from her nervousness that she only caught the last part of the introduction.

"We are so grateful that the life of our son—perhaps my own life, as well—was spared because of Holly's courage and take-charge attitude. We will surely never forget it. I thank the Lord every day she was there."

Applause thundered when they invited Holly to come to the stage. She was struck with a moment of intense déjà vu that made her feel as if she'd waited her whole life for this very moment.

The Belonger

When she arrived at the microphone, a local member of the ruling Cabinet handed her the plaque and read what it said aloud: "On behalf of Queen Elizabeth II, The Governor of TCI, and the Premier, we bestow this distinction for extraordinary bravery and service. With this, we also commemorate that Miss Holly Anne Walker is awarded the honorary title of 'Belonger.'"

Overcome with emotion, the best Holly could do was mumble into the mic, "Thank you for this honor—I love you all."

When another speaker stood up to give the second introduction, she bolted.

Byron followed her out the double doors leading into the black of the night.

When he found her, he asked, "What is it, Mom?" and handed her several tissues.

She appreciated that he knew enough about her to have come prepared with Kleenex.

She wiped her eyes and blew her nose, unable to speak. After a minute, she took his arm and moved with him to the open doorway to watch the rest of the ceremony.

During a break between recipients, she prepared herself to explain her tears. But she couldn't.

"You're crying because we're finally home," Byron said, a beaming smile on his face. "Look at you, Mom. A Belonger."

She thought how in a few months all the Trombleys would be coming. She and Anthony had already decided that as soon as they left, the two of them would head out on their sailboat adventure; they planned to return on Christmas Eve. Byron was happy he would have the chance to show her he could handle the business on his own.

She looked over at him. His face reflected the golden spotlights that illuminated the stage; his bright green eyes shone with curiosity for what the recipient currently onstage would say.

"I'm not going to tell you I don't really deserve this honor," the man joked. "My wife has already said so many times."

Holly and Byron cracked up.

Still chuckling, she put a hand on his arm and stood on her tiptoes to whisper in his ear, "I better go back and get set up. A lot of these people will be coming to the Sand Dollar after."

"I'll come and help you," he said quickly.

She shushed him. "Stay and watch . . . I'll see you later."

The truth was, Holly wanted to walk back home along the seawall alone. The moon was just rising, and the dome of stars tonight was brilliant. The waves, with their luminescent crests, would entertain her, and she was sure that a wild donkey or horse or dog would pad alongside her and keep her company. She longed to feel the mist of the ocean spray. In fact, she thought she might sit up there on the wall and linger for a while. Maybe she would try to retrace all the steps that had led her to this jubilant time and place.

One thing she knew for sure in this moment: of all the wonderful and difficult things in her life, discovery had turned out to be the best teacher of all.

Acknowledgments

I joke that my husband and I have the perfect marriage because while Tom's out golfing or scuba diving, I have the time to write. That is, of course, an oversimplification. He sacrifices plenty while I am absorbed by the written word and lost in my stories. Thank you, my love.

Additional appreciation to:

My greatest cheerleaders, my three sons Bruce, Jonathan, and Thomas. Special gratitude to my eldest, Bruce, for loving Grand Turk as much as I do, reading an early draft of *The Belonger* carefully, and giving me honest feedback. To Jonathan, for teaching me all he knows about crafting a story arc (and he knows a lot). And Thomas, for being interested enough to ask intelligent questions. You all make me a better writer.

My pod, my crew, my posse—Brooke, Carey, Chuck, and Susan—life is just better with you in it. We hold each other up, no snarking, no jealousy. When one of us wins, we all win.

Deborah Vieira, for orienting us to the balmy island of Grand Turk. It is she who sold us our first house there and helped us to rebuild it after hurricanes Irma and Maria knocked it down with a one–two punch in quick succession. Also, for the many nights of too-much fun and showing me where all the best food is at.

Deb's daughters, Tonya and Katya Vieira, the owners of Sand Bar Restaurant and Manta House vacation bungalows (where I wrote much of the novel). Mother Deb and daughters are three of the formidable women I dedicated this book to.

Tonya's husband and our builder, Tereze James, and his brother, architect Ricky James. What you created for us went beyond our expectations.

The dashing Tim Dunn, who mentioned that he was a descendant of pirates and set this story off and running.

All the friends and tradesmen-who-became-friends who helped in our darkest hour. Particularly: Arthur, Bradlio, Conrad, Desius, Frankie, Henry, Joab, Kingdry, Kristin, and Marvin.

Editor and best-selling author Marley Gibson, who was instrumental in developing this book. She has been a constant resource, supporter, and friend. When are you coming down to dive on Grand Turk?

Best-selling authors James M. Tabor and Kris Radish—your mentorship keeps me striving to be as good a writer as both of you are. Turks and Caicos's own educator and author, Debby-Lee V. Smith Mills, for consulting on language and culture. And lastly, best-selling author Kerry Schafer, for her invaluable advice.

And many thanks to the team at She Writes Press/SparkPress. Your unshakable belief that I have stories worth telling keeps me writing away. Brooke Warner, Samantha Strom, Krissa Lagos, and publicist Crystal Patriarche—you always point me in the right direction.

About the Author

Photo credit: Brooke Cunningham

Mary Kathleen Mehuron lives and teaches in a ski town in Vermont where everyone calls her Kathy and she and her husband raised three sons. She has a weekly column in her local newspaper, *The Valley Reporter*, called "Take Me Back." The Vermont Arts Council recently gave her an artist development grant and she is using it to grow the column into a nonfiction book whose sales will benefit the Mad River Valley historical societies. She is the author of two previous novels, *Fading Past* and *The Opposite of Never*. When she's not writing or exercising, she's hanging out with her husband, her three dogs, or her long-time posse of friends. You will also find her at any local event that has live music (she's the one out on the floor dancing). She takes extended time to work on her novels on Grand Turk Island and in Vermont's Northeast Kingdom.